W9-DFK-192

1861

A

TIME

FOR

GLORY

THE CIVIL WAR SOLDIER SERIES

BOOK ONE

1861

A TIME FOR GLORY

R. B. GREENWALT

BLUE/GRAY PRESS, LLC

FIRST EDITION

Library of Congress Control Number: 2005911334
Proposed Cataloging Data
    Greenwalt, Robert
        1861 A Time for Glory / R. B. Greenwalt - 1st ed.
        p. cm.
        ISBN 0977658201
            1. Campbell, Joshua (fictitious character) - Fiction
            2. United States - History - Civil War, 1861-1865 - Fiction
            3. Mississippi - History - Civil War, 1861 - Fiction
            4. Virginia - History - Civil War, 1861 - Fiction   I. Title

DEDICATION

To my loving, patient and understanding wife,

Mary Carol.

Le jour de gloire est arrive.

MAP OF BATTLE OF MANASSAS [ACTION AT GRIGSBY'S]

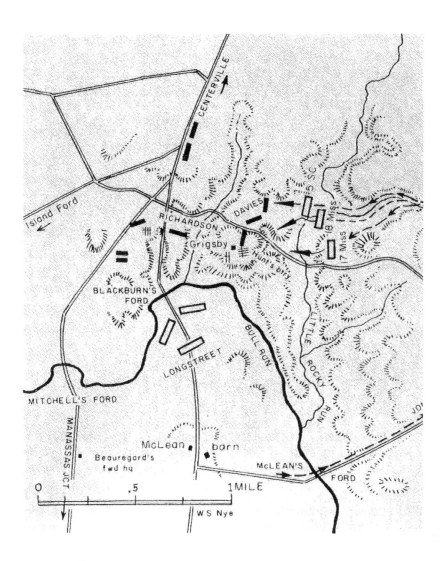

Map provided courtesy of Civil War Times

MAP OF BATTLE OF BALLS BLUFF

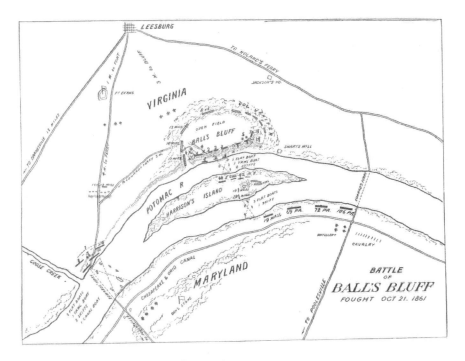

Map provided courtesy of Civil War Times

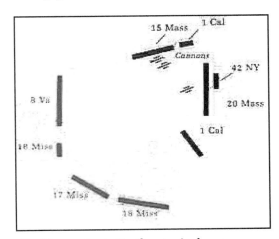

Positions prior to Featherston's charge

As a necessity, not a choice, we have resorted to the remedy of separation. . . . If a just perception of mutual interest shall permit us peaceably to pursue our separate political career, my most earnest desire will have been fulfilled. But, if this be denied to us, and the integrity of our territory and jurisdiction be assailed, it will but remain for us, with firm resolve, to appeal to arms. . . .

For purposes of defense. . . it is deemed advisable, in the present condition of affairs, that there should be a well-trained and disciplined army. . . .

Jefferson Davis, *First Inaugural Address, February 18, 1861*

I hold, that in contemplation of universal law, and of the Constitution, the Union of these States is perpetual . . . No State, upon its own mere motion, can lawfully get out of the Union, that . . . ordinances to that effect are legally void, and that acts of violence, within any State or States . . . are insurrectionary. . .

. . . [T]here needs to be no bloodshed or violence; and there shall be none, unless it be forced upon the national authority . . .

There will be no invasion - no using of force against or among the people anywhere.

Abraham Lincoln, *First Inaugural Address, March 4, 1861*

Holly Springs, Mississippi.—Sketched by Mr. A. Cooper.—[See Page 27.]

1

Nerves tensed along the gray line, polished rifles at ready, muscles tight in anticipation. Taut smiles creased fresh faces as soldiers watched cannoneers bend to their work. On command, a bone jarring, thunderclap roar shattered still morning air. Foggy smoke swirled and settled on those nearby, quiet prevailing until the effect of the single charge became visible. Though the ancient barrel had split, shearing spokes from a wheel and gouging the ground behind, the men in uniform could relax when smoke cleared. Civilians recovered their composure to resume a farewell to the company bound for war, though some of the women tended to casualties among the flowers and shrubs.

In a scene repeated throughout states both north and south this spring of 1861, departures of uniformed men were accompanied by ceremony. The Holly Springs, Mississippi version of late May began outside the courthouse in a town square bountifully decorated with red, white and blue. A musical contingent had been impressed to serenade the gathering with "Dixie" and "Ol' Susanna" among the favorites. The mayor, flanked by leading citizens and men of the cloth, loudly declared support for the cause from the town, the county and the State of Mississippi, with grand oratory. He promised a quick smiting of the mongrel Yankee foe and a glorious future for the Confederacy, not shrinking in his offer of blood from the young men before him to preserve and protect Southern honor.

The object of such festivities and praise were the
Mississippi Rangers, a company of 100 men raised among the
eager and willing of Marshall County. Outfitted in new uniforms
of gray with black trim, a signature navy blue flannel shirt
beneath their shell jackets, each of the Rangers sported the
compact and deadly Mississippi Rifle manufactured at Holly
Springs arsenal. Even the most rapscallion among them looked
solemn and purposeful amidst the cheers and tears of leave
taking.

The mayor concluded his remarks to polite applause,
orders resounded and a hundred bodies straightened. On
command, the company formed by two's to march in a semblance
of military order. The Rangers stepped off smartly for the train
station at the edge of town amid cheers and waves. By common
consent the crowd did not follow, farewells having been made
before formation, though a few of the youngest raced to catch
sight of the column from side streets.

As the newly minted soldiers began to march away,
thoughtful members of the crowd could not suppress an unsettled
feeling. Despite assurances from politicians and press of pride
and glory and easy victory, there was a sense that certainty was
not so certain. To some of those contributing fathers, sons and
husbands for this show of Southern military might came the
unspeakable and nearly unthinkable thought, that they had bid
farewell to their loved ones forever.

>< >< >< >< ><

Doubts and fears found no expression amongst the
Rangers. Eager anticipation reigned among these men, though
tempered slightly with the sadness of leaving home. Confidence
was high and the harsh realities of impending battle ignored. The
future held only glory. And the youngest felt these emotions most
keenly.

Among the youngest, just eighteen that spring, marched

Joshua Andrew Jackson Campbell, bearing the name of the prophet chosen by his mother, and the president at his father's insistence. Clear blue eyes full of youthful certainty, with a measure of adventure, danced with the sights about him. Just shy of six feet, he was taller than most in the company, affording him a good view of what lay ahead. Light brown hair, trimmed close above the ear, framed a youthfully handsome, full cheeked face. Unlike many others in the company, he was clean shaven despite repeated efforts to grow even the slightest mustache. Broad shoulders crowned his lean frame, hardened by daily labor on the family farm. That May day his shoulders carried the soldier's slings of war - rifle, chock full haversack, and canteen.

His most important possession, an eagle talon, rested safely inside his shirt pocket. Given to him by a Chickasaw Indian who lived near his home, the old man had presented it still bloody to an awe struck boy as a powerful charm. He carried the talisman into manhood, invoking a mystical power as needed for luck or protection.

Josh was proud that he was among men embarking on a glorious task. He cast his mind back to the beginning of the year. Talk of separation and war had blossomed with Lincoln's election the November before. Mississippi had been second to secede, after South Carolina, and Josh remembered a cool night in early January when the news was announced on the courthouse steps. He had cheered himself hoarse that night, though he had little idea what secession would mean to him or the State.

Immediately, talk abounded of forming militias and companies to defend the new Confederacy. Josh knew he wanted to be a part of this, but had kept his feelings private at home. His chance came with recruitment notices announcing formation of the Mississippi Rangers, the second company to be raised in Holly Springs. Joshua Campbell had been among the first to sign up.

First Sergeant Timothy Ferrall's terse instruction to close ranks ended the bittersweet remembrance. Josh concentrated hard to avoid the heels of the man in front. He switched the suddenly heavy rifle to his other shoulder, hoping Ferrall would not catch him. He glanced ahead to see they were near the station.

An officer shouted, "Company halt." The soldier behind bumped into Josh, knocking him off balance. "Keep still, lads," Ferrall cautioned men still lax about marching discipline.

"Hey, Riley, yer drawers're showin'," Ezekiel Owens whispered loudly to a soldier from beside Josh. Soldiers nearby stifled laughs and cackles, and Josh with them.

He and "Zeke" Owens were 'pards', had joined the company together. Their friendship went back to first school days and grew as they shared their lives. Zeke was a bit shorter and scrawny next to Josh, but sported a sparse mustache and chin whiskers, dark as his hair. Though a dead shot with his rifle, Zeke paid scant attention to military ways. He found life unremarkable and rarely complained about his lot, but could be a willing participant in any mischief.

A lifelong familiarity with horses gave Josh some thought to joining the cavalry, but Zeke did not ride well. With little regret or hesitation, Josh settled on the infantry. Having done so much together, he could not imagine this adventure without Zeke beside him.

Soldiers were divided by the officers and began to board the Mississippi Central Railroad cars, about thirty men in each. Josh and others in his group climbed aboard. He went to a bench seat near the back and began to stow his gear around the seat. He had loosened his jacket when Zeke nudged him.

"Hey Josh, yer gal's outside lookin' fer ya," he pointed. "She's yonder by the depot office."

Josh stumbled to the other side of the train and thrust his head out the window. "Becca" he shouted and waved. She turned her head toward him and waved once, then began to make her way toward his car. Josh forced his way out to speak with her.

Rebecca Tolliver was a complication in his life Josh was all too glad to leave behind. He had caught many a girl's eye, but

Rebecca had caught his. Not yet 17, she had the emerging body of a young woman, discretely camouflaged by the high neck fashion of the day. Her auburn hair fell in tresses just below her shoulder, framing an oval face with soft, rosy cheeks. Josh had been drawn to her hazel eyes, wide open and gay, though on this day reddened and moist.

They had met the evening before to say goodbye and she had pressed close to him just before parting. He could not deny the longing he felt for her and he had kissed her passionately. But he had avoided any commitment about the future, except to swear he would write, and she may have sensed his reluctance to declare his feelings. Now, she rushed to greet him among the embarking soldiers.

"Ah thought to see you one more time, Joshua," she stammered, turning her gaze downward as she spoke, though close enough he could smell her perfume. "I wanted to give you a remembrance." Her voice cracked as she fumbled with a handkerchief.

Josh wanted to console her, but he was conscious some of the soldiers were watching. He thought first to scold her, saying, "Becca, you ain't 'sposed to be here." She sniffled loudly at the rebuke and Josh could go no further. Instead, he tried to comfort her, placing his hands on her shoulders. "Look here, we'll whup them Yanks an be back 'fore you git a chance to miss me." He managed a half smile to raise her spirits.

She edged closer to embrace him, holding a lock of her hair bound tightly with a single strand, and looked up into his eyes. "You be sure to come back to me, Joshua Campbell." Her voice caught as she pressed the keepsake into his hand. Josh felt his throat tighten too. "An you bes write me like you promised," she added haltingly.

She seemed so forlorn, he closed his arms to hold her, watching eyes be damned, when he heard a squawky voice from behind. "Private Campbell, return to your car at once."

Josh broke from the embrace, thinking that damned Jasper

Welburn, fellow had a knack for turning up like a bad sore. He turned to face the company third lieutenant. Welburn was only a year older, but from the county's wealthiest family and his lack of military training was overcome by his father's influence. As long as Josh could remember, Welburn never failed to irritate for he was keen to laud his family's position over any one.

As even the lowest ranking officer, Josh knew to be careful in reply, though he tried to sound reasonable. "Jasper, I'll be on board 'fore we go. Jes sayin' mah good byes to a dear friend." He turned to Rebecca, caressed her quickly and kissed her tear stained cheek, then whispered "Bye". She swept the handkerchief to her face and walked away.

"You will address me as 'Sir', Private," Welburn shrieked. Josh turned back to see the now red faced Lieutenant advancing nearer.

Josh spat out the word 'Sir' without coming to attention or saluting. He was a head taller than Welburn and not about to show any fear to the upstart. He tensed, unsure what to expect, but the smaller man stopped short of arms length.

In the glaring silence that developed, Ferrall appeared between them with a half salute toward the officer. "Campbell's one o' my lads, sir, and you'll be knowin' he's aboard directly." The Sergeant grabbed Josh by the arm and hustled him toward the car. Josh was inclined to let Welburn know his feelings, but Ferrall's grasp was firm. The Lieutenant's belligerent cry that he would report Josh to the Captain faded as the two men boarded the car.

Ferrall pushed Josh on the train ahead of him. "Don't be stupid, boyo" the Sergeant growled. "So long's that popinjay wears them shoulder boards, you'll be takin' his guff with a smile on yer face. He kin drum you out o' this company in disgrace. Now be takin' yer seat and stay put." Ferrall propelled Josh toward his bench.

"Hey Campbell, don' worry 'bout that gal of yours, she'll find a real man quick to keep her warm at night," Lucius Bradwell taunted him and some men nearby joined in with a laugh.

Josh turned toward Bradwell, his face flushed with anger and humiliation. Bradwell's cold eyes and smirking face told him he would welcome a scrap right there. Anticipating a response, the offender rose confidently and stepped into the isle. The burly Bradwell was bigger and likely stronger, but Josh couldn't shy from a challenge in front of others. He took a step toward the menacing soldier, and was yanked backward by a hand on his collar.

"Campbell, you'll be takin' yer seat," Ferrall said sharply. "An' Bradwell, you'll be findin' yours," the Sergeant added evenly, facing the bigger man. Ferrall was short, but thick muscled and solid as a rock. Even the hulking Bradwell knew better than to challenge the older man and withdrew slowly into his seat. At that moment the engine whistle blew and the train lurched. Josh tumbled onto his seat next to Zeke.

"Hell's fire, Josh, ya got an officer an' Bradwell spoilin' fer ya all at once, and jes 'cause of a perty face," Zeke said. Josh turned on his friend with raw feeling, but realizing his predicament, both of them began to laugh at the situation.

On the bench opposite, Riley Osborne and David Crockett Williams looked at the two, trying to make sense of the humor. Osborne leaned toward Josh and said, "Don't worry none, Josh, we'll whup those Yankees an be back here 'fore the first frost. Ain't that right, Zeke."

"Long's we don' git back 'fore harvest time," Zeke added dryly.

"I jes hope to git a chance to shoot one of them Yankee dogs fore they turn tail and run," Davy put in. "If'n I have to, I'll chase 'em all the way to Yankeeland."

His three companions looked at the smallish Davy Williams and laughed together at the thought of him chasing anybody.

"Ya bes' watch out or one of them big Yanks'll pick ya up and put ya in his pocket," Zeke cackled.

Davy drew his wide bladed sword bayonet, saying, "One o' them cusses try, he'll git a belly full o' this."

This declaration stilled further comment and the four young soldiers fell silent amidst engine noise and chatter on the car. They settled into their journey, retreating to private thoughts or closing their eyelids.

Josh looked about the rail car. All around him were boys he'd known at school and others he knew from church or town gatherings. Some were good friends, like even tempered Riley and the always talkative Davy, who had agreed to be messmates with he and Zeke. He had come to know the rest as they became part of the company. A few, such as Bradwell and his friends from a small settlement north of town, he had learned to give a wide berth.

Though a couple were well off and a handful were poor, most were like Josh, somewhere in between, coming from farm families that did not lack for necessities, but knowing few luxuries. The majority did not own slaves, except for officers like Jasper Welburn, who was even allowed to keep a servant with him in the army. Despite material differences, Josh had no doubt they would fight together to defend the South.

Josh recalled the loudest drumbeaters for separation seemed to be slave owners. Robert Campbell, Josh's father, was a states rights man who denounced what he believed to be meddling by the federal government in local affairs. But his father had no love for the "aristos," as he called them, who made their money on the sweat and toil of slaves, and Josh accepted this attitude.

In his mind, though, the brewing war was more about letting people, and their states, decide whether they wanted to stay in the union or not. Mississippi had decided to leave the union and join the Confederacy and Josh reasoned the North had no right to oppose that decision. He thought anyone should have the right to live where he wanted, with whomever he wanted, and be part of any group as he chose. If his state chose to leave the union, he could understand no reason why it should not be allowed to do so.

Josh admitted only to himself that politics had nothing to do with his decision to volunteer. He had spent his whole life in Marshall County and figured this was his best chance to see the world outside of Mississippi. Besides, it was a well known fact the Yankees would run first time they saw Southern boys, so there seemed little danger in this enterprise.

The car became quieter as more men settled in for the journey to Tennessee. Some dozed and some simply gazed out the window. Zeke had nodded off and Josh hid behind closed eyes too, but sleep would not come easily. He was still troubled by the parting from his family.

Josh recalled the day he had revealed his decision to join the Rangers. After the evening meal, he waited until plates were cleared, then simply said, "I joined up to fight the Yankees." His parents both glared at him, without a word for the moment. His sister broke the silence with "Oh, Joshua!," though he could not then determine if she was happy or fearful.

After a lengthy silence, Robert Campbell cleared his throat before he spoke, glancing first to his wife. "I suppose yool not be talked oot o' this," he said, with his still prevalent Scots accent. Josh replied that his mind was set, and his mother had gasped at such insistence and promptly left the room.

Elsbeth Campbell was a woman of peace. She had been raised to loath violence in any form and to promote Christian unity in the Church of the Brethren, a group some called "Dunkers". She was uncomfortable with slavery, though even more disturbed by politics, and deferred to her husband on such matters. But her strong religious nature and lessons she taught her children had exposed firmly held beliefs in the value of human life.

Josh had known from the moment he signed up that his mother would not welcome or even accept this decision of her only son. He thought his father might express some reservations, but could be won over, might even feel pride that Josh had joined. And so it had been as winter turned to spring in 1861. An icy truce reigned in those months between mother and son, broken by an occasional clutching, wordless hug from her. Meanwhile, his father tried to prepare him for times ahead and gradually warmed to the idea of his son as a soldier.

Robert Campbell had not fought in war, though he was the son of a Waterloo veteran. His fight had come in forging a life for himself in a new land. Josh recalled his father's history easily. Robert had come to America from Scotland as a young man in 1839, leaving behind a hardscrabble farm and two older brothers with a greater claim to it. He had worked his way through Maryland to the Shennandoah Valley of Virginia, where he had met and married Josh's mother in a small Brethren settlement. Together, they established a farm in the lower Valley where Josh and then his sister were born. The Campbells emigrated to Mississippi when Josh was but three, on the promise of abundant, cheap land free of harsh winters. They left behind Elsbeth's family, none of whom Josh had ever met.

Robert Campbell began to raise beef cattle. A shrewd judge of livestock, his cattle flourished and he expanded to trade in horses. Josh could recall lean times, but never a time when they had gone hungry. His father had earned the respect of others, well known as an honest trader in four legged livestock. Robert had gained some standing in the community and could count planters, shop owners and tradesmen among his acquaintances.

As the train rumbled along the track, Josh remembered the many things his father spoke of in those warming spring months before the company was called up. He talked of courage in the face of adversity, of honor on the field of battle. He told Josh that a soldier would be bound to duty, to serve until the task was complete. Josh knew that none of this was based on first hand knowledge, but had been passed down to him from his grandfather through his father. During those times Josh felt a living link to the old Highlander, though he had never laid eyes upon him.

But his mother could not or would not soften her attitude. When she spoke to him, she would recommend Bible verses that invariably concerned peace or charity to others. His father had warned him that, having buried two babies, she would not warm to the departure of her surviving son. Josh had been proud to wear his new uniform, but did not force his mother to see him in it more than necessary. So he had spent the time before leaving hiding high spirits around his mother and letting his dreams rise around his father.

With news of the firing on Fort Sumter in South Carolina, expectations soared of mobilization for the company. Tensions increased in the Campbell homestead as every member of the family understood military confrontation would soon follow. Elsbeth became ever more distant as she fought against events beyond her control.

Until today, he reflected. Before his father drove him to town, he had embraced his mother to bid her farewell. She held her strong feelings in check, returning his affection and saying "God go with you" through a tight but loving smile on her face. His sister Rachel was less reserved and bawled so that she wet his collar when bidding him goodbye.

Then the drive to town with his father in near silence, Robert Campbell seeming to hold his feelings as tightly as the reins. Josh could not provoke much conversation, though his attempts were half hearted as he too felt a strange feeling of loss. They had parted at the newly built Presbyterian Church, a block from the crowded town square. As he stepped down from the rig, his father handed him a twenty dollar gold piece. "Fer yer kit," the elder Campbell said, and shook his son's hand. Then he struck the reins and pulled away. A sadness descended on Josh, and he walked slowly toward the gathering, steeling himself not to turn for a last glance at his father. With an effort, Josh suppressed his feelings as he made his way through the raucous group of soldiers and loved ones. His solitary spell broke only when Zeke called his name and pulled him to formation.

Now those memories he had worked hard to hide returned on the train, lending a melancholy air. Josh feared he might not shake the memory of family, that he might be branded homesick. He closed his eyes and willed the mournful feelings away. And he willed his mind to think of other things. *Marching, shooting, fighting, battle. Honor, glory, duty.* Of the unknown.

The rail journey to Corinth consumed the remaining day and extended into the night. Departing Holly Springs, the company traveled first north to Grand Junction, Tennessee to board cars of the Memphis and Charleston Railroad. This took no little time as delay arose in unloading baggage and equipment to transfer to the next cars. Baggage handlers could not be located at first, then only a few were found. Soldiers were not assigned such menial tasks and refused to shorten the delay by pitching in to help. Instead, they were under orders to wait in the station and area around the tracks.

Merchants from town came by to peddle food and drink to idle soldiers, though an enterprising seller of spirits was quickly run off by the officers. Men passed the time as best they could, but daylight faded to pitch darkness before boarding was completed and the journey continued. At a time when many might have surrendered to sleep at home, the train pulled out for Corinth. Josh found it impossible to doze as the jolting and bumping of the car kept him restless and the shaking was continually met by muttered curses.

In gray light of early morning, Josh glanced out of the window to see the town of Corinth. The train continued a bit farther to stop at a newly constructed depot south and east of town. Josh could discern rows of tents and a tall flagpole flying the flag of Mississippi in the middle of the grounds. Orders were shouted to disembark and the men made their way slowly out of the cars.   The company that formed beside the cars was a bedraggled lot, uniforms rumpled and hats askew. Tired eyes and morning stubble on faces bespoke a group of men whose sole desire was to stretch out on their bedrolls.

A stern but well turned out First Lieutenant Harlow Abernathy strode to the front of the group and advised them that sleep was not on the morning agenda.

The company was given one hour to retrieve their personal effects, find their tents, then report for breakfast. They were informed that drill would follow.   After claiming his satchel crammed with extra clothing and other items, Josh joined the group around Sergeant Ferrall. The Sergeant led them to an area of tents and designated groups of four to occupy each tent. Josh and Zeke were put in with the Tucker brothers, William and Walter. Riley and Davy had the next tent, with Hugh Driscoll and Charlie Akins.

Zeke drew the tent flap aside to reveal a dusty dirt floor. Tossing in their satchels, bedrolls, rifles and equipment, they stretched out to sleep until mealtime. Josh, Zeke and the Tuckers jostled for a place to lay until the morning drum roll, which sounded before any could doze. They followed an aroma of hot coffee to the cook fire where a large tarp spread over the kitchen area. With their tin plates and cups they joined the throng of men streaming into the area.

Passing through the line, Josh and Zeke found a grassy spot and settled down to eat. They were joined by the Tuckers and Riley Osborne.   There was little conversation as they ate, though there was general agreement the food lacked taste.

"Least it's hot" Riley said "though the coffee's burnt my mouth. You Tucker boys shur eat fast," he added, glancing at the two brothers who were wiping plates with biscuits.

"At our house, you eat fast 'fore its gone," William replied, his mouth half full. He was the older at nineteen, but Walter was nearer to sixteen. Word in the company was their father looked to be rid of two hungry mouths and never flinched when he vouched Walter as eighteen.

The hot coffee and cooked food seemed to revive tired spirits. As the sun burned off the light morning mist, the men could look about at the sea of tents around them.

"How many sojers y'all reckon're here," Will Tucker mumbled aloud between bites of biscuit.

"Must be thousands," Riley guessed.

Davy Williams joined the group at that moment. He took on an air of authority as he said, "I bin talkin' to some o' the fellows here. There's boys from Pontotoc, Panola and Calhoun counties here, an now us Marshall County boys. I reckon there's more'n enuf to make up a regiment." Davy paused to sip some coffee, but added one more bit. "Heard there's boys from Alabama here too."

Josh glanced at Walter Tucker who looked at Williams with open mouthed awe, the thought of so many men, and some from another state, in one place seeming too large for him to comprehend. Then he noticed the corporal of their group coming toward them.

"Ve ist ordered to march in der drill in ten minuten. Please to be ready quick now," the Corporal said, and moved off to the rest of his charges.

Josh smiled to himself at Corporal Himmelfarb's attempt to give an order. Everyone in the company liked "Dutchie" Himmelfarb, but he was not a person naturally given to barking his orders. He had been named a Corporal mainly due to his advanced age of twenty-six, older than most of the fellows in the company. Dutchie and his enormous wife Greta had arrived in Holly Springs a year before with their three children. A carpenter by trade, he was much in demand because he gave an honest days work for his pay. Although no one could remember him speaking out for slavery or secession, he had signed on with the company early. Everyone who knew him believed he joined to escape the constant barrage of abuse from a domineering Greta. Josh's only quarrel with him was the way he mixed languages when he got excited.

Josh and the others quick stepped back to their tents, stowed plates and cups, and retrieved their rifles to join forming ranks. An open area with the flagpole Josh had seen marked the parade ground. Officers shouted orders to form in two ranks. Sergeants passed among them to straighten the formation and to prod men into place. Standing near the center of the parade ground, the Captain and First Lieutenant surveyed the scene. When the formation was complete, Lieutenant Abernathy yelled "Rangers, ten-shun, shoulder arms." The men of the company straightened immediately, their rifles on their shoulders. At the command 'Right face' the men turned in ragged fashion and the lines were straightened once again. Finally, the order to march was given and the mass surged forward.

The company marched for a solid hour, rested, then marched again by squads for an hour. Tired legs bore weary troops around the parade ground, with officers and sergeants barking repeated commands to close ranks. While the men tolerated growling sergeants who engendered a healthy respect based on fear, they generally scowled at the bark of officers. Captain Columbus Franklin and First Lieutenant Abernathy maintained their distance during the drill, joined by the Second and Third Lieutenants when the junior officers were not scrambling along the marching column. Josh noticed other officers observing the drill and thought he recognized W. S. Featherston from Holly Springs at one point. Company officers were notably louder and more anxious during Featherston's brief appearance.

First Sergeant Ferrall was everywhere, telling Dutchie to keep men in line at one point and yanking a stumbling Walter Tucker to the side by the collar of his uniform. A recalcitrant Bradwell caught an earful. Though tiresome in the heat and dust, his rebukes were accepted by the company on his experience.

Finally, in the gathering heat of late morning, the company was halted and ordered to fall out. Men dragged themselves toward their tents on sore feet. They were allowed to rest for an hour, then orders came to fall in again to the sound of drumming.

Drill resumed with a long march outside of camp and back. Weariness weighed on the ranks and soldiers frequently bumped into those in front. Curses from officers and sergeants could not overcome the fatigue that permeated the company. When they returned to camp, Captain Franklin halted the column, dressed ranks and called roll before dismissing the men. The troops stumbled back to their tents and most flopped on their bedrolls without bothering to remove gear, falling fast asleep.

There was little enthusiasm for dinner and only about half the company lined up to eat. Zeke roused Josh to join the always hungry Tuckers. They obtained a dinner strikingly similar to their earlier meal of salt pork and overcooked greens from indifferent cooks, then flopped in a space beyond the cook fires.

"I'm wore out," Josh complained as he downed the bland fare. "Never reckoned on all this marchin' in one day," he added.

"Likely be more o' the same as long as we stay here," Zeke commented.

"You reckon they'll send us far away," Will Tucker asked in an uncertain voice. Josh realized the brothers knew little about the prospects of the Rangers.

"Yanks are gathering near Kentucky and Virginia," Josh informed them. "We'll likely be sent one place or t'other."

He gazed at Walter Tucker and realized the separation from home must be troubling to that youngster. Even with his brother along, home must seem a long way off. Walter was near the same age as Rebecca. Her name brought a picture of her face, and Josh brightened as he searched for the lock of hair in his pocket. His smile faded as Jasper Welburn strode into their midst.

"I'm glad to see y'all awake," the Third Lieutenant announced with a sly smile. "Company needs to provide guards and you privates'll stand first watch tonight.' Welburn ignored the responding groans and glared straight at Josh. "Report to Sergeant of the Guard on the hour, with your rifles," he commanded, then turned and walked away without waiting for salutes. Josh cursed the coming interruption to his long sought sleep, but Zeke seemed resigned to the chore.

At the appointed time, the four Rangers assembled with soldiers from other companies for first watch. The Sergeant explained in a gruff voice that guard duty lasted four hours and that they must challenge all who approached their post. He reminded them they could not fall asleep or they would be punished. Then he marched all of them to the perimeter of camp and began to station each soldier about 30 yards apart. He left them with orders to patrol the area between each post.

Josh was stationed between Will Tucker and a soldier he learned was from the Magnolia Guards. He walked his post periodically and a few times had to whisper to Will to be sure he was awake. The greatest enemy on this duty was boredom. Little stirred beyond the camp at night and no one approached the area Josh patrolled. He did hear a rifle discharge on the other side of camp and that reminded him to be more alert for a while. But the desire to lay down and rest was a constant temptation.

Fortunately, Sergeant of the Guard made enough noise each time he approached that Josh was not caught napping. Welburn made one appearance near end of the duty and attempted to startle him. Josh had just been alerted by a barking dog and was awake enough to challenge him with "Who goes there". Welburn's face knotted in disappointment with the challenge and the junior officer mumbled "At ease" as he walked past Josh. The exhilaration of spoiling Welburn's trick kept Josh awake rest of the watch.

At the expected time, their relief was marched to each post and first watch was marched back to the parade ground to be dismissed. The four Rangers trudged back to their tent without a word between them, more asleep than awake. It was after midnight when they finally lay down, pausing only to remove their equipment and shoes.

Lying abed, Josh tried to square his anticipation of army

life with the long day's experience. The company had been thrust in to camp life without a chance to adjust to their new surroundings. Drill was tedious and accommodations uncomfortably plain. His new home offered only endless rows of tents, stinking latrines and forgettable food. Honor and glory and adventure were sorely missing. He realized with some despair the Rangers might be here some time before they were needed. With his last thought, he prayed trouble would soon break out somewhere, anywhere, and the Rangers would be called to serve.

2

The days in Camp Corinth bore a marked resemblance one to the other. Reveille was early and roll called after breakfast. The company drilled together and by squads of ten. Drill resumed after midday break in the form of long marches or company parade. Dress parade was held before dinner and any orders issued in the final formation. The men were generally allowed free time after dinner, but guard and other camp duties occupied some of the evenings. As June replaced May, days continued to warm and nights provided only temporary relief.

Food was plentiful, but monotonous in similarity. The Rangers were immediately introduced to the mess system. Meat, vegetables, ground meal, coffee and other staples were issued to the group, though they were left to devise their own means of preparation. Each man had his own kit of plate, cup and utensils. Pots and pans were issued from company stores. With no other choice, men adjusted quickly to the system.

Josh's mess included Zeke, Riley, Davy, Walter and Will, Hugh and Charlie. Riley showed a knack from the beginning and assumed the role of cook without dissent. The rest divided themselves in meal fixing or cleanup after. Other messes organized in similar fashion, though quality of meals varied between campfires. Josh counted himself lucky to have a decent cook after the grumbling from some in the company. Remembrances of home cooking formed the foundation of many

Ranger conversations.

The principal topic of conversation, and a frequent part of the camp 'grapevine' gossip, was when and where the men would get a chance to fight Yankees. Rumors of impending movement were quickly dispelled as days passed. Additional companies arrived in camp, always with word of big doings soon to come. But the men gradually resigned themselves to drill and more drill, and even the officers seemed restless.

Little excitement was offered by the election of company officers early in June. The Captain and Lieutenants were elected as a slate and without opposition, having been accorded their titles unofficially when the company was formed in Holly Springs. Josh judged Captain Columbus Franklin a fair and honorable man. Abernathy was cut in the same mold, but Second Lieutenant Roscoe Barnett and Welburn were wanting in leadership qualities. However, there had been no real opposition to them, so Josh voted for all.

The Rangers were officially designated part of the newly formed 17th Mississippi Regiment. They were mustered in to the service of the Confederate States of America on June 7, 1861 and in company formation the men swore to fight twelve months for the Confederacy. The company welcomed news that the man appointed Colonel of the newly formed regiment was none other than W. S. Featherston from Holly Springs. Rangers were bold to point out to other companies that he was the best man for the job. Josh did not know the Colonel well, though Featherston had done business with his father.

With monotony at a high point, thoughts of many turned to some form of escape. Soldiers were under strict orders to remain in camp, but the town of Corinth became a siren song. Josh heard the stories around evening campfires, though it was unclear exactly what pleasures the town held.

Little Davy Williams had become operator on the grapevine telegraph for the mess and informed of the latest camp gossip. On the evening after the company was mustered in, he sang a now familiar song.

"I heerd some o' the Panola boys got caught tryin' to sneak back into camp las' night," Williams reported as they took their evening meal. "Had themselves a fine ol' time in town an' jes hafta stan' extra guard duty 'cause of it."

Zeke was game to try and had talked to Josh about an escapade several times. "That ain't so bad fer gettin' caught," he said. "Thar's plenty they don't catch. Lucius Bradwell and his crew go in town most ever night an they don't have no punishment. Bradwell's bin braggin' bout all the perty gals on ever corner."

"Well I'd shur like to see a pretty face and smell somethin' nicer than a bunch a sojers," Hugh Driscoll put in. Hugh was twenty-one, single and had an eye for the ladies. His wavy black hair, chiseled features and a pocketful of money to spend generally insured female companions. Josh couldn't recall a time Hugh was without a young lady at any town festivity. Hugh was a fun loving fellow, though vain of his appearance. His uniform was cleanest in the mess and he shaved and trimmed his mustache daily.

Charlie Akins did not join in the talk of leaving camp. He and Hugh were partnered up through some vague family connection, but different as day and night. Hugh was flashy and bold while Charlie was sober and serious. He was the same age and size as Hugh, though plain as a post with a pasty look to him. Charlie was married and very religious. He served as a deacon in his church, which earned him the nickname "Preacher". He had joined to fight against the godless Northerners and could quote scripture and damn Yankees all in one sentence. But he got along with the boys because he did not preach to every one and was a steady influence in the company.

Davy Williams spoke up quickly. "I say we give it a try tomorrow night. There ain't much moonlight and I know a place we kin sneak out," he said in a hushed voice.

"Riley won' go 'cause he's afraid o' gettin' caught," Davy

added to imply he had no fear. "How 'bout you Josh, you game to try?"

Zeke spoke before Josh could reply. "He's afraid he'll git caught, too," he said.

Josh flushed at the implied taunt by his friend. "I jes don' see the need. I don' want no spirits an' I ain't lookin' to git hooked up with no gal," he reasoned, then he tried a better argument. "Sides, y'all got to mind the Provost Guard. One of the Burnsville boys tol me the Provost caught two of 'em dead drunk in town and sent 'em home. I ain't gonna risk that disgrace."

"Can't no Provost Guard catch me," Zeke said, Davy and Hugh voicing their agreement. In the consensus of opinion, the Provost was old, slow and dull witted.

Charlie chimed in to support Josh, but in this discussion it did not help to be allied with the religious man. He could see no way to deter their plans and tried to change subjects.

"You hear any more 'bout that boy in the Guards," he asked Davy. A soldier in the Confederate Guards, a Marshall County company that included many from Holly Springs, had been sick with fever since that company arrived two days before. Charlie knew the man and replied before Williams could.

"He died, Josh," Charlie said somberly and the others looked to him for more information. "Surgeon tried to cure his fever, but he never got better. First one from town to die," he added glumly.

"Heard the surgeon might send one of our boys home for sick," Riley commented sadly. Sickness in camp was no way to end army service for any soldier.

"I'm gonna see to Will an' Walter," Josh announced, thinking of Walter in the talk of sick soldiers. Taking his leave of the campfire with some food, Josh made his way to the brother's tent. Walter had been ailing for two evenings now. He had missed the day's drill and had not eaten breakfast or dinner. He had done little more than lay about and moan in his bedroll while

‌‍‎‏

brother Will sat outside the tent with an anxious look .

"He ain't no better Josh," Will said as Josh neared the tent and handed him the food. Josh could hear the despair in his voice. "He don' eat 'cause his stomach hurts, but he ain't passed nothin' fer two days."

"Why don' you take him to the surgeon," Josh asked.

"He won' let me, 'fraid the doc'll send him home," Will explained. "But he sure ain't gettin' better an I don' know what ta do fer him."

Josh stepped into the tent and felt Walter's head. He was warm and sweaty to the touch. He had his hands wrapped around his gut and he moaned when Josh touched the area. The sick soldier peered at Josh with a vacant stare.

"Boy, you got to see the surgeon and git yerself well," Josh told him.

With a pained expression, Walter grabbed his arm, "No" he said, "No doctor."

Outside the tent, Josh spoke to Will. "When we couldn't pass nothin' at home, my Ma'd give us a tea of licorice root and sassafras."

"Only place to get that is town," Will sighed. "An' they don' give out no passes wit'out a load of questions."

"Well, we could give some money to one of the boys'll go in town," Josh said, thinking of who he could ask to accomplish the task. "But I don' know as I'd trust any o' them fellers ta bring what we need."

Josh paused in his reflection and glanced at Will. The distraught eyes pleaded with him and Josh swore silently when he realized what was being asked of him.

"I bes go my own self," he said resignedly and Will smiled in relief. "You got to stay with yer brother an' take care o' him. Try to git him to drink some." Josh turned to leave, but Will waylaid him.

"Josh, I ain't got no money till we git paid," Will told him, embarrassed at the brothers' lack of personal funds.

"I got 'nuf fer now an y'all kin pay me back later," Josh replied, to ease this additional worry. He walked toward the campfire struggling with how to keep the promise he had just made. He brightened a little with the thought that he could enlist a willing comrade on this ramble. Just short of the campfire circle he called to Zeke to give him a hand with some firewood.

Zeke walked toward him with a puzzled look. "We got plenty fer the evenin'," he said, but Josh pulled him a little farther away.

"Walter's still ailin' an I got to git sum medicine from town," Josh said evenly. "Thought you might like to tag along."

Zeke was about to protest when a grin of recognition slowly spread on his face. The grin faded slightly as he whispered, "You ain't foolin' me pard."

Josh shook his head. "I cain't see no other way to git that medicine, an I shur would like some comp'ny," he confided.

"Let me jes comb mah hair an we'll be off directly," Zeke said and trotted off to the tent.

Josh kept an eye on the others hoping to avoid any inconvenient questions and fingering the eagle talon in his pocket for reassurance. He would likely need some luck tonight to slip out and back in camp without being caught.

Zeke returned in a moment. "Oughtn't we to tell the others 'fore we slip out," he whispered to Josh.

Josh shook his head no. "Be hard fer jes the two o'us to git out 'n back without draggin' a crowd with us. An you know Davy'll have to tell near everyone in the comp'ny," he added.

Josh pulled Zeke towards the back of camp. "Let's slip out by the latrines. Nobody guards back there an we kin say we lookin' fer a good place to squat if asked."

They made their way in the declining light of dusk to the shallow dug slit trenches, keeping a wary eye for men on guard but sighting none. They worked around to dense undergrowth behind the latrines. It was hazardous work in the harsh smell, with the knowledge that a misstep could bring unwelcome consequences. They made it to the brush and worked their way through it. Emerging in a wooded area, they found a footpath leading away from camp. The trail led to two side by side dirt tracks cut by wagon wheels and they turned in the direction of the town.

Wordlessly both began to trot, keeping a wary eye and ear out for the Provost guard. The wagon road merged with a wider thoroughfare. They stopped a moment to catch their breath and saw a freight wagon coming toward them on its way to town.

The driver reigned up, his muscles bulging at the effort, and beckoned them on. "Y'all need a ride to town, hop in," the man said with a friendly smile, as if he had picked up many a soldier. Josh and Zeke jumped up on to the seat beside him.

The teamster introduced himself as Purdy and kept up a steady banter all the way to town, sometimes talking to his horses and in the same breath directing his chatter to his passengers. Josh and Zeke could hardly interject a word before they pulled up to a freight depot on the outskirts of town.

"Ah'll stand you two fellers to a drink," the man said as they all got down from the wagon. "Be jes a minute to git these hosses settled."

Zeke was about to set down and wait, but Josh spoke up right away. "We'd be obliged if you could direct us to the apothecary here. We come to git some medicine fer a friend."

The drover vaguely motioned the way to an apothecary he said was on the next street over. "Y'all kin git a snort when yer done yer business. I'll be over to Rainey's tavern, jes round the corner from the depot."

The two thanked him for the ride and hustled off toward the druggist. In near darkness it was difficult to sight the mortar and pestle signboard until they were almost on top of it.

Standing in front of the store they could see no lights on. Zeke pushed ahead and began banging on the door. Josh slipped off to the side and saw a light appear in the second floor. The light moved downstairs and moments later the door opened.

An older gentleman appeared in carpet slippers and a long house coat. He held his lamp high to get a good look at them.

"It's a might late to be bangin' on my door," the druggist said, glancing at his pocket watch.

"Sorry to trouble you mister, but we come to git medicine fer a sick friend," Josh explained. "We need some licorice root and sassafras tea."

The proprietor scrutinized them fully, then declared, "Y'all soldiers out to the camp," as if he were now satisfied. He led them in to the shop and walked behind the counter to face them. "What's ailin' yer friend," he asked, pulling on some jars arranged on the shelves.

"He ain't eatin' and he ain't passed nothin' fer more'n a day," Josh replied. "Bin layin' about the whole day an' holds his gut tight."

The druggist dug into one of the jars. "The licorice root'll help and the sassafras'll cut the taste," he said, adding a small pouch of the tea. He pulled a dark box from under the counter. "Give him one of these, too." He handed Josh two small packets marked "Doctor Wendell's Magic Elixir".

"The powder'll cut right through him, along with the root tea. If he takes that tonight, his bowels will move by mornin' and he ought to be eatin' regular by midday," the apothecary instructed.

"That'll be four bits," he told them.

"We obliged to you sir," Josh said as he handed him the money. He and Zeke headed out the door.

"We got time fer one drink with that drover 'fore we get back," Zeke said hopefully as they walked toward the freight yard.

"I reckon we got to be sociable," Josh responded doubtfully, "but we got to git back to camp soon's we can."

They found the Rainey tavern easy enough, lit by torches near the street. Inside was nearly as dark as the outside, only a few candles on the tables. As their eyes adjusted, they spotted a dusty, sweat stained Purdy seated in a corner.

"Its mah privilege to buy a drink fer our gallant sojers," the teamster declared as he poured two small earthenware cups full from the clay jug on the table. It was clear to Josh that the man had started before they got there. The drover raised his cup above his head.

"Here's to Jeff Davis and to hell with Abe Lincoln." The thick armed man knocked back his drink in one gulp.

Josh had never tasted hard liquor, for his father kept no spirits at home and his mother spoke strongly against the vice. He didn't think Zeke had much experience with it either, but Josh saw him take it in one swallow like their host. Josh took a sip and it burned him all the way down his throat.

"You got to drink that stuff like yer friend," the freight man told him. "It ain't fer sippin.'"

Josh swallowed the rest and it took his breath away. When he sat the cup down, his eyes blurred a bit.

"Much obliged, Purdy," Josh managed to rasp out in whisper, but the drover cut him off.

"Y'all cain't stan' on one leg," he said and poured them each another measure. "Let's drink to the finest state in the whole damned Confederacy. To Mississippi," he said and downed his drink in one gulp again.

Josh glanced at Zeke for some help, but he already had the cup to his mouth. Though he feared the result, he swallowed his drink slowly, but without removing the cup from his lips. His head spun slightly as the burning sensation seemed to extend to his feet.

Josh sat his cup down and waited a moment for his head to clear. He grabbed the table to steady himself as he started to rise. He managed to croak "Friend, we best be gettin' back to camp 'fore the Provost catches up with us."

The hard looking teamster seemed to ignore Josh's effort and rattled on about Yankees and Lincoln in a particularly venomous fashion. Josh searched for some way to converse with the man out of decency, but his thoughts were confused.   Time passed as their host spoke without pause.

Zeke remained seated, a silly grin spread across his face. He repeated a little ditty "Purdy ain't so perty" and giggled to himself each time.   Josh tried to rouse him by saying in a loud voice, "C'mon Zeke, we got to git back."

He reached for Zeke's arm, but lost his balance and fell back in his chair.   The teamster was pouring another round for each of them.

"Y'all got to have one fer the road," the drover said thickly.   He raised his cup again and said, "We'll drink this 'un to victory fer tha Cause."

The freighter spoke from far away and the cup seemed heavier to Josh.   Zeke mumbled "To vic'ry" and guzzled his drink. Josh knew he had to do the same, but he had to grip the container with both hands to get it to his mouth.   This time, the liquid did not burn so much going down.

With some effort, Josh rose determined to take his leave and pulled on Zeke.   As Zeke stood, he stumbled forward against the table.   Josh helped him to stand, but he felt like his own feet were in deep mud and the room continued to spin as he helped pull Zeke up.

The drover picked up the jug, shook it, then turned it over his cup to get a few more drips out.   "That's all thar is, boys."

Josh tried to puzzle out what he should say, but his tongue seemed too thick in his mouth.   Zeke was laughing softly to himself, though Josh had no clue what he found so funny. Leaning against each other they turned and made their way outside. The cool night air helped to clear the fog a little.

Josh heard Zeke trying to sing "Dixie", but he wasn't singing all of the words.   Josh looked for the road that had brought them in to town though he could not recall which one to choose.   He pulled Zeke with him toward the freight yard to get his bearings.

The road beside the yard appeared familiar and Josh

directed Zeke onto the dusty surface. Walking in a straight line was a mighty chore. Heading out of town, Josh cackled to himself as Zeke began to hoot like an owl. They were staggering beside a rail fence when a small wagon pulled by a lone horse came up beside them.

The driver was a young boy. "Y'all headin' out to the soljer camp," he asked, pulling on the reins to stop the horse.

Josh struggled a little with the question, but managed to nod "Yes" and asked if they could hitch a ride. The boy took a good look at them before he told them to hop on the back and they took off at a trot.

Zeke lay back in the empty wagon and let his lower legs hang over the end, his feet bouncing on the road at times. Josh pulled himself in a little further and lay against the low wood side, bracing against the constant bumping.

Zeke continued to sing lightly, having switched to "Old Dan Tucker" but eventually fell quiet and began to snore. Josh was feeling a little queasy from the jostling wagon. His head began to ache and he felt the need to relieve himself. He banged on the seat of the wagon and told the boy to stop.

The wagon eased to a halt and Josh jumped out and ran to some bushes at the side of the road. He pulled up at a tree and opened his trousers. Relief flooded out of him. He finished and made his way back to the wagon, his head clearing a little.

"Camp's rat over yonder," the boy said, pointing beyond a large grove of trees. "Jes a little further down this road is the train station fer the camp."

The news hit Josh like cold water. They were at the front of the camp where they arrived first day. There were sure to be plenty of guards near the rails.

He punched Zeke and shook him awake. Zeke rose slowly to sit up in the wagon. Josh pulled him on to his feet and kept him from sinking to the ground. He had to shush him because he began to sing again.

Josh thanked the boy and told him they would make their

way to camp from here on their own. The boy drove the wagon off on a dirt fork away from the camp.

Josh grabbed Zeke with both hands on his shoulders and shook him. Zeke stopped his singing and protested "What tha devil you doin'." He twisted out of Josh's grip.

"Zeke, you got to straighten out so's we kin git back to camp," Josh said sternly. "We're to the front o' camp and we got to git past the guards."

Zeke pulled on his face and shook his head. "Ah'm alright, jes lead the way."

Josh set off through a cornfield beside the road, angling to the right of the depot. Zeke kept up behind him, holding onto his jacket, as they made their way toward the tracks. The corn was shoulder high and someone would have to be perched above to see them.

As they neared the tracks, the corn gave way to some waist high bushes and they both crouched to get to the edge of the field. They stopped so they could survey the rail tracks just beyond.

Josh quickly noticed a sentry far off to their right who seemed to be staying in one place. He looked down the track to the left and saw another sentry coming toward them. About twenty feet in front of them, the man paused to light a pipe and take a nip from his canteen. They got a good look at the soldier in the dress of an Alabama company.

Alabama soldiers were a likeable lot and had no problem mixing with the Mississippi troops. But any soldier on guard could never let them pass without challenge, or face punishment himself. They would have to cross to camp without being seen.

Josh pulled Zeke back from the edge a little ways. "We got to git him away from here so's we kin scramble over the tracks," he whispered to Zeke. Zeke nodded, but could offer no means to accomplish the task.

Josh thought a moment, then said, "Let me go off to'rd the other sentry and create a little ruckus to draw him over. Then maybe we kin make a break cross the tracks."

"I'll see if I kin add to the distracshun" Zeke said with a sly grin. "We kin meet right y'ere and cross over whilst they're occupied."

Josh nodded and moved off to the right. He found a dog trot path parallel to the tracks behind the bushes. He brushed past a stick scarecrow, then stopped in his tracks. Josh thought he might use the scarecrow, complete with jacket and old hat perched on top. He pulled the scarecrow up from the ground and trotted off a few more feet until he found a part between the brushy hedge.

He crept to the edge of the bushes and held the scarecrow beside him. The Alabama soldier was well down the tracks and the other sentry had his back to Josh.

He managed to stand up and hollered "Halt" as loud as he could, then heaved the scarecrow on to the tracks. He turned without looking and ran onto the trail back to Zeke. He could hear some shouting behind him.

Josh heard the clink of something hit the iron rail and Zeke yell, "Hold yer fire." A little farther on he spotted Zeke and watched him skim a stone against the train track in the direction Josh had come from. Josh called his name low and Zeke joined him to move a farther left to the spot where they had separated.

They peered between the bushes and surveyed the tracks to their right. Both sentries were approaching the scarecrow with rifles pointed. They ducked as the Sergeant of the Guard ran past them with a torch, moving down the tracks toward the commotion.

Zeke looked left and, seeing no one, said "C'mon." The two burst through the brush and swung over the tracks in a crouch. Tent line was about ten yards farther and they ran low all the way. They got in beyond the nearest row and slid down to a stop.

Only then did they look back toward the rails. The torch held by the sergeant bobbed up and down and they could make out some angry shouts from that direction. Winded, they rose slowly and moved quietly off to their section of the camp, their heads clearing with the exhilaration of their effort.

Josh was concerned an officer might spot them and demand an explanation of their presence outside their company area. But they encountered none and those soldiers who noticed them as they passed by indicated no interest at that late hour. Once they got back among the company, they took a few moments to find their tent in pitch darkness.

Will was dozing near the entrance and Walter seemed to be sleeping. Josh nudged Will awake and told him to get Walter up so he could drink. Zeke had poked the campfire into a low blaze and had a pot with water on the coals. In a few minutes the water was hot enough. Pouring a cup full, Josh added the licorice root and sassafras tea to brew.

Sitting in front of the glowing embers, Josh felt the fatigue rise in his body. He seemed to give out all at once and it was a struggle to keep his eyes open. Will took the tea back to his brother and Josh began to relax with completion of his chore.

Josh saw Zeke flat on his back and snoring across from him. He longed to do the same, but suddenly remembered the powder for Walter. He fished in his shirt pocket for the packet, smiling when he touched the eagle talon in his search, thinking the charm had served him again. Josh walked over to the tent where Will was holding a limp Walter up to drink the tea.

"You got to git this in him too," Josh said and motioned for Will to hold the cup up. Josh tore open the pouch and dumped the contents into the cup. Will swirled the mixture around.

"Druggist said that powder'd help loosen his bowels by mornin'," Josh told Will. "Make shur he drinks all of it."

Will stared up at him. "Josh, you and Zeke done a good thing fer Walter. We owe y'all," he said earnestly.

Josh smiled in return and grabbed two blankets for he an Zeke from the tent. He made his way to the campfire and covered Zeke as best he could before spreading his blanket on the ground. A noise drew his attention and he noticed a shadowed figure for the first time. Sergeant Ferrall stepped into the light of the fire, giving Josh a start.

"A bit restless tonight, lad," Ferrall said as Josh straightened to speak with the man. He knew by Ferrall's look that the First Sergeant understood what had happened. Josh wondered vaguely if one of his friends had told on the pair. Since the dull ache had returned to his head, Josh did not trust himself to respond.

"You'll be knowin' there's many an eye in camp don't miss much, though I don't believe any officer tis the wiser," Ferrall continued. "You'll not be leavin' camp without my permission in the future," the senior man declared sternly, "though you'll not be punished this time."

Ferrall walked away into the night, ignoring the sound sleeping Zeke. Josh relaxed and lay down upon his blanket. He stared at the stars above for a moment, reminding himself to tell Zeke of the favor bestowed by the Sergeant, then closed his eyes.

The next thing he knew, dawn was creasing the sky above him. His tongue was swollen inside a mouth full of cotton. Josh roused himself to get a drink of water, noticing that Zeke remained snoring in his blanket. As he stumbled to the canteen hanging from his tent, Walter Tucker rushed past holding his gut, running toward the latrines. Josh smiled to himself that at least somebody would feel better this morning than he did last night.

3

The heat and humidity of a Washington June day made every one in the Capital uncomfortable. However, Member of Congress Elihu Hawthorne of Massachusetts was particularly disturbed. He had been to the White House that morning and found the President to be "otherwise engaged." He had then journeyed to army headquarters to speak with the newly appointed commander, Irvin McDowell. There he had presented his card to an orderly with the instruction to notify the general that the Congressman wished to see him. The orderly glanced at him without proper respect for his office, Hawthorne noted, and simply asked him to have a seat. The Congressman had now occupied that seat for more than thirty minutes, waiting with others of lesser stature.

He spied a young junior officer making for the door to the inner sanctum with a leather satchel. Hawthorne waylaid the officer by the arm.

"Excuse me young man, I fear that General McDowell is not aware that Congressman Hawthorne of Massachusetts is waiting to see him. Would you be so kind as to announce me."

The officer brushed past him with a surprised look, saying only "See the orderly." Hawthorne was perturbed at this behavior and immediately confronted the orderly.

"Sergeant, I have been waiting for more than one-half hour to see General McDowell. Please summon him immediately,"

Hawthorne demanded. The orderly stared at him curiously. "Sir, the General is extremely busy," he replied sharply.

Hawthorne thumped his walking stick on the floor, silencing the Sergeant. "I do not wish to hear excuses, sir, please deliver my card to the General at once," he thundered.

Just then, a captain appeared beside him, saying, "My apologies Congressman, the General can see you now. Please follow me."

Hawthorne followed the officer through a door behind the Sergeant to confront a scene of bustling chaos. Officers shouted instructions to soldiers of every rank. Maps were pinned to boards and even walls. An enlisted man walked past him with a sheaf of telegrams. He continued behind the captain through another door to a smaller room adjacent.

The captain closed the door behind Hawthorne and announced, "General McDowell, I have the honor of presenting Congressman Hawthorne of Massachusetts."

A mature man in well tailored uniform rose in greeting. His face bore little expression, although the Congressman noted the lines and creases of fatigue. The General emerged from behind his desk and offered his hand, which Hawthorne shook politely. "What can I do for you, sir?" McDowell asked, gesturing toward a chair in front of the desk.

"General, I sense that you are a direct man and I will come to the point of my visit," Hawthorne began. "This rebellion must be crushed and the scoundrels who have fostered it brought to justice. I have come to determine what efforts the military are taking to deal with these traitors."

"Congressman, you can be assured that we are making plans now to confront the armed forces of rebellion in the east," McDowell said wearily.

"General, I have been advised that an army of these rebels lies not 30 miles to our south in Manassas, preparing to strike the capital. Such impudence must be dealt with immediately, sir, and harshly."

McDowell suppressed exasperation. "I am sure you must be aware that troops are arriving every day in Washington and it will take some time to prepare this army for battle," he noted.

Gesturing to the pile of papers on his desk, the commander of the eastern army added in a tolerant tone, "As you can see, there are details of supply and equipment which must be considered every day. In addition, I must become acquainted with the officers and fighting ability of the various regiments that have arrived. I can not embark this army on any enterprise until I have been assured that such action will be successful."

Hawthorne leaned toward him. "General, every day without punitive action emboldens these rebels to continue the effrontery of their so called Confederacy. We must strike them now and run these scoundrels from the field of battle. A sound thrashing will put a quick end to this rebellion," he instructed.

"Congressman, you can be sure that I and every one on my staff shares your desire to end this matter quickly." McDowell rose from his seat to suggest that the interview was over. "And I am sure that the fine men of Massachusetts will be among those who help to suppress this rebellion."

Hawthorne was not placated so easily and remained in his chair. "General McDowell, you can be sure the good men from Massachusetts will do their duty. You can also be sure that my constituents want military action. I have not been convinced that the gentleman in the White House is resolved to prosecute this matter thoroughly. Therefore, I look to you and the army to vanquish these traitors."

Hawthorne finally rose from his seat. Pointing the head of his cane toward McDowell, he said, "Today is the 10th of June. My constituents will expect a confrontation with these rebels before the month is out." He touched the brim of his hat with the walking stick in parting to the General.

"We shall make every effort to deal with the rebels as soon as possible," McDowell said, coming from behind the desk to guide his visitor to the door. "If you would be so kind as to find your way out, I have some tasks for the Captain."

Hawthorne added a "Good day to you sir" without turning. The Captain closed the door behind Hawthorne, just in time to prevent him from hearing the commanding general of the Union forces utter a string of obscenities directed to politicians in general and Massachusetts' Congressmen in particular.

>< >< >< >< ><

Joshua Campbell was having a hard time writing home. He had put off the task for some time, though his failure to send word had nagged him since arriving in Corinth. His mother would be anxious for news. But he was lost at how to begin or even what to relate.

Letters and news had arrived from Holly Springs with some regularity through various visitors to camp. Mostly clergy and a few well to do citizens who could afford the time and effort to travel. They would eat with the officers and perhaps watch the company drill. Visiting parsons always contrived to lead a prayer service. Though generally careless of religious activities, to a man the Rangers welcomed letters and parcels from home. Cakes and sweet breads were valued more than letters, though the letters survived longer to be savored over and over.

Josh had received a package through the minister of the Presbyterian Church in Holly Springs. Largely foodstuffs, his mother had included a two page letter with the admonition to remember his Christian upbringing and relaying the hope he was in good health. He knew he had to reply, if only to reassure the family he was fine.

Josh had envisioned letters home full of glory and excitement, filling his family with pride and, perhaps, envy. The reality of army life was hardly inspiring. Days were filled with drill and drudgery. Many of the men in camp had become careless of personal hygiene. Vices such as liquor and gambling had infiltrated the camp and, together with the monotony, led to raw feelings and occasional scraps. It was impossible to translate the world around him into a letter that would not be fearful or plain boring to his family.

He had related the escapade with Zeke in a short letter to Rebecca and managed to filter some information about military life in a way that should have impressed her. Of course, to Rebecca he could write of how she was in his thoughts and how he missed her, things a young girl would like to hear. That would not do to satisfy his folks.

There was little time left in the midday break and Josh had still not scratched a word when Davy Williams rushed in to the group near the campfire.

"Y'all gon to git a chance now to shoot some Yankees! We leave for Virginny tomorrow, to join the army up there."

Riley Osborne stepped closer to him. "You ain't foolin' us," he asked. Davy looked him in the eye. "Pard, I swear by the good Lord it's true. I heard the Cap'n tell the officers and sergeants. The whole regiment is goin' north."

Josh was convinced by Davy and he noticed cheers from other parts of the camp. He looked about to see men in little groups all over.

Williams told them afternoon drill was cancelled to allow for preparations. Davy did not know their exact destination, but he told all of them he thought they were going to Richmond. Hugh Driscoll reminded him there were no Yankees in Richmond and they would likely be going closer to the Virginia border with Maryland. The others expressed their agreement with Hugh and Williams got irked and refused to say any more. The group broke up as they wandered off to handle personal matters before leaving.

Now Josh had something to write home about and he knew he'd have to get a letter off that day. He sat down and wrote quickly, starting with the big news about their departure for Virginia. He added some limited information about camp and told them he was in good health and spirits. He wrote about some of the boys they knew and made sure to say that he had visited with the Presbyterian minister. He concluded by saying he would write from the new camp and tell them where he was. The letter was little more than a page, but it was a chore accomplished and he did not dally with afterthoughts. He slipped the letter into an envelope and trotted off to the camp dispensary, which included the posting office.

At the dispensary he encountered a fellow he knew from Holly Springs in the Confederate Guards

"Y'all hear the news, Josh," Lemuel Morse asked him, "we headin' fer Virginia."

"I heard," Josh said, "but I ain't heard where we goin' exactly."

Morse looked around before he spoke and leaned closer to Josh. "I got a cousin is one o' the Colonel's adjutants and he told me we goin' to a place called Manassas Junction up near Washington City. There's a whole army formin' there and the 18th Mississippi's leaving today fer the same place."

"The boys're itchin' to go and fight Federals," Morse said. "Course, we got a few that's too sick to go. I'm glad to be shut o' this place. Guards is down five men since we come here."

"Yeah, we lost a few to sickness too," Josh rejoined. "They'll likely git better and join us up north. But we got plenty left to fight."

Josh bid his friend goodbye and began the short walk back to his company area. All about him were indications of departure. Soldiers were packing gear and cleaning firearms. A few had washed clothes and hung them on lines to dry. Enthusiasm for the move north bristled through camp.

Josh had learned the Regiment would be shipping ten companies. Officially, the colorful company names had been replaced with letters A through K. Still, most soldiers identified themselves by company name and county in northern Mississippi.

In addition to the Rangers, the Samuel Benton Relief Rifles and Lem Morse's Confederate Guards also hailed from Marshall

17n 1 5wrs

County. The Quitman Grays and the Rough and Ready Volunteers called Pontotoc County home.

Chickasaw County had sent the Buena Vista Rifles and the Burnsville Blues were out of Tishomingo County. DeSoto County had contributed the Pettus Rifles and the Magnolia Guards had been raised in Calhoun County. The Panola Vindicators included their home county in their name.

As the day gave way to night, a mood of celebration passed through the camp, accompanied by fiddles, banjos and homemade instruments. Hard liquor appeared at many campfires. Whether from libations or pure relief, patriotic songs and cheers circulated among departing men to the envy of those remaining.

Josh had celebrated with the others, but declined any spirits. The big head he had suffered after his night in town was fresh in his mind and he did not want to risk one for the coming train ride. Besides, he was overcome by exhilaration of the moment and needed nothing else to enliven him.

The celebration carried well past midnight and sleep was near impossible, if not hazardous. Those who tried to catch a few winks were roused if spotted, often by a douse of cold water. Eventually, though, the carousing died off and soldiers attempted a few hours of shut eye.

Sergeants moved through the companies before dawn rousing men. Ferrall had awakened his charges and Dutchie followed a short time later to be sure no one had retreated to his bedroll. Josh, Zeke and the Tuckers cleared their tent and rolled their blankets. Leaving their gear behind, they stumbled off to the breakfast being served for the regiment.

Josh noticed Zeke's hat askew. On closer look, the cap was different than the one he'd worn before. Josh asked his friend about the new headgear.

"Some damned bandit stole mah cap las' night," Zeke noted irritably. "I appropriated this un from one o' the Guards."

Josh checked an impulse to laugh. Zeke was always

particular about his hats, making sure they fit just right and kept in good repair. He had worked with the Rangers kepi for some weeks until it perched just so on his head. The model he wore now had been carelessly used.

"You got any suspects fer this terrible crime," Josh asked with a chuckle.

"I'll be keepin' mah eye out," Zeke replied and Josh could see his friend was in no mood for jest. "I catch one o' the boys with mah cap, he'll be sorry," Zeke declared.

Josh laughed at Zeke's determined tone, but Zeke saw no humor in his situation.

"You watch yerself next time you go celebratin'," Josh cracked. "You best wear a bonnet so's you don' lose this un." Josh gave in to the belly laugh that shook him. Zeke simmered with disgust.

The morning meal was a hurried affair as everyone tried to eat at once. The troop train had arrived at the depot and boarding was set to begin soon. Josh managed to get some coffee and biscuits and Zeke shared some of his bacon. Josh stowed a biscuit against infrequent meals on the long train ride.

As they made their way back to their gear, Dutchie appeared with instructions.

"Ve ist to board der train soon. Please to bring der bags quick now."

Josh and the others grabbed their satchels and equipment to follow the Corporal. As they formed by company, Josh was struck by the loading operation. Lines of soldiers waited to board cars of the Memphis and Charleston train. Enlisted men were assigned to cars and boarded with their belongings, officers designated to separate, less crowded, cars. The Regiment was now complete with band, medical men, and staff officers. Room was found for all. Freight cars bore equipment, baggage, officers' horses and those servants who would remain with their masters. The train was longer than any Josh had seen before.

The Rangers squeezed into two of the cars, with the

quickest securing enough bench space to sit. Despite inadequate room for all there were few complaints among soldiers in anticipation of departure. The whistle sounded and the train began to move.

The 17th Mississippi departed from Corinth bound for Stevenson, Alabama, where the men, equipment and baggage were transferred from the Memphis and Charleston to the Nashville and Chattanooga rail line. Continuing across Alabama and part of Georgia, the Regiment would ride the N & C all the way to Chattanooga, Tennessee. At Chattanooga, the 17th was to board cars of the East Tennessee and Georgia Railroad for the comparatively shorter journey to Knoxville, Tennessee. In Knoxville, the train then converted to the rails of the East Tennessee and Virginia line for the run to Danville, Virginia. Once in Virginia, the troops were to be transferred to the Virginia and Tennessee Railroad for transport to Lynchburg. The Mississippians would board the last cars of their journey in Lynchburg, those of the Orange and Alexandria Railroad, to their final destination, Manassas Junction on the O & A.

Through Alabama and Georgia, people hailed the Mississippi troops as brothers in a patriotic struggle, freely exhibiting their support. Rail stations were draped with the Confederate national flag, two bold red stripes and single white stripe. Some stations sported the newest version with eleven white stars for each state, though the seven starred flag was still displayed. Civilians offered food and drink when the train stopped, and occasionally a band would appear to entertain, at which time the Regimental band was ordered to reciprocate.

Josh found little remarkable in the trip through Alabama. As they neared Tennessee, the landscape changed. Zeke was awed by the mountains near Chattanooga, clinging to the window and pointing to the highest rises. Josh grew tired of his friend's commentary and longed for a quiet ride.

The 17th found a warm reception in Chattanooga. Men were allowed to leave the station area as materials were switched to the East Tennessee & Georgia cars. Nearby eating and drinking establishments were flooded with rail weary soldiers. Many hours later, with some basic needs satisfied, men accommodated their confinement as the journey resumed.

There was little patriotic fervor in eastern Tennessee and stops along the E T & V were met largely with indifference. An incident in Knoxville puzzled the Rangers who witnessed it. Halted at the station for a little while as cars were added from a siding, men were confined to the train though officers were allowed to disembark. Restless soldiers crowded windows for any view of the town or inhabitants. Hugh spotted a young, light haired beauty escorted by an older woman and tried to attract her attention with calls and whistles. She and her escort resolutely refused to look toward the train as they walked by.

Driscoll was bold enough to holler "Darlin', that shur is perty dress fer a Southron lady." The young woman snapped her head toward him and cried, "I'm not one of your rebel hussies."

She took a step toward the car to the astonishment of everyone, including the motherly woman with her. "You disgrace our country with this rebellion and offend our heritage," she screamed to the now quiet cars. "You will see the error of your ways end in hellfire, and the Union emerge triumphant."

She seemed ready to say more, but her guardian managed to coax her away from the train. Hugh was silenced, but others who heard her paused only a moment before retaliating with jeers and whistles as she retired. Shortly after, the train lurched into motion away from the station.

As he settled in to his seat the strong emotion of the woman chilled Josh with the weight of prophecy. He just naturally assumed everyone in the South supported the Cause. Josh had not conceived that a native Southerner could be against Southern independence. The incident troubled him, but it seemed a solitary note of discord on the journey and the unsettled feeling dispelled with the miles. He wrote off Knoxville, Tennessee in his mind as an inhospitable place and one to which he would not willingly return.

The welcome turned much warmer in Virginia as the entire populace embraced arriving soldiers. Young ladies in some towns bestowed flowers and handmade keepsakes on the warriors. To the chagrin and envy of older soldiers, they demurely declined invitations to kiss any but the blushing drummer boys. These exhibitions of gratitude and pride heartened all of the men and relieved the tedium of a seemingly endless train ride.

On June 17, 1861, the Regiment disembarked at Manassas Junction, Virginia. The 17th Mississippi had arrived at the eastern front in the War Between the States.

4

The extensive rail yard at Manassas teemed with hordes of drovers, freightmen, laborers and slaves in a constant motion. Rail cars were relieved of military supplies as quickly as they arrived. Wagons moved in a constant stream away from the yard toward a field of white called Camp Walker. Soldiers of the 17th retrieved their gear and formed ranks beside the tracks. As Lieutenants shouted "Forward", the men moved off in step toward the canvas covered plain.

They marched nearly a mile to arrive at their designated camp site. As they passed, soldiers in camp stopped to look at the arriving troops. Near a group of men beneath the flag of Virginia, Davy Williams called out "Mississippi is y'ere, boys." Sergeant Ferrall immediately called him down, but the Virginia troops waved and cheered in greeting. A little later, the Rangers passed men who said they were from North Carolina. Riley taunted them, "What're you tar heels doin' here."

"Told us to make sure you Mississippi boys stick on the battlefield," one of the men responded.

The 17th bivouacked near the 18th Mississippi. Wagons bearing their camp equipment had already arrived and the soldiers were issued tents. Zeke got one for Josh and the Tuckers. Officers supervised placement and tents began to sprout on poles and ropes.

A group of men found themselves without tents and began

to complain to an officer. Josh saw the group break up and scatter about. Some of these men fit in with others, but some were bound to spend the early days in camp sleeping under the stars.

As their tent began to rise, Dutchie came by to tell them to draw rations. By agreement, the arrangement started in Corinth was to hold in their new camp. Charlie went to obtain the food while Riley began preparations. The Tuckers set off to secure firewood. Davy and Hugh had vanished to explore their surroundings.

Josh and Zeke tended to their belongings, then drifted over to the 18th's area in search of a distant cousin of Zeke in the regiment. They didn't locate him, but talked with a tent mate named Tom.

"How long y'all bin here," Zeke asked the sleepy eyed soldier.

"Jes got in early yesterday," he replied. "Ain't had much time to settle in. They's a regiment from Sou' Carolina jes over there," he pointed to some conical tents near the 17th's area. "Men from all over the South here."

"Whar's the Yanks," Josh put in with a smile.

"Ain't seen none yet," Tom grinned. "But I heard sum o' the Sou' Carolina boys run into 'em north o' here in a place called Vienna and a few of them Federals won' be no more trouble. That regiment's lettin' ever one know they drew first blood," he added.

"At one of the train stops, fellow told us 'bout a battle at a place called Big Bethel in Virginia. Said the Yanks 'uz sent packin' in that un too," Zeke remarked.

"Yea, we heard 'bout that'n. But Big Bethel is clear t'other side of Richmond, perty far from here."

They chatted on a few minutes about acquaintances in either regiment until Josh reminded Zeke they had to get back for dinner. They took their leave of Tom with a message to tell Zeke's cousin they had called to see him and a sketchy description of where their company was located.

When they got back to the mess, Riley had already started

the dinner meal. Charlie Akins was boiling coffee while Will
Tucker chopped firewood. Zeke pitched in with Will and Josh
helped Riley with the food.

They were blessed this meal with fresh beef and potatoes,
a nice change from the salt pork and crackers issued during the
train journey. Riley had some corn meal baking in the coals and
coffee to drink. The hot food tasted good and nurtured a kind
feeling toward their new home.

After the meal, Davy got stuck with cleanup and the others
tended to camp chores and personal matters. Many in the 17th
visited with the 18th and some of the 18th came over to mix with
the new arrivals.

Just as night fell, some of the South Carolina soldiers
bivouacked near the 17th filtered in to the camp. These men were
from the 5th South Carolina Regiment and sported tall black
campaign hats adorned with palmetto tree sprigs. Their dress
uniform was a frock coat of light gray with two rows of brass
buttons. The Mississippi uniforms seemed plain in comparison.

Josh found the South Carolina boys likeable, but boastful.
They were quick to remind their state was first to secede and to
claim first northern blood. The soldiers from the 5th had seen no
hostile fire at Sumter or anyplace else, but were ready to
appropriate the actions of their brethren as their own.

The Palmetto State troops came bearing cakes and pies,
and the Mississippi soldiers were pleased to partake of the
delicacies. They seemed to have plenty, including a generous
supply of spirits, which were toted about by servants.

While munching on a slice of apple pie, Josh heard the
routine at their new home, Camp Walker, from a Carolinian
named Matthew.

"Y'all going to march a couple o' miles each day,"
Matthew said. "We generally march out of camp a mile or so and
halt for firing drills. Then we march round some more and come
back to camp after midday."

"There's a little stream called the Bull Run just north of

here and we get to scout the fords on occasion," he added. "It's a fair march to the stream, but the officers let us a take a little break and cool off in the water."

"Y'all be detailed to stand your share o' guard duty, though we really trying to keep the boys from slipping out," Matthew continued.   "No hostiles have been spotted hereabouts. Sundays are for services and such devotions, but there's no duties on that day and y'all can do as you wish, though you ain't s'posed to leave camp."

The talkative South Carolinian paused, but another one responded to Zeke's question about what there was doing around the camp.   "There's a town at the rail junction for those willing to risk the ramble," a smallish fellow with a big knife on his belt said. "The sutlers come by each day with food and spirits, though the prices are right high. And towards the back of camp, there's some friendly ladies that'll do your wash," the short soldier added with a wink of his eye.

The soldier named Matthew started up again. "We get plenty of visitors each day. Politicians and preachers are thick as flies and just as worrisome, but they are often accompanied by young ladies eager to meet the South's finest."

Matthew drew breath long enough for Riley Osborne to put in a question.   "How many men you reckon're here," he asked.

Another South Carolinian, clearly affected by spirits, answered in a loud voice. "Must be 20,000 men, and more comin' each day.   We got boys here from Alabama and Georgia, Louisiana and North Carolina. And more damn Virginians than we need. These Virginia boys stick to themselves and act like they don't need no help to fight the unionists."

The other Carolina soldiers muttered their agreement to these sentiments and conversation slowed. When Hugh Driscoll asked who was in command, the drunken South Carolinian shouted "Beauregard, Hero of Sumter." A toast was offered to the general and the visiting soldiers began to move off toward other campfires.

"Y'all be good, but not too good," the fellow named Matthew said in parting.

Josh had grown tired as the evening wore on and took this chance to slip away to his tent. Cool night air helped sleep came easily. As he drifted off, Josh felt content that he had arrived among friends and wondered how, with so many soldiers around, the Yankees could dare to attack.

Marching and drill consumed the days following the 17th's arrival as predicted. Drills became more complicated as regimental formation was added to company drill. In battle order, skirmishers were advanced in front as companies formed two ranks behind. Inevitably, companies vied for the same place or gaps occurred in formation, and arguments developed amongst the officers. Forming ten companies of men seemed more than the officers could handle. Colonel Featherston bluntly made his complaints known to the Captains and Lieutenants, who in turn barked at the line soldiers. Only after several days of hard drill beneath an unforgiving sun and the hard glare of officers did men form and advance as a regiment.

The Rangers were often ordered forward as skirmishers and thus avoided the blundering. As skirmishers, the Rangers spent more time looking to their rear at the chaos behind them, than they did looking forward. Josh despaired of battle when the men might have to form ranks with the added element of enemy fire.

The heat and constant drill created a steady stream of casualties from the ranks. Overcome with exhaustion, some of the men would stumble off to find shade or make their way to the sick tents. The exodus of soldiers during drills contributed to disruption in the ranks and angered their superiors. But the heat respected no rank and even officers swooned under its effect.

Josh was worn out each evening and had little energy to do more than help with the dinner meal. He needed to relax by the campfire just to gather strength for the following day. But

Zeke was among some in the company who spurned quiet evenings in favor of searching for whatever the camp had to offer.

Along with Hugh Driscoll and Davy Williams on occasion, Zeke wandered about nightly and usually returned to sleep late with the smell of spirits about him. Josh had been sickened by his first encounter with liquor, but Zeke had remarked on the good feeling it gave him. Spirits, and drink that passed for spirits, seemed plentiful in camp and Zeke had joined the imbibers.

One evening during dinner, Zeke settled down to eat with Josh.

"Ya got some time for yer old pard," he said.

"Thought maybe you was too busy each night fer me," Josh replied with a little edge to his voice.

"Ah wisht you'd come along with me and t'others, there's a lot to see round this camp," Zeke went on. "All you wanna do is sit round the fire. I figure on havin' some fun each night, cause I sure ain't havin' no fun in the daytime."

"I ain't lookin' to fill my gut with spirits fer a good time, if tha's what yer sayin'," Josh put in.

"Well the spirits jes help the good times along an take the edge off the day," Zeke said evenly. "An I'm gettin' to meet some fellers from all over the South each night. Those Alabama boys know how to tie one on," he remarked.

"Yer burnin' the candle at both ends, Zeke, an somethin' has to give," Josh said, looking directly at his friend. "You bin suckin' water durin' the drills and you had to fall out on march yisterday."

"Aw, I kin look after my own self," Zeke said flatly. "Sides, you ought to roam 'bout with us stead of sittin' here all moped up each night," Zeke added to goad Josh a little.

"I got enough to keep me busy, if I want to," Josh said defensively.

"Well, Hugh and I figure to check out them washer ladies at the back of the camp t'night. We hear they right friendly to'rds us sojers."

"I'll let you know what we find out," Zeke said as he rose with an empty plate. "Say, you ain't got a spare dollar or two till pay day?"

Josh dug in his pocket and flipped Zeke a dollar coin. "I'm a little short mah self till we git paid," Josh told him.

Zeke wandered off to join Hugh. Riley and Charlie offered some company this night as they always did, but Josh stowed his mess kit and slipped off toward Sergeant Ferrall's tent.

Since the regiment had begun to prepare for battle, Josh sensed there was more to soldiering than carrying a rifle. He had assumed that officers would direct all movements on the battlefield. But watching the chaotic placement of companies in line and hearing misdirected orders, he began to think it would be healthy for him to know a little more about what he was supposed to do.

He naturally gravitated to the one man in the company he knew had some fighting experience, Sergeant Timothy Ferrall. The compact Irishman seemed to know what he was doing and a keen sense of what others, even officers, should be doing. Josh sought out the Sergeant to learn what he could expect if and when firing started.

The talkative Irishman could be found every night in front of the tent he shared with the Second Sergeant. He was a genial fellow by nature and tended to orders without raising his voice. But he was thick muscled and solidly built. Every man in the company, even bigger men like Bradwell, instinctively knew the Sergeant was not a man to cross.

Ferrall could spin a story and Josh had usually found it hard to extract the information he wanted. He had learned about the Sergeant's early life as a boy in Ireland. Josh knew he had been orphaned early and served as an apprentice in a mill. The back breaking work had developed a boy's body into that of a man, but he had been ripe to fall for the pitch of a British army recruiter.

"Fact is, I lied to the recruitin' sergeant about my age so's I could join," Ferrall had recalled. "Those lads in their red blouses looked fancy and well kept to a hungry boy from County Cork. So I took the shilling and served her majesty in the 95th Derbyshire Foot," Ferrall had explained more than once.

This night Josh hallowed his First Sergeant and squatted near the fire. He hoped to hear more of the lessons Ferrall had learned in the British army. The older man had told him he was sent to the Crimean War within two months after he had enlisted. Josh had only a vague idea of where Crimea was and it's location on the globe held no importance to Ferrall. His only comment was that it was far from Ireland.

"Sergeant, you was tellin' 'bout that Crimea War las' evenin' fore you got called by the Lieutenant," Josh said in opening. "How much trainin' y'all have fore you went to battle," he asked.

Ferrall took a long pull on his pipe before he spoke. "The Brits force new recruits to follow orders and load and fire quick like. I could do both by the time I landed in the Crimea courtesy of the meanest son of a bitch on God's green earth.

"My Sergeant Jameson was a big Englishman who'd been in the army his whole life and hated all Irishmen. He cussed me every day until he was killed at Sevastopol. Truth is lad, I was more afraid of him than I was of the Roosians," Ferrall noted wistfully.

"You think we done 'nuf trainin' yet fer a battle," Josh asked, keen to get a fix on Regimental readiness.

Ferrall glanced around before he spoke to make sure that no one was within listening distance. Then he leaned toward Josh and fixed his eyes directly on the younger man.

"Lad, this Regiment ain't ready to fight. The line officers don't know how to fight, and they'll disremember what they learned when the bullets fly. Half the men will probably run when they catch sight of a Yankee and the other half are likely to shit themselves." Ferrall could not have issued a lower assessment.

The comment stung Josh hard, and though he was not about to speak for officers, he tried to salvage some respect for the ranks. "We all of us kin load and fire our rifles in volley, Sergeant, and we doin' better ever day at formin' ranks."

"You'll be knowin' there's a difference tryin' to get off a shot when someone is shootin' back, lad," Ferrall said with a note of exasperation in his voice. "We've yet to get through commands to load and fire without one of the lads fumblin' with his rifle or losin' his rammer. And the rest of the ranks snickerin' at the culprit."

An awkward silence intruded as Josh realized the low opinion Ferrall had of the regiment included him.

"You were thinkin' the lads'll fight to a man," Ferrall guessed and Josh nodded his agreement. "There's aplenty of what my old sergeant called 'piss and vinegar' among the lads. But you'll soon find spirit wears off when the lead flies."

Ferrall leaned toward Josh and clapped him on the shoulder. "When the shootin' starts, lad, you stay by me, I'll see you through. You'll want to run, but fight the urge, and do as I do. And learn to load and fire that weapon so's you'll be doin' it in yer sleep.

"Don't worry too much, young Campbell, the Federals are just as likely to run first," the wily Irishman added with a wink.

The veteran fighter's comments had touched a sore spot and Josh searched for understanding.

"How come you to join the comp'ny if you thought we wuz all wet behind t'ears," he challenged.

"Colonel's the only reason I'm here, riskin' life and limb," Ferrall declared. "That man has treated me kindly in the past. He asked me personal to be First Sergeant when the company was formed."

The older man leaned back on his stool with a thoughtful smile. "After the war in Crimea, my regiment returned to England. By then I'd had my fill of soldiering.

"So when we landed in the great port at Liverpool, I

slipped away from my mates and roamed the docks. I found an old cutter bound for America that needed a crew and a captain who asked no questions. I signed on and worked hard until we dropped anchor in the city of Baltimore."

Josh had heard of the Maryland city to the north of Washington.

"I took my leave of that ship when the old captain was in his cups one night," Ferrall continued. "Baltimore was not a friendly place for the Irish and the copper's were on my tail soon as I set foot in town.

"By a stroke of luck I happened on a fellow hirin' for the railroad. It was hard work totin' rails to replace track, but so long as I did my job and took the bosses guff, I had a place for my head and a jingle in my pocket.

"I took leave of the rail crew in Holly Springs on no more than a hope to settle in one place. By luck again, I met Featherston my first day in town. A word from him gave me a start in the livery business."

Ferrall paused as if remembering something that brought a smile to his face. "I'll not hear a word against that man. When he asked me to join the company, I could not say no."

Though Josh held some interest in the narrative, he had come to find out about the Regiment's readiness.

"How long you reckon we got 'til we fight the Yanks," he asked.

Ferrall gave a short laugh when he spoke. "You best put that question to an officer, but you'll be meeting the elephant before the summer's out, lad."

Josh was about to ask the Sergeant to explain his meaning when Ferrall interjected. "You'll not be familiar with the expression 'seeing the elephant', lad, but you'll soon know," and refused to explain more.

Puzzled, Josh wanted to question further, but Ferrall continued his earlier response.

"The generals figure out how we fight, but the politicians

tell us when we fight. The high and mighty started this war and they won't be letting two armies full of men set about fer too long without some blood on the ground," the Irishman remarked somberly.

"Fightin' Yankees got to be better than drill ever day," Josh declared boldly.

"You'll soon get your wish, though you'll be dreamin' of quieter days after you've had yer fill of battle," Ferrall cautioned. He was interrupted by a drummer boy with a message that the Captain needed him. Josh wandered back to his tent with his pride dented, but much to think about.

Ferrall's words haunted Josh in the following days as men and officers of the Regiment continually proved the Sergeant right. Josh had resolved to take drills more seriously and doubled his effort to load his rifle faster. But the others proved far less serious and little inclined to improve their skills. The men could see no value in constant, repetitive drill and longed to meet their foe, fearing that drill would dull, rather than sharpen, readiness.

Davy brought the mess news one evening that a photographer had set up at the edge of camp. He went on about soldiers who had pictures made to send home to family and sweethearts. He had seen some of the results and noted the impressive military bearing of the subjects. Josh decided a picture would be a good keepsake to send home and readily agreed to join Zeke when his friend asked.

One afternoon when the company was dismissed early from drill, the two men went in search of the photographer. They spotted a canvas covered wagon parked in a grassy field, 'Ellis Fitch - Photographic Artist' emblazoned boldly on the side. A sizeable tent was pitched nearby and men lined up at the entrance. Zeke and Josh piled in behind a dozen others, but the line moved steadily.

A sign just under the tent flap set forth the price, two dollars each man. Zeke and Josh had talked of having a photo together, but decided during the wait to have individual pictures.

As they stepped in to the tent, the photographer's assistant explained the basic picture was something he called a 'carte de visite', a picture mounted on a thick paper card. The assistant collected their money, pointed in the direction of a pile of weapons and told them to take a pick.

Besides the pistols, rifles, and swords available, Josh noticed large, thick bladed Bowie knives. He disdained the impractical weapon and instead stuck a pistol in his belt and grabbed a bayoneted rifle to hold. However, with a bold smile Zeke scooped up the big knife in one hand and added a pistol to the other.

Photographer Fitch was a short, balding man of perpetual motion. He beckoned Zeke to a place in front of a blanketed wall, between two standing columns. Slipping behind the camera, he peered through the instrument and motioned Zeke slightly to the right and forward. Zeke straightened and hefted the knife and pistol across his chest, assuming a stern, scowling look Josh thought unlike his usual countenance. The photographer pulled the camera cover over his head, making some noises with the camera, all the while reminding Zeke to stand still. After a few minutes, the photographer emerged and told Zeke to put the weapons back in the pile. Then it was Josh's turn.

Josh smoothed his hair and straightened his uniform, then stepped to the place where Zeke had been. He decided to hold the rifle across his chest with both hands and tried to assume a fierce scowl like Zeke. But it was not in Josh to look so and he could only manage the expression with effort. As the photographer fooled with his camera, Zeke pulled a face and caught his friend's attention. Josh's harsh look softened and he only stifled a broad grin with great effort. The camera man cautioned him again to stay still as he took the photograph. Finally, the man emerged from behind the camera and dismissed his subjects.

They made their way back to the company area expecting to return next day for the finished picture. Zeke rattled on about how mean and warlike they looked and how impressed family and friends would be by their distant warriors. Josh was less enthused, though he nodded agreement with Zeke. The confident, warlike posture, complete with costume weapons, of the photograph contrasted sharply with Ferrall's comments that the men of the 17th would likely falter when they encountered the Federals. His Sergeant's low opinion nagged at him and stuck in his mind in a way that was hard to ignore. With some relief, Josh realized the camera could not picture his troubled thoughts.

5

To commemorate the Confederacy's birth a grand parade had been scheduled for the fourth day of July. Dignitaries from Richmond joined Generals to review the regiments at Manassas. The public was invited to this show of Southern military might, dotting a low hillside beside the parade route. Regimental bands competed to provide a concert of martial airs and patriotic songs. "Maryland, My Maryland" received an enthusiastic response as an invitation to the sister state to join the Confederacy.

Since the Magnolia State Regiments were placed near the end of the march, Josh and Zeke decided to catch a glimpse of other regiments before being called to formation. Midday heat rose with the sun and, with others from the mess, they sought a shady spot on the hillside at the beginning of the parade route.

"I shoulda figered them Virginy boys would lead off," Zeke remarked as the review began while they settled on a grassy spot. "Them boys do have a shine about 'em," he added.

Josh could see the Virginians fairly sparkled in the bright sun. Most had silver breast buckles where the leather straps crossed their jackets. Their polished rifles gleamed, though they were many different makes and styles. Virginia regiments favored gray frock coats that were drawn around the waist and ended about mid thigh. Pants were usually gray or light blue, although a very few units wore white. Headgear was most often the kepi or forage cap in the home state regiments, with some affecting the cloth covering called a havelock for their neck.

"Sum o' those boys is wearin' blue uniforms," Josh pointed out to Zeke. "Might not be too healthy if they get mixed in with them blue coated Yankees," he noted.

Following the Virginians · came the proud South Carolinians. These men also wore gray frock coats, but with a grander design employing double rows of brass buttons on the chest. White dress pants were more in evidence on these fellows along with the tall, wide-brimmed campaign hat marked by the palmetto sprig.

"Them boys look too perty to do much fightin,'" Zeke commented dryly.

As the parade wound on, the regiments from Alabama, North Carolina, Arkansas and Tennessee appeared in succession. They were fewer in number and wore plainer outfits than the men from Virginia and South Carolina. Soldiers from these states tended toward coarse woven battle shirts instead of jackets. Shirt colors went from red for some of the Alabama troops to a light buff color for North Carolinians. Rather than upright hats, these troops tended toward slouch hats with wavy brims to shade the head. There was little evidence of brass in these regiments.

Riley Osborne gave a low whistle and pointed to the next group of men. "Wouldja look at them fellers," he said.

"That's Wheat's Tigers, Luziana troops," Zeke commented. "Them boys might dress peculiar, but their hellacious fighters," he added in a tone that made Josh wonder if his friend had encountered some in his nightly wanderings.

The Tigers wore the most unusual clothing in the army. Styled on the Zouave uniform from France, the outfit consisted of a short navy blue jacket with red trim over blousy blue and white striped pants that ended below the knee. For headgear they sported a sort of red stocking cap. Many wore a belt holding a fearsome looking long knife and they all held the Mississippi rifle.

"I see the 17th is formin' up," Riley said, rising from his seat. "We bes be gettin' back to the company."

"Aw, we'll be 'nother hour 'fore we step off," Zeke said without moving from his reclined position.

"B'lieve I'll stay awhile, too," Josh said to Riley. Osborne shrugged his shoulders and trotted off to join the rest of the company.

Josh noticed that the Washington Artillery would be in line behind his regiment. He admired the artillerymen from New Orleans greatly, judging them the finest looking soldiers in the army. They were attired in blue frock coats with a single row of brass buttons down the front. Cuffs and collars were trimmed in bands of red and their light blue pants bore red stripes on the sides. Each man wore a solid red kepi and each had a badge on his chest with the motto "Try Us".

"I could stay here all day," Zeke sighed, stretching full out on the ground. "I had mah fill o' marchin' in midday heat and I don't reckon to be missed in that crowd."

Josh sympathized with the thought and leaned back on the hillside. He noticed two figures making their way toward the shade to his left. As they approached, he could see a little girl leading a young woman. The young lady held a parasol above her, but seemed unsteady on her feet.

The two settled in shade about twenty yards from Zeke and Josh. The girl began to fan the young woman who appeared to be in some distress, then she got up and started down the hill toward a water wagon holding barrels of water for the troops. Leaning on his elbow, Josh spoke to her as she walked by.

"Y'all git mud on that fine dress if you go down to that wagon, little miss," he said.

"Mah sister has swooned in this heat and she dearly needs a drink of water to calm her," the little girl said, her voice betraying some anxiety.

Zeke had noticed the girl by now and spoke up. "We got some water you kin take over to yer sister," he said, rising and handing the girl the canteen he had brought with him.

The youngster accepted the canteen and ran to the young

woman reclining beneath the parasol. Josh and Zeke made their way over to the ailing woman.

As they approached, Josh could see the little girl pour water in to a cup and offer it to her sister. The young woman beneath the parasol wore a light crinoline dress fluffed with numerous petticoats that made her position on the grass seem awkward. The young girl fanned her sister ardently while she drank. As they approached from behind, neither man could see the face of the reclined young woman.

When they were very close the little girl said, "Annie, these are the soldiers who gave me the water."

The parasol swung to the side and Josh beheld the profile of a stunningly beautiful young woman. A faint smile creased her soft, round race, framed with auburn hair falling in curly rolls to her shoulders. The heat flush brought a becoming red color to her cheeks, reflecting the pink color of her dress. Her long eyelashes fluttered over hazel eyes as she turned her head toward them. She spoke in a tone just above a whisper that softened her Virginia accent.

"Ah am obliged for your assistance, gentlemen. Ah fear ah have been careless with tha heat," she said, moistening her brow and cheeks with the wet cloth.

"Ah am Anne Marlow and this is my sister, Mary, whom you have met," she noted as the two Mississippians stood mute. "May ah inquire as to tha regiment you serve," she said with a faint smile that invited a response.

Josh glanced at Zeke before he replied. Zeke stood dumbfounded in the presence of the Virginia belle. Josh cleared his throat to compose himself.

"The 17th Mississippi, m'am," he managed to croak.

"Well Mississippi can be proud of her gallant sons, and ah am most grateful for your courtesy to me," she said, pointedly smiling at Josh.

Josh pulled his cap off and introduced the two. "Joshua Campbell and Ezekial Owens at yer service, m'am."

Before she could say more, a shrill male voice just behind them brought Zeke and Josh out of their stupor.

"You privates will return to the comp'ny, now," Jasper Welburn said sharply. Then he noticed the two young ladies seated on the ground and removed his cap, transfixed by the beautiful Anne.

"My apologies m'am, these men are needed in the ranks," he said, bowing slightly. "Perhaps an officer can be of greater assistance to you."

"Jasper, we kin handle our own selves y'ere. You ain't needed," Zeke said crossly.

Welburn straightened, turned and glared at Zeke. Josh could see by the look Zeke returned that his friend was not in a compromising mood. He grabbed Zeke's arm and turned him aside. "We bes be gettin' back to the regiment, pard" he said, looking Zeke squarely in the eye.

As Anne spoke, all three turned toward her. "Ah feel refreshed by the water," she remarked with a voice that seemed to caress her words. "Perhaps you will allow me to repay your kindness. If y'all are evah near tha town of Leesburg, y'all would be most welcome to visit our family home, Mountain View." Josh grinned dreamily as he thought she spoke directly to him.

She rose without assistance, smoothed her dress and took the little girl by the hand. "Ah am quite recovered now. We must return to our hosts."

Her smile was radiant and the three soldiers stood transfixed as she turned under the parasol and walked in to the crowd along the hill.

"I ain't fer shur where Lees burg is, but I aim to find out," Zeke muttered.

Welburn regained his authority and turned toward the insub- ordinate Zeke. Josh pushed Zeke off toward the forming regiment as their Lieutenant spoke.

"Private Owens, you will address me with respect," Welburn called after them. But whatever else Welburn had to say was lost in the air. Zeke and Josh quick stepped all the way and made it back to company ranks well ahead of the Lieutenant.

As they joined the regiment, Josh thought the Mississippi boys were plainer than the South Carolinians, but still well turned out. Their uniforms tended toward waist jackets and pants of gray, both trimmed with black. A few companies wore different styles, such as the Pettus Rifles of the 17th who had gray frock coats trimmed in red. The Rifles sported tall gray campaign hats, though the kepi or forage cap was more common in Mississippi ranks.

Zeke and Josh stumbled in to place just as the order was passed to march. A smartly dressed Colonel Featherston led the regiment out, sitting grandly atop his horse. Soldiers were ordered to keep eyes front as they marched. Others stole glances toward the honored guests, hoping to glimpse General Beauregard, commanding General of the Army and the hero of Fort Sumter. But both Josh and Zeke searched the hillside looking for a particular member of the Virginia gentry.

As they neared the end of their route, Josh heard Zeke whisper to him. "That Anne Marlow has my canteen. Ah'm jes gonna hafta go git it one o' these days."

Josh whispered back, "I bes keep you comp'ny if you do jes so's you don git lost."

Zeke turned to his friend with a sly grin.

The day ended with a patriotic speech by a local member of the Confederate Congress whose name was lost in the crowd noise during his introduction. He promised victory over the godless Yankees and pledged the blood of every Southern soldier to repulse the Northern invaders. Then a cannon for each state of the Confederacy was fired in sequence to celebrate a second American revolution.

A more somber mood marked the Fourth of July in

Washington City. The large number of soldiers gathered in the city had precipitated some carousing and these men raised glasses in local watering holes to the future of the republic. With Congress called to session, Representatives and Senators assembled to watch a small contingent of troops march before them, their banners only stirring with movement. Yet, a suppressed calm reined in the City, not entirely due to the oppressive heat. Those who resided in the Capital remembered more lively celebrations of the nation's birthday in previous years.

Congressman Hawthorne, too, was affected by the city's mood as he made his way to Capitol Hill on the following day. The special session of Congress, requested by the President, had been a point of hope in recent days. Hawthorne believed the energy and resolve of Congress could be translated to the White House and military.

Though the ceremonial opening had occurred on the fourth, a message from Lincoln greeted Congress on July fifth. In a manner some members thought wordy and overly legalistic, the President placed blame for the current conflict on the Southern states. Without asking Congress for approval, the President defended the steps he had taken since assuming office. Calling the conflict "essentially a People's contest" he established the prime issue as whether a government "of the people, by the same people" could defend itself against "domestic foes."

The President issued a call for an army of 400,000 soldiers and asked Congress to appropriate Four Hundred Million Dollars to support the army. Lincoln could anticipate full support from Republican majorities in both House and Senate on this measure. Seceded states were no longer represented and those from border states such as Kentucky were generally ignored. In fact, Congress would exceed the request in typical fashion, approving Five Hundred Million Dollars for an army of 500,000 men.

As he left the session near the end of the day, Hawthorne was troubled by a feeling the rebellion would not be crushed quickly. The President's implicit message had been that more men would be needed for a longer time to end the conflict. Hawthorne noted that this request had been made before any clash of arms established the need for a larger army.

The gentleman from Massachusetts seethed at the prevarication of the military. The excuses he heard for inactivity were varied, and seemingly inexhaustible. They accumulated like flies and were equally tiresome.

His thoughts found voice as he encountered the burly Senator from Ohio, Benjamin Wade, on the Capitol steps. After they exchanged pleasantries, Wade seemed inclined to talk with the Bay State member.

"Perhaps a Republican Congress can prod this army into action," Hawthorne declared, "now that we are rid of the southern Democratic influence."

"One can only hope, my good man," Wade responded guardedly.

"I have been told by everyone from the President on down that we must trust our military leaders in this crisis," Wade continued dismissively. "But our volunteers are fit and eager and every resource has been made available. I fear there are darker purposes that stay our generals."

This last statement immediately intrigued Hawthorne. He too had heard the counsel of caution and faith from the highest levels of government. "I have tried to retain my trust in our military leaders, but it seems they are paralyzed with the task before them," he replied evenly, in hope that the Senator would enlarge on his statement.

"McDowell and that old war horse, Scott, have grown stale," the brusque Wade noted. "Our brave soldiers need vigorous leaders who are also good Republicans. When we have men who are not afraid to offend southern feelings, you will see the rebellion crushed."

"Surely, sir, you must exclude the President from your indictment," Hawthorne questioned. "I believe that his caution is borne from inexperience with military affairs. Mr. Lincoln has been bold to act in political matters," he assured the senior Senator.

"The President has not grasped the true objective of this struggle, an end to the abominable disgrace of slavery," Wade retorted, his voice gaining in strength.

Wade continued in an impassioned manner. "We have the instrument to erase this evil for ever, armed and waiting in camps about the City. But there is no resolve in our generals and the President has lost his nerve on this issue. I heard no pronouncement from Mr. Lincoln to end slavery in his message to Congress."

"My dear sir, there are many of us who wish to see an end to enslavement of the Negro," Hawthorne inserted. "Our foremost objective, though, must to be to restore the Union and the President has been quite clear on that to Congress."

Wade arched an eyebrow at this comment and Hawthorne feared he might have alienated the influential Senator. He quickly returned to the threat imposed by a common enemy.

"These military men are insufferable, Senator, and I have heard that Mr. Lincoln has urged movement before the ninety day enlistments expire."

Hawthorne placed a friendly hand on the Senator's arm and drew closer to him. "A story was relayed to me how McDowell had protested to the President the army could not fight because the men were too green. Lincoln noted the inexperience of the other side and said 'You are all green together'," the Congressman laughing again at the anecdote.

Wade had heard the story from other sources and could muster no smile at hearing it again. "Our President is good at pointed comments, but it will take more than clever rebukes to make our dithering military move," he said with some exasperation.

Hawthorne continued in a confidential tone. "I have also heard, Senator, that there are efforts about to find a young and able leader for the army. The name of George McClellan has been mentioned often. Perhaps you have heard of our 'Young Napoleon' as he is called."

A wry smile creased Wade's face. "Surely you know there are no secrets in this town, Hawthorne. Yes, I have heard McClellan's name, but I fear that he is not of Republican persuasion."

"However," Wade continued, "you can be sure that McDowell has heard such talk and perhaps that will be enough to spur the horse. In my experience, nothing provokes the use of power than the threat of losing it."

Hawthorne smiled in agreement. "With Congress now assembled, the generals will be hard pressed to ignore the combined will of the President and Congress. The people have provided a 'terrible swift sword' and now we must be sure to use it."

"The military wish us to be like the maiden on her wedding night, to submit without protest and trust that the result will be satisfactory," the earthy Senator rejoined. "They will find that Congress is not so easily dismissed.

"Scott and McDowell are riding high at the moment, but memories are long in this city. I will continue to press our generals to move. And I will not forget those who have placated the rebels by their idleness," Wade added sharply, preparing to take his leave.

"I, too, shall be active in urging the army to move," Hawthorne hurriedly added to the departing Senator. "I pray our efforts will soon be successful.'

On his way home, the Congressman reflected on the Senator's bellicose mood. Even in his best moments, Benjamin Wade was not a kind or forgiving man. He could be a dangerous and aggressive foe to those who crossed him. The army commanders had clearly tried the Senator's patience and he had openly hinted their recalcitrance might be treasonous. The generals had aroused a formidable enemy if they did not soon satisfy Senator Wade.

Hawthorne was sympathetic to the Ohioan's frustration and felt a full measure himself. Yet he had not thought of McDowell's reluctance to attack as anything more than timidity about the outcome. Indeed, the army was larger than had ever been assembled and there was surely inexperience at every level, including the field commanders. Problems with delivery of military supplies compounded matters. Hawthorne had privately resolved to ignore these otherwise valid excuses while prodding the generals to move against the rebels. Aggressive military action, even with such 'green' troops, was the only way to end the rebellion and seize the traitorous leaders of secession.

Inevitably, Hawthorne must consider his own political future. He had wondered if he was right to criticize the military and to date, his complaints had been made directly to the military powers. Wade had now informed Hawthorne that he was watching the military closely. The Congressman sensed an ill wind blowing from Capitol Hill toward the War Department. Those who allied themselves with the military leaders or excused their dawdling might find themselves separated from the powerful Senator. Prudently, he had embarked on a path that agreed with Ben Wade's politics and Hawthorne could perceive no disagreeable consequences if he were allied with the Senator.

He paused near his rooming house and gazed about him. Hawthorne could glimpse the Virginia side of the Potomac. Soon, very soon he hoped, McDowell would lead the army to Virginia and play hell with the rebels. Or there would be hell to pay on this side of the Potomac.

6

The lengthening days of June had now been replaced by the languid days of July. In Camp Walker life continued on a schedule of drill and marching during daylight, picket duty and chores at night. Rumors circulated daily on the intentions of the Yankees and varied little in substance - the Yankees were coming and there would be a battle soon. Of course, such predictions had not yet proved true.

Josh had been anxious at first each time he heard another rumor. Then he became suspicious of the frequency and resigned to the fact that all proved false. Finally, in mid July, he had become exasperated with the 'grapevine telegraph', figuring that since the Yankees were still miles away, summer would pass without a battle.

Josh believed the Regiment was better prepared for a fight. The men were able to deploy from marching ranks to form line of battle. There were fewer mistakes and lately, little had been heard from Colonel Featherston during drills. The Regiment had even fixed bayonets and stepped forward in a charge, though the uniform of a fellow from Panola County had been holed by the man behind him.

Efforts to make men load their rifles faster had met with limited success. Commands to load and fire were given in nine separate steps. Soldiers privately, and publicly, ridiculed the number of commands as unnecessary. Officers barked a sequence from "load" through "handle cartridge", "charge cartridge", "draw rammer", "ram cartridge", "return rammer", and "prime". Finally, the command to "ready-aim" came just before "fire".

Soldiers were required to perform each step in unison with the result that it took over a minute to load and fire one volley. Ferrall had told Josh a man should be able to load and fire 3 rounds in a minute, though it hardly seemed possible. But Josh continued to practice in his spare time and could load his piece in about half a minute.

Josh had not been able to talk much with Ferrall since the First Sergeant seemed so busy of late. One day after the noon break, Josh had tried to catch a quick nap before the afternoon drill. As he lay dozing on his bedroll, Ferrall was suddenly above him calling his name and prodding his side.

"Campbell, you'll be needin' to come with me."

Josh pulled on his footwear and struggled to his feet. He wondered again if Ferrall ever needed rest.

"What'd I do, Sergeant" he said sleepily.

"You've done nothin' wrong lad. The Colonel's horse has taken sick and needs some lookin' after," Ferrall explained. "You'll be havin' some experience with the creatures workin' your father's farm, so I've offered your services." Pausing, the Sergeant fixed an eye on Josh. "You'll not be lettin' the Colonel down, now, lad," he commanded.

They walked toward a barn near the railroad tracks. Entering, they threaded their way among stalls and equipment to find Colonel Featherston. A young Negro stood with the officer before one of the stalls.

"This is the lad I spoke about, sir, Private Campbell," the Sergeant said after saluting. Josh offered a hand to his forehead in imitation of Ferrall.

"Mah trusted friend advises you are a good man with horses, Private," the Colonel began. "Your family name is known to me for I have purchased numerous drays from your father in the past, and always found my purchase sound."

The Colonel paused and glanced about before he continued. "I fear the care for animals is not of the level to which I prefer. And Marcus is not mah regular groom, having little experience with the animal."

Motioning inside the stall to the horse laying on its side, the Colonel said, "You would oblige me to take a look at Sir Ivanhoe and see if you can detect the cause of his distress. Mah boy Marcus tells me the horse will not take feed today and appears quite anxious."

Josh stepped close to the horse and grasped the head with both hands. He gently guided the head toward him so that he could look directly at the horse. He noticed its labored breathing. Then he stroked the forehead, muttering some soothing words in a low voice.

Josh peeled back the lips and peered inside the mouth. Then he moved his hands toward the flank, gently stroking the back. The coat was wet with perspiration. He paused to tap the belly twice, causing the horse to raise slightly and turn its head toward his tormentor. Continuing to speak to him in a low voice, Josh ran his hands along each leg and gently lifted each hoof. As he moved back toward the head, the horse nuzzled his shoulder.

Josh stood to face the Colonel. "Has a touch o' the colic, sir," he told the worried officer. "He's perty wet an' turns his head to the flank. He likely has some gas." Josh paused. He caught Ferrall's nod to continue and added, "I reckon his droppin's is smaller than usual."

Featherston turned to the servant, a full sized young man just younger than Josh. "Marcus, have you noticed any of what the Private says," the Colonel asked sharply.

"Suh, I's seen the small droppin's this mawnin' and he been frettin' an won't eat none," Marcus said hurriedly keeping his eyes averted humbly. Josh noticed the dark skinned man seemed to shrink from the Colonel.

"Colonel, he more'n likely picked up colic from his feed," Josh put in. "Likely, he's eatin different than usual, an' that'll cause colic most ever time."

"What d'you suggest as a remedy, Private," Featherston asked evenly.

"Sir, bes remedy is to git some chamomile leaves or valerian from the apothecary. Mix that in with his feed twice," Josh said as he bent and stroked the horse's neck.

"I'd give him some fresh hay and alfalfa, chopped up real good, fer feed. No corn right now," Josh continued, looking at Marcus. "He ought ta be walked a bit till he gits rid of that gas. In a few days, I'd mix some sprigs of mint in his feed."

Josh turned and spoke directly to the Colonel. "This'll pass right soon, sir, but once't they git the colic, they like as not to git it again."

"Private, ah am surely obliged to you for seeing to my stallion," the Colonel said, smiling graciously. Josh felt a little uncomfortable with the officer's gratitude.

Featherston turned to the young slave and, handing him a slip of paper, said, "Marcus, find the apothecary in town and obtain the herbs on this list."

The servant took off at a trot and the Colonel ushered Josh from the stall. "Would you do me the kindness of checking mah horse when you have the time, Private," Featherston remarked. Josh knew he had been dismissed and turned to leave the stable with Ferrall beside him.

Outside, Ferrall said, "I hope you know what yer doin', lad. The Colonel sets great store by that horse, he does."

Ferrall appraised the young private. "How'd you come by yer knowledge of horse care," he asked.

"I learnt a good bit from my Pa. But we also had us an ol' Chickasaw Indian 'roun who showed me a lot. He give me this eagle talon fer good luck," Josh said, fishing in his pocket for the talisman to show Ferrall.

"Well, there's no harm in a little luck with your doctorin'," the Irishman remarked with a knowing smile. "The Colonel'll be well and truly in yer debt if his horse gets well," he added.

"I reckon might be handy to have the Colonel on my side one day," Josh mused. They had reached the area of Josh's tent and Ferrall, noticing some commotion in the company, broke away without another word.

As Josh made for his tent, Dutchie came up beside him. "Ve ist to drill mit der rifles in ten minuten. Please to follow me."

Josh wearily retrieved his rifle and cartridge belt. He joined the others to trot along behind the corporal. A broiling afternoon sun did not promise to be kind. Josh remembered the cool shade of the barn and figured that maybe the Colonel's horse might need his constant attention.

Zeke had to stop and cough after a few paces at quick time and Josh noticed his friend was sniffling. Zeke had not seemed well during morning drill and had complained of the heat even though that morning had been unusually cool.

The Regiment drilled that afternoon with rifles. They had been fixing their sword bayonets to the Mississippi rifle in recent days. A group of soldiers would level their rifles about waist high. Then, with one hand behind the stock, they would thrust the bayonet into a hay bale target on command. They extracted the bayonet and stepped back in ranks as others followed.

The bales of hay were decorated with faces and placards identifying them as Northerners. There were some cackles if a hay bale fell against one of the men as he withdrew a bayonet. Yet the men took the drills seriously for little imagination was required to understand the bayonet's effect on a foe

When afternoon drill ended, the men were marched back to their camps. Josh saw that Zeke was having a hard time walking and struggled with a hacking cough. As soon as they got back to their tent, Zeke flopped onto his bedroll.

Josh busied himself with dinner preparations, allowing his friend to rest. When the meal was ready, he went to wake Zeke. He noticed the sleeping man's shirt was wet with sweat. His hand grazed Zeke's neck and he could feel the fever.

"Pard, yer burnin' up," Josh said as Zeke stirred. "An yer

face's red as the devil."

Zeke tried to speak, but his voice caught in a hacking cough. He used an old rag to cover his mouth, then wiped his nose.

"I feel poorly, pard, an ain't gittin' no better," Zeke croaked in a voice little more than a whisper.

Josh noticed Zeke's hands bore the same red blotches that showed on his face. He knew his friend was terribly sick.

Ignoring his dinner, Josh told his friend that he would get the surgeon, and he tried hard to hide the fear in his voice.

Will Tucker was eating nearby and Josh called him over, explaining that he wanted Will to stay close by Zeke in his absence. Will settled down without question and resumed eating outside of the tent. Josh ran off toward Regimental headquarters area.

Among the officers tents he encountered a Lieutenant who pointed out the surgeon's tent. Josh made his way to it. The men had been instructed to see orderlies or the assistant surgeon for health matters, but Josh could see no one else about.

He paused outside to see if any one was within and heard the rustle of clothing on a chair.

"Sir, Private Campbell to see the Regimental Surgeon," Josh said, straightening his body to attention. Josh recalled the man's name as Isom, though he had never spoken to him.

The doctor emerged from the tent with his uniform coat unbuttoned. He was a middle aged officer with keen eye and a pleasant, bearded face.

"What seems to be the problem, Private," the doctor asked.

"Mah friend's awful sick, sir, he's coughin' real bad and burnin' with fever," Josh related hurriedly.

"He must report to the sick tent," the surgeon declared.

"He's dreadful sick, sir, and I don' think he could walk on his own," Josh cut in on the officer.

"What is your company, Private, and where are y'all camped," the surgeon said slowly, in an effort to calm Josh.

"We in the Rangers, sir, an' I kin take you right to him," Josh replied excitedly.

"Let me get mah case and we'll see to this man directly," the doctor said to Josh's immediate relief.

Surgeon Isom ducked back inside his tent and emerged with a worn leather satchel. He called to a nearby soldier that he would be away for a time. Then he followed Josh through the headquarters area toward the tent where Zeke lay. Josh kept up a good pace and the doctor did not lag behind. On the way, Josh tried to relate the previous days symptoms that he had noticed.

Will Tucker was still sitting outside the tent, but Walter and Hugh Driscoll had joined him. They all saluted the officer, but he ignored them and pushed in to the tent.

Josh waited outside with the others. No one spoke, anxious for the doctor to give his opinion.

In a few moments, the man emerged and drew a notebook from his satchel. Four faces turned to him expectantly. The surgeon wrote something in the book and closed it before he spoke.

"Your friend's likely got the measles," the surgeon said finally. "He may look poorly now, but the disease is not usually fatal."

"I will send orderlies over to carry him to the hospital area," the surgeon added. "He must be put in quarantine until the disease runs its course." He started to leave.

"Anythin' we kin do fer him," Josh asked.

The surgeon put a comforting hand on Josh's shoulder. "No need to fret. He'll be looked after and should be back in ranks with y'all in two week's time." Nodding to the other men, Isom walked off toward his tent.

Josh looked in on Zeke, but he appeared to be resting peacefully. With nothing else to be done, Will, Walter and Hugh wandered away.

It was but a short time before the orderlies came with a stretcher and carted Zeke off to the hospital area. They told Josh they had tended men from several companies with the same sickness.

Josh rolled Zeke's blanket and piled his friend's gear with his own. It struck Josh that he and Zeke would be separated this night, the first time since they had mustered into the company. He consoled himself that it would only be a few nights.

Josh slept fitfully that night and busied himself with drills and camp duties through the next days. Word had reached him through Ferrall that Zeke was about the same. The fever had declined and he was eating regular, but he still had the red rash and coughing.

To turn his mind away from Zeke, Josh checked his horse patient frequently. Each time he saw the horse, the slave Marcus was tending to the animal. Josh tried to instruct the young servant on how to care for horses. Marcus always listened respectfully, but Josh thought the slave too carefree to be concerned about the Colonel's horse.

Josh sensed the horse no longer needed his care and he thought to look in for a last time one evening after supper. Josh usually entered from the front, but this time he had come in from the rear of the barn, closer to the Colonel's stall. He could hear someone speaking in a confident, soothing voice as he got closer, saying 'You gots to be ready when the time is right.'

Just beside the stall, Josh's shoes crunched some hay and the voice ceased abruptly. The face peering around the corner belonged to Marcus.

If not quite surprise, Marcus wore an expression of some concern. His voice returned to the sing-song lilt familiar to Josh.

"He's doin' real fine, Mistah Josh, real fine," Marcus said and resumed brushing the animal.

"I reckon he's shut of the colic fer now," Josh noted, patting the horse on his flank. The stallion turned toward Josh and nuzzled his hand. "He eatin' all his feed," Josh asked the servant.

"Yas, suh, he sho' eats his fill now," Marcus said.

"He'll be alright then, an' I won't need to come roun' here no more," Josh said as the horse seemed to perk up his ears.

"Y'all sho' nuf fixed him up," Marcus put in, though without looking directly at Josh. "Colonel, he's real happy now, yaaas suh," Marcus said with emphasis.

Josh turned to the slave and looked directly at him. "Colonel allow you to ride Sir Ivanhoe, Marcus?" Josh tried to make the inquiry innocent, but it still sounded hard.

"Yas, suh, ah gits to take him fer mawnin' exercise," Marcus said proudly. The young black man seemed willing to talk. "We rides all over the fiels an' roads, an' he gots a little jumper in him."

Josh was about to ask the slave how far he was allowed to ride from camp when he heard the rustle of sword and spurs. Colonel Featherston appeared at the front of the stall and Josh instinctively offered a salute. Marcus retreated some distance to the back of the stall.

"Private Campbell, you have given mah horse some fine personal care," the Colonel said, acknowledging Josh's salute with a wave of his hand. Josh smiled at the compliment, but the older man seemed distracted by other matters.

"He will need to be in good form, for I have just received word that the Yankee army is marching this way."

Marcus stopped brushing. As the smile faded from his face, Josh swallowed hard to moisten a suddenly dry throat. A thousand questions leapt to his mind and he chose one at random.

"How long till they git here, sir," Josh said, remembering to add the respectful title.

"We lie just a day's hard march from where they are, though I doubt they can move that fast," Featherston told him. The Colonel knitted his brow as if Josh's question had provoked a new worry. "For now, Private, I suggest you return to your company while we await General Beauregard's orders."

The Colonel's words signaled no further questions would be welcome and Josh straightened to attention. He saluted and left the stall, walking with a purpose out of the barn toward his campsite.

Word was spreading fast. Small groups of soldiers clustered here and there in silence, an uncertain future written on their faces. The usual noise and chatter of an evening had declined noticeably.

When Josh arrived at camp, the boys were huddled together while Charlie Akins finished a short prayer. He ended as Josh arrived.

"I reckon y'all heard the Yanks're comin'," Josh said flatly.

"Davy heard about it from Lieutenant Abernathy and jes come by to tell us," Riley said. For once, Davy Williams seemed stunned into silence by the news he delivered.

"We have prayed to a merciful God fer forgiveness and strength in the coming days," Charlie said, glancing toward the sky.

Will Tucker had his arm around the shoulders of his brother to console him. Walter, his head down and staring at the ground, seemed to be shaking a little.

Hugh Driscoll tried to make a joke. "Ol' Zeke's gonna miss the show, he don' git well real soon."

Although he too had been stunned on first hearing the news, Josh was surprised at the somber mood of his mates.

"Ain't this what y'all signed up fer," Josh said firmly. "We bin lookin' to'ard a scrap since we got here.

"We bin drillin' fer months now an we're ready to fight," he went on. "The good Lord willin', we'll lick 'em good an we kin all go home."

They were all looking at him, even Walter Tucker had lifted his head. Josh suddenly felt a little foolish for speaking out, but the others seemed to take heart.

As usual, Davy recovered first. "Them Yanks is in fer a thrashin'."

"Lads, you'll be needin' your rest tonight," Sergeant Ferrall said as he unexpectedly entered the group. All eyes turned to the calm and steady Irishman.

"Lay yourselves down and rest while you can. We've a long day of it tomorrow and for days to come." The Sergeant paused and waited for the mess to disperse. As they shuffled off, he went on to the next group.

They moved to their tents and blankets, but restful sleep was to be an elusive companion this night.

Some few miles away, young men from Northern towns and cities were finding peaceful rest a common enemy.

7

Drummers beat an early reveille and dawn was creasing the sky when Josh awoke. Dutchie was outside the tent moments later. "Quick mit der eating, ve ist to marching," he said.

Josh pulled on his shoes and grabbed his jacket. He emerged from the tent into a whirl of activity. Riley and Davy were already at the camp fire rousing it to life. Hugh and Charlie were assembling gear and rolling their blankets. Even the Tucker boys were fully dressed, not their usual morning custom.

Josh pitched in on the breakfast of bacon and johnnycakes that Riley fried together. As ordered, they used up the last of their rations so there was plenty to eat. Anticipation had dulled Josh's appetite, but he saved two of the corncakes for his haversack.

Young Walter gave voice to the thought of everyone. "Whar you reckon we goin' to," he said between mouthfuls to no one in particular.

"I 'spect we goin' to meet the Yankees at that Bull Run stream," Davy Williams said, his confidence having returned overnight. "I hear the Gen'ral wants to block all the crossin's," Williams declared, as if Beauregard had confided in him personally.

"Wherever we goin', we likely to do a lot of marchin'" Hugh put in. "Whilst the calv'ry gets to ride all day," he added.

"Aw, they jes git their blisters in a different place," Riley said, to a round of laughter.

The drummers beat assembly and the men broke apart for last minute preparations. Josh slung the cartridge pouch over one shoulder and looped his haversack and canteen over the other. He looped his rolled blanket over a shoulder and grabbed his hat and rifle.

As he was about to leave the tent, he caught sight of Zeke's kit piled to the side. His close friend would not be along this trip, not beside him when they saw the Federals. On impulse, he grabbed a handkerchief Zeke used to shade his neck in the sun, and stuffed it in his haversack. Josh was comforted that if Zeke could not make it back in time, something of his would go along. Charlie trotted by and said "C'mon, Josh," breaking his daydream and he hustled off to the forming company ranks.

Lieutenant Abernathy called roll and marked a list as he moved down the line. Sergeants checked men to be sure they carried necessary equipment. The Rangers mustered some eighty men this day, ranks reduced by sickness, though that list likely included a few 'beats', as the men referred to shirkers.

Other companies were in place and in short order the Regiment was formed and ready to march. Colonel Featherston and his staff rode to the front of the ranks. Someone hollered 'Atten-shun' and the 17th came to order. Minutes before, sounds of men and equipment had carried through the air. As men snapped to, an uneasy stillness pervaded the scene.

"Men, we have been ordered to a position on Bull Run Creek," the Colonel said in a voice that pierced the morning air. "Y'all know the Federal army is marching toward us."

The senior officer paused with dramatic effect, checking his suddenly restless horse in an expert manner. "General Beauregard has placed this Regiment in the Third Brigade, which includes our friends in the 18th Mississippi, and the 5th South Carolina. We will be under the command of General Jones.

"The Brigade will form a line behind McLean's Ford on the creek, and stay there until ordered elsewhere," the Colonel announced.

He paused again, surveyed the lines from left to right and raised his voice higher. "The time is near when you will be asked to do your duty. Remember always - - that you are sons of Mississippi."

Featherston's voice seemed to crack and he stopped abruptly, reining his horse to turn. Lieutenant Colonel John McGuirk glanced at his Colonel and ordered the men to stand easy. Then the officers and staff trotted to the right while the troops remained in formation.

A slight commotion rose left of the line and all eyes turned in that direction. A soldier holding a long pole moved in front of the Regiment. The soldier, wearing a jacket of the Rough and Readies from Pontotoc County, unfurled a bright, new Confederate flag. He marched along the front of the Regiment, flying the 'Stars and Bars' flag for all to see, stopping on the extreme right at a point that would assure he was head of the column. Josh was surprised, but delighted, to see that the Regiment would have a battle flag.

They remained in ranks longer than expected. Marching orders placed the 17th behind the 18th. The 5th South Carolina had the Brigade van. But they had to wait for another brigade of four regiments to clear the road ahead and that delayed the start of Third Brigade.

A broiling July sun baked the morning air, rendering a tense wait most uncomfortable. After standing in ranks for endless minutes, officers apparently believing the order to march imminent, word was passed the 5th was on the move. Men of the 17th relaxed slightly with the knowledge they would soon follow.

Captain Franklin was summoned to the Colonel as men mumbled they saw movement in the 18th. A moment later, the Captain returned and ranks were dressed a final time. Josh could see a moving column ahead to his right as the 18th entered the road out of camp.

Finally, the Captain and Lieutenants took their place in line. From the head of the column, Josh heard a call repeated down the line, 'Face right, column of fours'. The men turned and shouldered their rifles. Then he heard the now familiar, 'For'ard, march', and the column began to move.

Though some grumbled quietly about the delay in marching, there was little talk in ranks for the first half mile. However, marching was 'old hat' by now and as they relaxed into routine, a bantering chatter began to flow through the ranks. Challenges were hurled at the Yankees and between companies. One company behind Josh mounted a short cheer that he could not decipher. These outbursts brought only halfhearted rebukes from officers privately pleased by the show of spirit.

Before noon they were ordered to a halt without breaking ranks. Craning his neck, Josh could see a side road up ahead and barn nearby. Soldiers broke out canteens as the relentless sun bore down upon them through a cloudless sky. A commotion up ahead signaled movement and Josh could see the South Carolina flag leading men onto the side road. The 17th began to march again a few minutes later.

When they approached the side road, Josh noticed a homestead opposite the entrance to the lane. A middle aged man and woman were seated on the porch while two children frolicked about. The children called and waved to the soldiers, but the couple did not stir as they passed. The man wore a troubled expression.

The column marched for some distance along the lane before halting once again. Josh caught a glimpse of flowing water ahead, the Bull Run. They had reached their destination.

The 5th and 18th were posted right of the road in a clearing bordered by sparse woodland. The 17th deployed left of the road, among the tall trees there. A small 'lean to' cabin stood near where the road cut through the creek bank. The road continued on the other side of the stream, through a low, wooded area like that on the near side. Farther to his left, Josh noticed the ground rise on the opposite side where the stream made a bend. On his right, the 5th faced a steep bank and wooded hillside across from their encampment.

Men were dismissed from ranks and clustered in company groups, searching for soft ground. The commissary had not been brought up so there was no meal to fix. A few soldiers wandered down to the stream to refill canteens. A company of South Carolina troops splashed across the shallow ford and continued down the road out of sight. Josh figured these fellows had been detailed on a scout.

The Rangers secured an area well back from the stream, but near the Ford road. Second Lieutenant Barnett walked by and Hugh was bold enough to ask if this was the end of the day's march.

"This is McLean's Ford, Private, and we shall remain here through the night," the Lieutenant said. Although usually abrupt with the men, Barnett seemed inclined to answer questions.

"Sir, you reckon the Yankees'll be here today," Charlie asked.

"I've not heard that the Federals reached Centreville as yet, so I would not expect them today. When they do reach this area, they will likely try to cross first at the ford north of here, on the Centreville road," the Lieutenant declared. He paused a moment longer and left when there were no more questions.

"Wonder why this place is called 'McLean's Ford'," Will Tucker said. Davy Williams was ready with the answer.

"Heard Abernathy say that was old McLean back yonder, watchin' us pass by. He owns the ground 'roun here," Davy explained.

Day passed to evening before the commissary wagons arrived. The Regiments were issued foodstuffs by company and cook fires came to life. Most had not eaten since breakfast, so there were few complaints about the chewy salt beef and hard crackers provided for this meal.

Ferrall assembled a squad for guard duty and Josh was included. He was posted up stream a little ways and got a closer look at his surroundings as dusk faded to night.

The shallow and slow moving Bull Run was bordered by a low bank on his side. Trees and underbrush dotted a low slung landscape as far as the eye could see. What Josh would have called a creek seemed about twenty feet wide along its distance.

On the other side across from his post, a small stream meandered along a hillside and emptied into Bull Run. The hill rose dramatically from the little stream, and though wooded, a person standing atop it could have a good view of the Southerners' camp. The rise continued opposite, stretching to the left so that the bank was impassable. A marshy area extended right from the little stream to the road from the Ford.

Hardly a sound came from the opposite bank and his watch passed without incident. The day's excitement had dissipated to the tedium of solitude. When he was relieved Josh surrendered easily to sleep in the cool night air.

The next morning dawned lazily with still no sight of the Yankees. Cavalry scouts rode through camp and disappeared on the other side of the Run. Breakfast turned out to be coffee and hard crackers from the night before, causing the Tucker boys to speak fondly of the fare in their previous camp.

In early afternoon, an officer on horseback galloped across the Run from the other side. General Jones had established his headquarters to the rear of the 17th, though Josh had yet to see the man. All eyes followed the officer as he rode up to the tent and dismounted, evidently with important information. The General emerged from a meeting with the Colonels of each Regiment. Featherston of the 17th, Colonel Burt of the 18th and Colonel Jenkins of the 5th gathered with General Jones to hear the courier's news.

Minutes later, Josh watched the horseman remount and ride off toward the Centreville Road. Jones and the three Colonels stepped into a tent with other staff officers. Moments later, the meeting broke and officers returned to their Regiments.

Everyone in camp detected at once that something was stirring. Josh noticed his friend Lem Morse standing in a small group and walked over to see if they had heard anything.

"Pickets out on the Ford road spotted Yankee cavalry," Lem said. "Guess they're just tryin' to find out whar we are."

Further speculation ceased as drummers beat assembly. Josh returned to his company, secured his rifle and equipment, and fell in with the others.

The company sent to scout the previous day had been recalled earlier and South Carolina troops were deployed along the bank on either side of the road. The Mississippi regiments were placed farther back from the Ford in a reserve position. Men of each regiment grew tense after these maneuvers, anticipating Federals would appear before them at any moment. Tension eased as time passed through the hot, sticky afternoon and sergeants circulated among the companies to insure readiness.

Late in the afternoon, men of the Third Brigade could hear the repeating pop and rattle of rifle fire to their far left, well north of their position. Instinctively, heads turned in that direction, though it was clear the firing was some distance away. Lone, loud blasts revealed that artillery had joined the fray.

Josh kept an eye on the headquarters tent and watched the couriers come and go throughout the afternoon. General Jones and his staff turned at the sound of firing, but the General did not show great concern. Josh knew nothing about the Brigade commander, only that he was from South Carolina. Even Davy Williams could provide no background on the small, wiry man in the immaculate uniform and tall campaign hat. The question foremost among the ranks was whether the South Carolinian would prove to be a fighter.

As the sun dropped in the sky, it seemed less likely that the 17th would see any fight this day. Finally the men were retired from battle formation and returned to their previously secured portions of ground. The now familiar crackers and coffee were issued for evening meal since the day had passed without resupply.

Josh and the others gathered about a fire to boil coffee.

Williams had not appeared since they had been relieved. For once, Josh would be glad to find out anything about the days events, since information was scarce as fresh meat. Davy returned just before dark, the campfire highlighting his face as he began.

"I got the whole story, boys," he said in opening. "Let me git a swaller of coffee an' I'll tell y'all what happened."

He was handed a cup of coffee and took a good pull, then settled down cross legged on the ground.

"The firin' we heard was Longstreet's boys up at Blackburn Ford. They had a regiment across the stream when the Yanks appeared on the Centreville Road. Those boys caught some hell from the Yanks until the rest of Longstreet's Brigade helped out."

He paused to catch his breath and drink more coffee, holding their undivided attention. "I heard twas hot 'n heavy for a little while, but the Yanks got a bellyfull and retreated back to'rd Centreville."

"How'd you find all this out," Hugh questioned. "We ain't heard much roun' here."

"I went on out to the Centreville Road while y'all ate yer dinner," Davy explained. "Beauregard's got his headquarters at the McLean place, an' I heard everthin' from one o' the sentries.

"They brought in some of the wounded whilst I was there," Davy continued. "One of them boys tol me tha Yanks run like scart rabbits when that artillery lit in to 'em.

"That feller said he'uz in a Virginia comp'ny that charged cross Bull Run and pitched into them Federals." Davy smiled. "He come close to stickin' one of 'em 'fore he got hit in the arm. I shur hope we git to see some fightin'."

Josh was relieved to hear the Northerners had run off when pressed. He pondered whether the Federals would now have enough of fighting and go back to Washington.

Davy finished his coffee and went off to other campfires. He was generally welcomed as a reliable source for news outside the Regiment and this information would only enhance that reputation.

    Josh broke away to look for Sergeant Ferrall with the hope of getting his perspective on the day's events. He didn't turn up Ferrall, but he was surprised to encounter Marcus tending to a group of horses, including the Colonel's stallion.

    "I didn't think you was s'posed to be near the fightin', Marcus," Josh said in greeting. With the prospect of battle, many of the servants had been forced to stay behind in Camp Walker.

    "I tells the Culnel I's gwon wif da hoss," Marcus replied, with a touch of self-importance. "Culnel says if I go, I gots to tend to all de officers hosses."

    "Well you bes keep yer head down when the shootin' starts," Josh remarked with a laugh. "Sir Ivanhoe looks to be in fine shape," he noted, patting the horse's flank.

    "Yas, sir, he doin' fine. Culnel is real proud of that hoss," Marcus answered, returning to his grooming.

    Not wanting to hold Marcus from his work, Josh made his way back to turn in. Some of his friends still talked about the cook fire, but despite the excitement of this days events, he quickly fell in to a deep slumber.

    Rumors flew next day by the minute. Ears perked for more firing, but nothing was heard in any direction. Ferrall came by during the morning to say the day would likely pass without incident, but cautioned men to keep their rifles handy.

    Tension in their situation found expression first in a large measure of grumbling. The hard, tasteless crackers had been consumed, leaving only coffee for the troops. The Confederate commissary was damned more often than the Yankees. As the day wore on, petty disagreements arose among the men. Confined in readiness for an enemy crossing of the Ford, men were forced to stay in place without even the relief of drill. Josh saw an argument arise between Bradwell and a man from Tishomingo County. Others rushed to support either man, but it was quickly halted by the sergeants.

    Waiting and uncertainty had frayed nerves. Even Hugh

and Charlie exchanged words over some imagined slight and stormed off in separate directions. Josh began to hope the Yankees would show up just so there would be something to do.

Late in the afternoon, the commissary wagons arrived with ample rations for two days. The smell of meat and potatoes cooking had a calming effect. With hunger abated, men relaxed during evening hours. The bands of each regiment helped feelings by treating the soldiers to a number of lively tunes, conveniently ignoring any slow, sad songs.

Although he had done little all day, Josh was hard put to stay awake after his supper. He slept, but awoke in early morning to shots from nervous sentries. Muffled curses from a Sergeant told him there was nothing to fear, and he dozed off again. He awoke in daylight to a commotion upstream from the Ford.

Josh saw Corporal Himmelfarb trotting toward him. "What's all the fuss, Dutchie," he asked.

"Der Yan-keys ist here," the Corporal said without breaking his stride. Josh pulled on his shoes and followed him to a crowd of men at the creek bank.

It was impossible to get close enough to see the object of the commotion, so Josh climbed a tree to get a better look. What he saw shook him momentarily. The Federals had managed to place two cannon on the steep hill he had noticed when he stood guard. Long, dark gun barrels were visible and he thought he could make out some soldiers scattered about the hilltop.

Josh had to acknowledge the Yanks' daring. It would have taken some effort to drag those guns there, through woods and up a hill. They were in good position though, since the steeply wooded banks would make attack very difficult. The little stream below the hill formed a V with the Bull Run, so any attack would also have to cross water. The guns were sighted directly on the Ford to disrupt easy movement.

Colonel Featherston and Colonel Jenkins arrived with staff officers in tow and pushed to a good vantage point. The officers tried to disperse the men, but only succeeded in moving them back from the bank a little ways. The two senior officers conferred a while and then walked back to headquarters. Those able to overhear the Colonels reported that nothing would be done about this threat immediately. Josh stayed in his perch nearly an hour, but the situation remained unchanged and the crowd eventually wandered off.

The Federal guns became the sole topic of conversation at every gathering of men. There being no orders to march or assemble, soldiers from each regiment made periodic trips to check on the Northerners.

A cheer went up at midday when a battery of the Washington Artillery arrived. The men hoped to see an artillery duel. But the landscape easily defeated such an idea. Unless they were rolled out and unlimbered in mid-stream, it would take a full days work just to get the pieces sited. Daylight faded without any artillery engagement.

As dusk fell, Josh wandered down to the bank to look at the Yankees. No shots had been fired by either side all day. The troops had accommodated the gun emplacement, but it remained a curiosity. Josh saw one of the South Carolina soldiers cup his hands to his mouth.

"Hey, Yank, y'all best not fall asleep t'night, we might come up to see ya," the Southern soldier yelled.

"Come on up, secesh," a voice yelled back, "we got somethin' for you." The sound of laughter followed down the hill.

The soldier from the 5th had no rejoinder and Josh had to hide a smile at the Federal's audacity. He turned to walk back to his fire and spotted Lemuel Morse running through the wood just ahead of him. Josh called out and Morse cut toward him. His friend had to catch his breath when he came up to him.

"What's got into you, Lem," Josh said.

"I jes heard the whole Brigade is goin' to cross Bull Run an' attack the Yankees tomorrow," Lem said. His breathing was under control now and he slapped Josh on the arm. "I got to tell my comp'ny."

Josh was too stunned to bid his friend good bye as Morse took off running. Josh found his way to the campfire and the relaxed posture of his friends indicated the news had not reached them. For once, Josh had heard something before Davy Williams.

"We're movin' out first light, boys," Josh announced in opening, and immediately got their attention.

"Hell you say," Hugh Driscoll barked. "How you know that."

"Heard it from Lem Morse in the Guards," Josh said proudly. "Whole Brigade is movin' up to attack."

It was clear Davy's pride was bruised this time. "I ain't heard that," he said.

"Well maybe you don' hear everthin' first," Josh taunted.

As they spoke, cheers arose from different parts of the camp. The words to 'Dixie' drifted up from the South Carolina troops. Ferrall came by shortly after to confirm the news and tell them the Regiment was gathering beside the Ford road. Josh and the others hastened over to the crowd.

Men clustered around Colonel Featherston in ragged formation. Officers were mixed in with the lower ranks and everyone edged close to hear what he had to say.

"Men, we are directed to march across the Ford at daybreak," the Colonel began. "General Beauregard has resolved to attack the Federals and Third Brigade will take part in that attack.

"The moment has arrived for us to drive these Yankee invaders back to Washington." Featherston paused, passing his resolute glare across the men before him. "Tomorrow, we fight for our families, our homes and the right to be free men. May God preserve our Confederacy."

These hundreds of men stood perfectly still, until someone barked 'Dismissed' and the Regiment dispersed. Josh followed his friends wordlessly back to their camp. As men returned to campfires though, the whole area buzzed. Josh idled nervously, joining the chatter of his mess in speculation on the morrow's events, distracted by his own thoughts. Eventually, conversation gave way to private reflections and the men began to wander off to their blankets. Sleep would not come easily this night.

Lying atop his blanket, unable to find a comfortable position to sleep, Josh tried to take stock of his feelings. He did not think himself afraid of the coming fight. He thought he could perform as a soldier after so many days of drill and he had always handled his rifle well. He was still unsure about what would happen in a battle, but he was sure he could load and fire his rifle at the Yankees when the order came.

He did feel a sort of relief that the battle was finally near. After all the days of preparation, sleeping and eating rough, and the generally dull military life, maybe tomorrow would bring the big battle everyone expected. He remembered that Yankees had already run from Southern troops at the Blackburn Ford just days ago. If the Southerners could beat the Northern troops in a full battle, the Yankees would have to quit the fight and leave the South in peace. *If* he thought, I can't think of *if*, I have to think we will.

Repeating this conviction sounded more and more like a prayer.

8

From everything Elihu Hawthorne had learned, the 1st Massachusetts Regiment would not redeem its reputation on the 21st of July. The 1st Massachusetts, with the entire Fourth Brigade of the First Division, was to be held in a defensive position around Centreville during the coming operation.

The Congressman was disturbed by this turn of events, but privately could not refute the logic of the decision. After the awkward engagement a few days earlier, the 1st Massachusetts would have to prove its worth to the army commanders.

Hawthorne had arrived in the Regiment's camp late on the 19th, after an arduous ride from the Capital. He had secured an aging hack and an equally aged horse to cover the distance to Centreville immediately upon hearing of the fight at Blackburn's Ford. Descriptions of the engagement did not give much credit to the 1st Massachusetts Regiment.

The Congressman drove directly to the Regiment's camp and confronted its Colonel, though the man was unknown to him. The Colonel provided a more detailed description of events and termed the fight a skirmish. He also indicated that the men retired in good order. The Lieutenant Colonel and a company Captain at headquarters echoed these sentiments.

Hawthorne was relieved by this explanation and satisfied that his excursion had been well founded. He retired that evening with a more confident feeling the Regiment had acted appropriately in the circumstances.

He was unsettled the next day, however, when he chanced to meet a Sergeant he knew from home. The Sergeant relayed a tale of bumbling officers, indecision as the enemy was engaged and a retreat that was more a mad scramble. Hawthorne believed the man, though he realized the soldier spoke from inexperience with battle. However, there was little doubt his story reflected the impression in the ranks.

Hawthorne decided that a journey to army headquarters was in order to speak on behalf of the 1st and to discern McDowell's plans for renewing the attack. The rebels were close by and battle was inevitable. His reception at army headquarters, however, had been decidedly cool. McDowell could not, or would not, see him. No other officer that he spoke with would divulge any plan for action. He had departed without any information on when or where an attack would take place, and whether the 1st Massachusetts would be included.

As he was leaving the headquarters enclave, fortune at last smiled upon him. He spotted the son of a political ally, now serving as an officer in the 5th Massachusetts Regiment. Hawthorne hailed the young man, thinking initially only of being sociable.

"Good to see you, Robert, though I shall have to call you Captain Lowell in these surroundings," Hawthorne said, grasping the officer's hand warmly. "I trust your father is well."

"Very well, when I last saw him," Lowell replied, a little surprised to see a member of Congress with the army. "What brings you to headquarters, sir?"

"I had journeyed to the camp of the 1st Regiment and I thought to pay my respects to General McDowell," Hawthorne commented. "He is, however, too busy to see me at this time."

"Indeed, I should think so," the young Captain declared. "We are to attack the rebel army tomorrow and he must be extremely busy," the officer said.

Hawthorne nearly leapt for joy. He had stumbled on an

officer who not only knew of the army's plans, but might be willing to talk about them. He hastened to prolong conversation.

Steering the Captain by his arm, Hawthorne pleaded in a friendly manner. "Perhaps you could walk with me to my buggy, just over there," he added, pointing.

"I would assume the 5th will be in the thick of things," Hawthorne ventured evenly, trying to hide his peaking curiosity.

"Yes, sir," the younger man declared proudly. "We will be part of the attacking column.

"Our Regiment is in Heintzelman's Third Division," the junior officer continued. "Our orders are to march by 3:00 A.M. to the Sudley Church on our right, with the object of turning the rebel left flank." Robert Lowell went on to detail the disposition of the Brigade containing the 1st Massachusetts in a reserve position. Hawthorne believed that Lowell was repeating orders almost word for word.

"The attack is set for tomorrow morning then," Hawthorne said as they neared the buggy.

"We shall surprise the enemy just after dawn and drive them before us," Lowell said with youthful confidence.

"I would dearly love to see those traitorous scum soundly thrashed," Hawthorne declared passionately. "In your opinion, where might I secure the best vantage point to watch the battle," he prodded.

Lowell hesitated. "It may be dangerous for you near the battle lines," he warned. "A place about the Warrenton Turnpike as it nears Bull Run should be relatively safe and would offer the best viewpoint," the Captain said thoughtfully. They had reached the buggy and Hawthorne climbed aboard.

"I bid you 'Gods speed', Robert, and I am confident that you will achieve a glorious victory on the morrow," Hawthorne exclaimed, pumping the Captain's hand once again.

He waved the young man goodbye and shook the reins to start the horse. Smiling to himself, he reflected on his good fortune. He had undertaken this journey because he feared the 1st

Regiment had sullied the state he served. Now, the 5th Regiment had been given an opportunity to bring glory to the state. Massachusetts would be well represented at this decisive battle, including a Member of Congress. Elihu Hawthorne had been too long in the political wars to miss a share in the glory of complete victory. Though he would do no fighting, his presence near the field of battle would insure a contribution he would most certainly manipulate to future advantage.

Joshua Campbell awoke in the early light of dawn on July 21st to a whirl of activity about him. Noise had interrupted a fitful sleep during the night. Sometime in the early morning he had managed a deeper sleep. With a start, he awoke to find he was the last person abed in the 17th Regiment. The Tucker brothers seemed to find his awakening comical.

"I wuz thinkin' we'd hafta git one o' them cannon to wake you, Josh," Will Tucker said, between fits of cackling laughter. Walter was chuckling right along with him, sharing a joke that must have started as Josh lay sleeping.

"You bes git some food 'fore we douse this fire," Riley called to him. Josh could see Riley also wore a grin.

"I guess y'all was gonna march off an' leave me," Josh grumbled. But as he looked about him in the gray light, he had to laugh at himself. There was as much noise around him as two thousand men could make.

He grabbed some bacon and coffee. He ate and drank quickly, not knowing how much time he had to complete the ritual. Everyone in his mess was dressed, with rifles and gear ready, their eyes and ears keen for the call to arms.

He swallowed the last of his coffee and grabbed a cold corn cake for his haversack. He rolled his blanket, pulled on his jacket and leather pouches and found his cap. He was slapping the dirt off his headgear when he heard assembly drummed.

Josh fell in to line with the others as roll was called and officers reviewed the ranks. Glancing to either side, he could see the company lines had thinned since their first muster in camp at Corinth. But he thought those present sufficient for the task ahead.

The soldiers were ordered into marching column of fours and strung out along the McLean's Ford road. Josh could see the South Carolina in front again. The 17th was last of the Brigade, the Washington Artillery forming the tail end. Peering to the front, Josh could make out General Jones and the three regimental Colonels in conference. Jones seemed to be checking a pocket watch. He motioned to a rider, handing him a message and moments later the rider passed the lengthy column toward the Centreville Road.

Sunlight brightened the road as the morning wore on. All was in readiness, but minutes passed without an order to march. The troops gradually became restless.

Captain Franklin wandered back along Ranger company ranks, gently checking that the men stayed in line. A rumbling sound, like distant thunder, could be heard to the rear and far west of the Ford. The Captain perked his ears in that direction with a puzzled look. He checked his pocket watch and snapped it shut with some disgust.

A courier on horseback rode past the column at breakneck speed and Josh saw him rein up before the General. Jones took the message he was handed, and turned to a subordinate. In less than a minute, the command was given to shoulder arms, and then to march. Josh heard a soldier behind him say it was half past eight.

The column lurched forward and the South Carolina troops prepared to get their feet wet. Suddenly, the Federal artillery on the hillside to the left opened fire.

In the rush of morning preparations, Josh had nearly forgotten about the Yankee cannon on the hill. A murmur went through the Regiment when the guns opened. Seconds later, he saw two great splashes of water in Bull Run. The South Carolina troops weaved to the right instinctively, away from the guns. Officers screamed and shouted for men to remain in formation until they continued to the other side.

The Federal battery fired another round in the direction of the road far behind the column. Josh thought he glimpsed the cannon ball in flight, but lost it among tree tops. He did not hear an explosion after the ball passed.

As Josh now approached the Ford, he was anxious that another artillery round might be fired at the column. Strangely, only one round had been fired in their direction. Josh closed on Bull Run and prepared to get his feet wet, every man in the Regiment looking anxiously upstream.

When he reached the creek and could see the hilltop, Josh saw the Yankees had apparently limbered their guns and drawn them away. There was no sign of cannon. It occurred to Josh the Federals had been posted only to detect any movement across the Ford. Having spotted the crossing, they threw out a few shots and returned to a safer place.

The bank on the far side of Bull Run was slippery and the men struggled on the low slope in now wet shoes. Josh made it through the muddy mess, supporting Walter Tucker so that he did not fall. They had crossed Bull Run into what he had come to think of as Yankee territory.

From the beginning, something seemed to slow the march. Just over the Ford, the column halted briefly, then started again. Full daylight now covered the road and a glaring sun bore down as the column stopped and started along the road.

After about two hours of slow progress, Josh could see a road ahead veering off to the left of their route. The troops were allowed to fall out where the roads divided and sought shade under nearby trees. They pulled canteens to wet parched throats.

Lieutenant Abernathy told them they were awaiting further orders. Another courier arrived and went straight to General Jones. Minutes later, orders were passed to form up, and the men prepared to resume their march. Unexpectedly, the head of the column was turned to the rear, and began to march back the way they had come.

When Captain Franklin passed along the company ranks, he confirmed what everyone had surmised. The Brigade had been ordered back to McLeans Ford.

The Brigade returned more quickly, with men in a sort of exasperated silence. Everyone had expected a fight, but they had not even seen a Yankee. The rumbling continued from the west and it seemed the fight was occurring elsewhere.

A dispirited group trudged back across Bull Run and resumed old positions on either side of the Ford road. The Washington Artillery did not halt and continued out of sight toward the Centreville Road. With a little envy, Josh figured they were headed for the fighting to the west.

When men were ordered to fall out, they staggered off to find shade and lie down. Josh was getting comfortable on the ground when Davy Williams slipped in to their midst.

"What'd you find out," Riley asked.

"Attack's been called off," Davy began. "Abernathy tol' me the Yanks have attacked on the left an' we jes sposed to hold the Ford fer now."

"We marched all that way fer nothin'," Hugh grumbled.

"Souns like we might not see no action today," Charlie said evenly.

"Not unless the Yanks try to cross Bull Run here," Riley noted.

Josh had mixed feelings at the news. He was ready to be part of the battle, but after the tiring, hot march earlier, he was glad to have a chance to rest. He removed his damp socks and shoes to dry.

Sergeant Ferrall joined them. "Don't be getting too comfortable here, lads. The day's not yet over."

They all looked hard at the Sergeant. "You may yet get yer wish to see some shootin'," he added, and walked away.

"I'll see if I kin rustle up some food," Riley said, rising and following after the Sergeant. Josh roused himself to get some firewood.

Thunderous rumbling in the west had grown continuous and been joined by sharper sounds. The noise continued for a while, then died away about noon and everyone figured the fight was about over for this day.

Josh and his friends found little to do as they waited, though they managed to scrape together a hot meal of boiled grits. Some played cards or gambled, a few wrote letters. Josh had resolved to take up pencil and paper when another courier raced by going to General Jones. Within moments, orders were issued to form up and prepare to march. Resignedly, the men struggled back into their equipment and took places in line as the drummers beat the familiar cadence.

"I guess we goin' fer 'nother little walk," Hugh said without much enthusiasm.

"I shur don't like gettin' my feet wet all the time," Will Tucker joined in. "Mah shoes 'bout wore out from all the marchin' we done since we got to this Virginia."

Grumbling was put aside as the column started off without delay. A grueling afternoon sun made progress especially hard, and choking dust fouled air for the 17th at the rear of the column. This time, the march continued without pause to the crossroads, past the spot they had stopped before. The column stepped on to the road veering left, halting a little farther on at the farm of a man named Croson.

Josh looked ahead and saw the command party astride their horses clustered at the head of a ravine to the left. Given the route they had taken from the Ford, he figured the ravine led north and west, probably toward Centreville. He watched as a scout on horse emerged from the ravine and rode toward the General. The soldier spoke briefly to the Brigade commander, saluted and returned the way he came. Seconds later, the head of the column turned into the ravine and orders were passed for quiet in the ranks.

Exhausted soldiers slowly comprehended the meaning of this maneuver. Not only were they entering new territory, but they were likely to close on the enemy. As Josh quickened his step with the others, he noticed there was plenty of daylight left for a fight.

When the 17th entered the ravine, Josh could see it bore on relatively straight ahead. Grassy hillsides bracketed the depression, dotted with the occasional tree. Where the ravine began to widen, Josh noticed the flag of the 5th South Carolina veer to the right around a small rise in front. Men of the 18th started to ascend the rise and the 17th was directed farther left in the ravine. After some 200 yards, the 17th was also marched upwards to the crest of a hill. A wagon road appearing to their immediate left.

As men of the 17th Mississippi deployed from column of fours to rank and file, Josh saw what he both feared and desired. Across a small valley, on a hilltop opposite, flew the Federal stars and stripes. It was well protected by a full battery of artillery, though there seemed to be no infantry visible.

Josh tried to see all about him as lines were formed. The 18th Mississippi was strung out to the right of the 17th. The 5th South Carolina was out of sight, beyond the 18th. He noticed General Jones and his staff to the rear of the 18th, and watched couriers take off toward each regiment. With a shudder, he realized they were about to attack.

Congressman Hawthorne had grown increasingly uncomfortable under the broiling Virginia sun. Coat and cravat had been removed, sleeves rolled and a fan employed through the early afternoon, but as yet no respite. His water supply was nearly depleted and his pocket watch read 3 o'clock on the dial. He could only hope the battle was nearly over so that he could politely depart for some relief.

Hawthorne had arrived in mid morning on the small knoll just off the Warrenton Turnpike. He had dodged military vehicles and troops to gain this spot and it had proved to be well situated. He could see across the Bull Run to a small rise with a farmhouse atop. A passing officer had informed him that the farm was owned by someone named Henry, according to the officer's map.

His was apparently a very good viewing spot and it was steadily populated after his arrival by citizens from the Capital. People of all ages in carriages and on horseback arrived to join him. Clogged with abandoned conveyances, the Turnpike had become impassable beyond this point to Bull Run.

People had brought picnic baskets of food and drink. The Congressman accepted an awkward invitation from a War Department clerk to share some food. Hawthorne recognized the man as someone he had dealings with when the first Massachusetts' regiments arrived in the Capital. He strained to remember the fellow's surname as Johnson and that he had been helpful in securing some needed camp supplies, but he hesitated to make extensive contact with a mere clerk. However, the invitation was cheerfully extended and their food seemed plentiful, filling a need the Congressman had overlooked in his preparations.

"I do not wish to intrude on your family meal," Hawthorne politely protested when the invitation was made.

"Nonsense, my dear sir, we would be delighted to have you join us," Johnson replied.

"Perhaps a few morsels and something to drink would suffice," Hawthorne countered, doffing his hat to the wife as he sat down. The plump, smallish woman did not speak or look directly at him when she handed him a plate.

"You'll find this squab most enjoyable, Congressman," the pretentious Johnson boasted. "I had my man at Willard's prepare a basket for me from their kitchen.

"We are in for a most satisfying spectacle, sir," the clerk continued. "The rebellion could well be over by sundown."

When Hawthorne finished his meal, he lingered with the Johnson family. The crowd had thickened so that if he moved, he could not have secured another place to sit on the rise. He had brought along a field glass and peered through it frequently to observe the battleground.

In speaking to the officer earlier in the day, he learned the Federal troops were advancing against the rebels. As day passed, the advance seemed to progress from his right to the area in front of him. Curiously, the sounds of battle had diminished after noon as he lunched with Johnson.

Now, as he checked his watch, their attention was drawn to the hill around the small house he had noticed earlier. The thump of artillery began to increase and rifle fire crackled intermittently. Hawthorne consulted his looking glass and watched Federal troops occupy the Henry house hill.

"We seem to have the high ground, Johnson," the Congressman commented. "I see little of any rebel resistance."

"This is a day we shall long remember, Congressman," Johnson said excitedly.

"You can be sure that treason will not go unpunished," Hawthorne declared loudly. "Congress will see that Davis and his cohorts receive the highest penalties."

Hawthorne turned back to his telescope. He watched as Federal troops formed in lines atop the hill. He looked in vain for the 5th Massachusetts flag.

Hawthorne detected a shift in the lines as the rebels surged forward. Southerners seemed to swamp the cannon in their wake and the Federal lines were pushed back. A damnable rebel flag waived triumphantly near the damaged house.

The Congressman had little time to reflect on this while he relayed developments to the Johnson family and those nearby. Some time passed, then the rebels appeared to be giving ground. More blue clad Federal troops occupied the hill and Hawthorne thought he glimpsed the flag of the 5th Massachusetts. The Regiment was now in the thick of the fight.

Dense smoke engulfed the field for some time and it was difficult to determine which side possessed the hill. The crackling rattle of rifle fire came in waves toward the spectators from the other side of Bull Run. This was clearly a hotly contested fight.

Hawthorne mopped his brow and rechecked his watch. It was now approaching four o'clock and the smoke began to clear as he peered through the field glass. The sight that greeted him was stunning. Rebels occupied the Henry hill and more units seemed to arrive in his sight. The Stars and Stripes were not to be seen.

At this moment his attention was drawn toward the road. On the crowded turnpike below, bluelcad soldiers were running through the obstacles and shouting wildly. Hawthorne detailed Johnson to find out the source of the mayhem. He turned back to scan the field on the other side of Bull Run.

The rebels were still in possession of the hill. He now noticed the lack of rifle or artillery fire from that quarter. He was puzzling over this development when Johnson rushed toward him.

"We are lost, Congressman, our troops are in retreat," a flushed Johnson said breathlessly. He shouted for his wife to gather their things and the formerly sedate woman jumped in to action.

Hawthorne grabbed the frightened man by the arm. "What do you mean, Johnson. Surely the army has not broken."

Johnson wrenched free of him. "See for your self, man," he shouted and fled with his wife toward the carriages.

Hawthorne looked to the Turnpike. A sea of blue seemed to flow from the direction of Bull Run toward them and on toward Centreville. There seemed to be no order, no one to take charge.

The Congressman grabbed his coat and raced toward his carriage. His horse strained restlessly in the harness. Unarmed Federal soldiers of every rank ran past him, a look of wide eyed terror on most.

Hawthorne jumped into his carriage and struck the horse

with his whip. The horse responded eagerly. Fear stricken troops were nudged to the side by the steed, but the Turnpike was extremely crowded. Progress would be slow in this horde as he reined the horse sharply every few moments.

His earlier route to the Turnpike had been by a side road from the camp of the 1st Massachusetts. Hawthorne now turned on to that side road and found it nearly open. The horse increased its pace and they met no delays in their progress. Although he saw Federal soldiers, the men were preoccupied with their own safety and paid him scant attention.

He struggled to remember the several turns and connections in his route that morning. Hawthorne kept to a general sense of direction and determined to head northeasterly. With some luck, he would return to the camp of the 1st on the edge of Centreville. He would be safe in their midst.

Suddenly, Hawthorne heard cannon fired to his front, the direction in which he traveled. Rifle fire followed closely after the booming artillery, indicating the rebels may have gained a crossing of Bull Run. He could not see any soldiers ahead, but instinctively slowed the horse to a trot lest he find himself in the middle of a battle. The road ahead turned and rolled with the landscape. He feared what he might find on the other side of any crest or around any bend, but he did not encounter troops of either side. The noise of battle flared ahead.

Hawthorne was about to stop and get his bearings when he saw them. Two soldiers were standing in the middle of the road looking toward the sound of the firing. They wore gray uniforms of a cut far different then he had seen in the Federal camps. The Congressman believed he had somehow veered into rebel lines!

Without hesitation, he struck the horse hard and the animal responded. The Southerners noted his presence too late as the carriage bore down on them. They turned just before the carriage struck them and dove wildly to the side. Hawthorne whipped the horse furiously, expecting any moment to hear the sound of firing from behind.

Hawthorne breathed easier as he rounded a bend in the road, leaving the rebel soldiers in his wake. The sun was lower in the sky now, and he was confident that his direction was north to Centreville. If he remembered correctly a wider road lay just ahead. Bearing to his right, he spotted a crossroad. Surely he had reached the Centreville Road.

He reined up a short distance from the intersection. The road before him was filled with horse drawn artillery. Closely following were Northern troops in good marching order. He was relieved by the sight, but the mass of troops would impede his progress.

Just at the intersection, two Federal soldiers stepped into the roadway and leveled their muskets at him, ordering him to halt.

"I am Congressman Elihu Hawthorne of Massachusetts," he announced as he reined the horse. "Please let me pass."

"I don't give a damn if yer Abe goddamned Lincoln," the taller one barked. "You'll not pass this way today."

Hawthorne allowed his horse to step toward the men and both cocked hammers as they leveled their rifles. To his immense relief, he yanked the reins, turning the horse away slightly.

A captain appeared without bothering to identify himself and took in the situation quickly. He rode up to Hawthorne's carriage and explained the Congressman could not continue until the road was cleared. The busy captain gave those orders to the soldiers, saluted Hawthorne and was on his way. Hawthorne resigned himself to wait.

The Congressman watched dispirited Federal troops marching back toward the Capital and knew the rebellion would survive this day. Unlike the scene to the west, these soldiers exhibited no panic, merely resignation.

Finally, the ranks began to thin and the sentries prepared to take their leave. The taller one turned toward Hawthorne.

"You best stay close behind, there's nothing but secesh

back that away."

Member of Congress Elihu Hawthorne was now the rearguard of a retreating army.

9

Soldiers of the 17th Mississippi stumbled into line with their eyes riveted on the hillside opposite and the shouts, curses and commands of officers could hardly focus them to the task at hand. Men bumped into each other and rifles were dropped. Little of what they had practiced in drill was now remembered in the presence of the enemy.

Josh took his place in ranks without conscious effort. The sights and sounds of battle preparation became a blur to him. He thought he heard Walter Tucker gasp for air. Davy said something like "Goddamn", and he heard Charlie Akins next to him asking for God's mercy. Ferrall's booming voice penetrated his mind and he turned to the sound dumbly as if to a bright light.

"Stand in ranks, lads. Dress yer line," the First Sergeant repeated over and over. He pushed some into place and stiffened others with a slap to the back. Second Sergeant Haskins merely cursed and barked excitedly, but Ferrall's cool persistence gradually brought the Rangers to order.

Company officers took their positions behind the men. No orders were issued once the Regiment formed and troops stood stock still, all eyes fixed to the front.

In the lull that followed, Josh had time to take in the sight before him. Southern troops occupied a crest of ground separated from the Yankee position by more than 200 yards. The Federals had fortified the top of a hill with logs and pointed sticks.

Between the lines, the ground dropped to a shallow depression. Tall grass covered the slopes, though trees grew thickly farther right. Josh could see the shimmer of a narrow stream snaking its way through the low ground. He counted 6 cannon barrels spaced about the Federal works. Looking harder, he could now see blue coated infantry forming behind the artillery. The three Southern regiments outnumbered the Federal soldiers he could see, but artillery more than evened the odds.

The day was dripping hot and Josh had wet every part of his uniform during the afternoon march. Now he felt a chill on his back. His gut stirred with a queer sensation. Josh fought the sick feeling by swallowing hard. He willed himself not to break from ranks and run to the rear for relief. Raising his cap, he wiped his brow quickly to keep sweat from stinging his eyes. He checked his shirt pocket, fingering the eagle talon and praying that he would not disgrace himself this day.

Not for the first time since he awoke, Josh thought of Zeke and despaired of his missing friend. Ferrall's voice sounded and he recalled the Sergeant's words to stay by him during the fight. With that thought to comfort, and a strange lack of activity, Josh relaxed tight muscles slightly.

Suddenly, officers shouted to load rifles. Nervously, men conducted the drill that had been drummed in to each. Cartridges were pulled from pouches and torn by dry mouths now tinted with the grisly taste and smell of gunpowder. The metallic clink of ramrods against gun barrels rattled through the Regiment as they poured powder and balls down the barrel, then rammed the charges home. Rifles were leveled and caps placed by sweaty hands, every soldier anxiously awaiting the order to attack.

Josh heard a crackle of rifles to his right in the area between the 18th Mississippi and the Carolina boys. Instinctively, all eyes turned that way, but woods obscured any clear view. Smoke drifted from the trees where Josh caught a glimpse of the 5th South Carolina flag. Indecipherable shouts and sounds reached the area of the 17th and the firing ceased quickly.

Abruptly, the Rangers were ordered out as skirmishers. The men stepped out of ranks and spread along the forefront of the Regiment. The 17th's color bearer came forward with an escort and formed just behind the skirmishers, the flag hanging limply in the still air. Josh feared this movement might draw attention from the Federals. He calmed a bit as Riley and Hugh stepped in at either side and Ferrall took his place just a few feet away. Officers placed themselves in front of the line, though Josh could see Jasper Welburn hunkering down to diminish an already small body. When the formation was complete, every Ranger tensed for the order to advance.

Just then, the entire 18th stepped off to their right with a cheer. As their skirmishers neared the small stream, that Regiment was staggered with Federal cannon fire. The ground erupted in several places as a thunderous roar passed over the hillside. Josh heard desperate cries of fright and pain from the 18th and noticed groups of men trailing in the wake of the still advancing regiment.

"Forward men, eyes front," Captain Franklin shouted and pointed the way with his sword. The Rangers turned their attention to the field before them. Josh moistened dry, cracked lips with his tongue and stepped off with the company, gripping his rifle with both hands. The ground descended some 50 yards to the stream and men began to quicken pace downhill. In a few minutes, the company reached the winding stream without incident.

Puffs of smoke above them marked another round of fire from Federal guns and this time missiles arced toward the Rangers. Ground just to the right of Josh erupted in dirt and smoke and Hugh pushed hard into Josh so that he stumbled against Riley to his left, barely holding onto his rifle. Josh heard someone cry out as he struggled to right himself.

Josh looked right and saw Lucius Bradwell standing erect, his hands empty and uniform spotted with dirt. The two men on either side of him lay sprawled on the ground in unnatural shapes. Ferrall rushed to the spot and prodded stunned survivors around the men. Bradwell wore a strange, half smile look on his face, hesitating just a moment.   Then he grabbed the nearest weapon and moved quickly across the stream. Without orders, Bradwell defiantly raised his rifle and fired toward the Federal troops. Josh caught a glimpse of the wounded before he crossed the stream, now writhing in pain.

As the company crossed the stream and started to climb the hill just beyond, they met rifle fire from Yankee infantry placed in and about the battery. The Rangers instinctively halted, kneeling or crouching to return fire. Federal fire was not accurate and seemed to hit the ground in front of the skirmishers. Bradwell and a few others remained erect, boldly challenging the enemy.

From one knee, Josh took aim up the slope for his first shot at the Yankees, but could see no distinct form. A sliver of blue appeared through thickening smoke. He held his breath and pulled the trigger. The rifle exploded loudly and kicked against his shoulder. He had to stop a moment to clear his head and remember what to do next.

"They ain't hit nothin' yet," the soldier next to him shouted over the crackling battlefield noise. Josh looked at the strange, grimy face and was ready to reply, but the man did not seem to notice him.

His arms felt a hundred pounds each as he began to reload. It must have taken an eternity to pour the powder, place the ball, ram the charge and cock the rifle. He tasted powder again on his tongue and inhaled the smoke of his previous shot. Then he raised the rifle to his eye, ready to shoot. This time he saw a cannon barrel and fired at a place just behind the barrel.

The Mississippi Rifle took a 'buck and ball' cartridge, consisting of one large lead ball and several pieces of smaller buckshot. The ammunition was only effective at close range, contents dispersing over a wide area, and were apt to hit the enemy only within eighty yards. The Federals barricaded above the Rangers were at the edge of this effective range. Neither the 'ball' nor the 'buck' were doing much damage in this confrontation.

Josh heard officers shouting to the men to keep moving, but none of the skirmishers stirred. Over the call of a bugler, he heard Dutchie screaming strange words he had never heard before. He looked for Ferrall and found him a few paces to his left, calmly loading his weapon. Josh gravitated closer, decreasing the distance between.

Suddenly, Josh sensed others beside and behind him. A rifle fired near his head. He turned and saw that the Regiment had come forward to the skirmish line and stopped as the men advanced no further. It was impossible to reload without bumping into someone.

Federal artillery had been occupied in the direction of the 18th during the exchange of rifle fire. Now with the 17th stopped in a group, the cannon turned toward them. Cannon balls soared overhead. The hill behind them exploded in several places. This had the immediate effect of pushing men at the rear into those in front. The front line became a wavering mass while men fought to steady themselves and get a clear shot at the Yankees. Regimental fire slackened with men crowded so closely together.

Another round from the Federals brought a rushing, windy noise that sounded to Josh like a swarm of bees. This time some in the forward line were hit, as well as those farther behind. Josh had no idea what type of weapon the Federals were using, but he heard the cries of more wounded.

An officer from another company Josh did not recognize bolted to the front, pointed his sword toward the enemy and shouted for the men to follow. He immediately tumbled forward grasping his arm while the sword fell to the ground. Two men from the ranks raced forward to help the stricken man.

Among the pop of rifles, Josh heard voices shouting to "Fall back". Soldiers began to move back across the stream and return up the hill. Josh was uncertain whether to join them, but he saw Ferrall shoulder his rifle and lope sideways to the rear, keeping one eye on the Federals. There seemed no order to the movement, but neither was there widespread panic. The men appeared to tolerate this retreat as a temporary interruption. Josh could see that the 18th had already begun to pull back from their forward position. The enemy seemed to encourage a pullback as they ceased consistent firing.

When Josh turned he saw Colonel Featherston dismounted and his staff clustered on the crest of the hill. Just beyond the Colonel and overshadowed by the horse, Marcus held Sir Ivanhoe at the ready.

Suddenly mindful that he had his back to the enemy, Josh turned sideways in imitation of Ferrall. He scrambled awkwardly toward the top of the rise where the assault began. He reached the crest winded, but now in the relative safety of the Regiment.

The 17th settled at its starting point with fewer in the ranks, having now experienced enemy fire. With the exhilaration of survival, men knelt or crouched on the ground, though many remained standing, facing the Federal position. Though firing had ceased on both sides along the entire Brigade front, officers cautioned men to be ready.

Josh gathered his feelings and looked around. He felt relief and a little pride to have survived the short fight, though he calculated he had only fired twice, three times at most. He quickly spotted the Tuckers, Riley, Davy, Charlie and Hugh. All appeared to be without wounds, though likely feeling as tired and dazed as he did. He also recognized Ferrall speaking with Captain Franklin, both of whom seemed untouched. Lucius Bradwell moved about the hilltop, wearing a fearful expression and anxious to renew the fight immediately. Reclining soldiers generally ignored the hulking Bradwell, though Josh had to admire the man's aggressive determination.

As he looked behind and down the hill on which they stood, Josh could see the bloody result of the quick encounter. He counted twelve men prone on the ground, brought to medical care by regimental bandsmen. The surgeon and his assistants moved among them, bandaging and treating their wounds. Josh could hear moans etched with pain and pleas for water. Two of the forms, their clothing askew and dirty, lay stock still, ignored by the medical men.

Josh was transfixed by the wounded. Despite his shock at the sight, he could see no one he immediately recognized among the casualties. Yet he knew he could just as easily be down there, stricken by a painful wound. Ferrall's voice broke this morbid feeling and Josh turned to face his First Sergeant.

"You're alive, lad, and be thankful for it," the smiling Irishman whispered. The confident, assured nature of the man infected and comforted him. Josh allowed a guilty grin play across his face.

"We may yet have more work this day," Ferrall added in louder voice. "Check yer rifles, lads, and count yer cartridges. There's more to be had if you need 'em."

Josh did as he was told and judged his ammunition sufficient. He felt his sweat soaked shirt clinging to his body and opened his jacket for some relief. Grabbing his canteen, he tilted it high to quench a powerful thirst, the warm water tasting better at that moment than a cool drink. He spit some water to drive the bitter taste of gunpowder from his mouth. He suppressed the hunger forming because he knew food was unavailable, but he noted the sun was much lower in the sky. The fight could not last much longer as evening descended.

Davy cried out excitedly, "Them Yanks're runnin'."

Josh looked to the other hill and saw that he was right, the Federals were hooking guns to wagons and pulling back from the breastworks. Soldiers of the 17th rose and worked forward to get a better look, pointing and yelling with relief. Some of the men were foolish enough to taunt the Yankees, though the enemy soldiers paid no attention. A few of the Pettus Rifles started down the hill toward the Federals and had to be called back by officers.

Josh looked expectantly in Colonel Featherston's direction,

half fearing and half hoping for orders to advance. The Colonel was dispatching a rider, and Josh guessed he would need orders to advance the Regiment.

Just then he heard shouts of "Halt" and "Stop him!" near Featherston's.   A horse reared on its back legs and dashed off toward the ranks.   As the animal broke through the Regimental line, Josh recognized Marcus crouched low atop Sir Ivanhoe. He was driving hard toward the Yankee side.

Shots were fired after the galloping horse, but it raced down the slope and bounded cleanly over the small stream. In a matter of seconds, the horse gained the crest of the other hill, Marcus clinging to its back.   Then both rider and horse disappeared on the road toward the retreating Northerners.

Josh turned his attention back to the Colonel, who had by then run ahead of the Regiment. Featherston stood and glared toward the opposite hill as if demanding his horse return. Finally, he turned in disgust and walked directly to where the Rangers were gathered, staff officers in tow.

"Colonel 'pears to be a might upset," Hugh Driscoll muttered to Josh as the officer came toward the company. Featherston stopped in front of the Rangers, a hard look on his face.

"The Regiment will pursue those Yankees," he declared, his voice straining with anger. "This company will resume as skirmishers and follow closely on the heels of those devils."

He turned as if to leave, then returned with a glare along the entire line of Rangers. "And get mah horse," Featherston hissed sharply, snapping a salute to Captain Franklin and pausing to fix his eyes on Josh before he continued down the line.

By now the entire company was ready to move and Franklin simply hollered "Forward", taking off at the double quick. Shadows had lengthened so that the valley between the hilltops lay entirely in shade. The Rangers trotted down the hill, jumped the stream to a man and climbed toward the Federal works. Passing their earlier stopping point, Josh reflected that the climb was much easier without enemy fire.

Then they were within the redoubt. Not a Yankee soldier remained. In the gathering dusk, there was no sign of Federals ahead, though much had been left behind. Company officers paused to reform the men and pressed on to the road the Federals had taken, still at the double quick.

"Them Yanks prob'ly run faster'n us," Charlie said hopefully.

"We best watch out they don' have a li'l surprise fer us up the road," Riley countered.

Josh squinted hard to see if any dark shapes waited ahead.

>< >< >< >< ><

The horse collapsed shortly after Hawthorne was allowed to proceed. Probably lame, he realized, since the animal had not responded to the whip. With Federal troops disappearing rapidly before him and the hour growing later, he decided to abandon the buggy and the troublesome steed to walk the rest of the way. He prayed it would not be far to Centreville.

Even with daylight waning, the heat continued and Hawthorne quickly found he could not keep pace with the now vanishing soldiers. In short time, he was completely alone and unarmed.

Thirty minutes into his walk, a dispatch rider came pounding up behind him. As the rider slowed, Hawthorne detected the bars of a lieutenant on his uniform. The soldier offered a quizzical look as he reined up beside the bedraggled walker.

"I am Congressman Elihu Hawthorne of Massachusetts," Hawthorne said through parched lips, "and I am need of some assistance."

"What in hell are you doing on this road," the Lieutenant said after a pause, surprised to hear the northern accent on a Virginia road. He did not offer his name.

"I was forced to abandon my conveyance some ways back and I am trying to reach the camp of the 1st Massachusetts near Centreville," the weary politician replied.

"You have a good walk ahead of you, sir," the soldier rebuked. It was clear the Lieutenant did not intend to shorten that walk. "I am on military duties and can not carry you with me," the officer said, softening his tone slightly. "I will alert the 1st to your presence on the road," the man added, preparing to resume his ride.

"What road is this, young man," Hawthorne pleaded, his dry voice cracking, hoping the officer would not leave him alone again.

"You are walking on the Island Ford road. Continue on this road until it ends at the Centreville Road. Then turn north to the town." The lieutenant tried to be helpful.

"I would judge you have more than an hour's walk to the town," the officer continued. "Be careful of the secesh, they have crossed Bull Run and are likely not far behind."

The warning shook Hawthorne, and quickened his step. Since he had seen no one for some time, he had assumed danger from the enemy to be far behind him.

"I can stay no longer, sir, I must deliver the messages I carry." Sympathy tinged the soldier's voice and he tossed his half full canteen to Hawthorne. "Godspeed, sir," he said and galloped off. The Congressman wasted no time in continuing his walk, draining the canteen as he traveled.

He neared the Centreville road a short time later and paused a moment to wipe his brow before continuing. The sound of hoof beats reached his ears and he saw a rider approaching the intersection from the south. With an effort in the dimming light, he determined that it was a small black man and he waved his arms to bring him to a halt.

The rider reined up beside him, fear and wariness etched on his face, peering closely for a weapon. Hawthorne spoke before the dust settled with an expectant proposition.

"Boy, I will give you a silver dollar for the use of your mount to Centreville," he said.

The rider shied to create a greater distance between them, fearful of any quick move by the stranger. "Mister, you the first man I seen on mah way to freedom and I don' want to be hurtful," Marcus explained to the odd talking white man. "But I got's to get away from them gray sojers. They catch me an put me in shackles, an I wants to be done with slavin'."

Hawthorne had no desire to stop the young slave's flight, but he sorely needed transportation. He took a step closer to grab the reins, but the young man was quick to turn the animal's head.

"We can ride together," the Congressman shouted desperately, but the wary rider had already dug his heels into the horses flank and galloped off. Hawthorne watched them go with a sinking feeling. Full dark was less than an hour away with no sight of the town ahead. He resumed his journey despondently, willing his feet onward.

Something hit the ground before him, startling him from his dull state of mind. As he looked to see what had caused the noise, he heard a crack and pop behind him. He turned around, puzzled as to the meaning of this disturbance, then halted when he saw the source. A dozen gray clad men were running toward him with rifles leveled. Hawthorne was so exhausted that it did not occur to him to run.

Bradwell fired at the dark human shape without a word to the others. They were ordered to catch retiring Yankee soldiers, but had so far spotted none. The man some distance away was indistinguishable in near darkness as friend or foe and was the first person they had encountered in their pursuit.

Mississippians had left the Yankee breastworks on the run, chasing a foe retreating to its strength. The Rangers quickly arrived at a crossroads, and it was not immediately clear which road the Yankees had taken. Captain Franklin reckoned north toward Centreville, but split the company to cover both paths. Josh and his mess were detailed with Ferrall on the road to Centreville, First Lieutenant Abernathy in charge.

As they double quicked up the road, they began to pass the debris of a hurried enemy. Knapsacks, blankets, canteens and even rifles had been tossed aside. Josh was tempted to retrieve a keepsake, but Ferrall had already warned them against straggling.

A grassy path led through woods to the right of the road at one point and it had evidently been well used. The First Lieutenant could not ignore a possible escape route and detailed a group of men to explore the path a ways. Abernathy remained at the road where the path diverged and ordered Ferrall to continue down the road with a squad of men. Josh fell in with his group.

There had been no sign of the Regiment in support and Josh knew the group was too small now for an encounter with the Federals. The light of a summer evening was fading fast, and Josh figured pursuit would be halted shortly.

Riley Osborne was the first to see the human form ahead and called out to the Sergeant. Bradwell had fired before Ferrall could even reply. The stunned man, clearly a civilian, stood perfectly still as the Mississippians approached and surrounded him.

Josh thought he looked a poor specimen, clothes dusty and unkempt. He had a look of fright on his face, but he did not bolt. He wore no uniform of any kind and carried no weapon, though his very presence on the military road aroused suspicion.

Ferrall pushed his way to the man. "Who might you be and what is yer business here," the Sergeant commanded.

"I am Elihu Hawthorne, member of Congress from Massachusetts," Hawthorne declared in a hoarse voice, trying to muster some dignity and composure.

"Hoo-ee, we done bagged us a Yankee Congressman," Davy Williams cried out. The men hooted and whistled at the news. Most let their weapons rest on the ground, since the unarmed man clearly presented no threat.

"You are a prisoner of the 17th Mississippi Regiment, sir," Ferrall said over the commotion.

This was troubling news and Hawthorne spoke up to put these rebels in their place. "I am not a soldier, Sergeant," he said stubbornly, "and I will not be treated as a prisoner."

A fellow named Joe Crawford stepped menacingly close to Hawthorne and said, "Mister, y'all ain't in Yankeeland, an yer gonna do what we say."

Hawthorne recoiled from the direct threat, then felt an anger born of humiliation stir in him. He straightened his body and said defiantly in clearer voice, "I might expect a rabble not to know the difference between civilians and soldiers. I demand that you take me to your commanding officer."

Josh caught his breath apart from the cluster, and as the civilian spoke, he noticed Lucius Bradwell working up behind the man. Ferrall would not see him in the near dark and the others had their attention on the prisoner. Bradwell had his sword bayonet held low and was ready to strike the man from behind.

Josh dodged a soldier and slipped in behind Bradwell. Bradwell said aloud "I got the best med'cine fer this Yankee scum." He reached for the prisoner's shoulder to turn him around, ready to shove the blade in his gut.

But Josh was quicker because he had determined exactly what Bradwell was going to do. With his left hand in a fist, he reached around the burly man and chopped down on his left arm. In the same motion, he grabbed the other arm with the bayonet and twisted it backward. Josh hooked his right knee behind Bradwell's and pulled him backward, spilling the man face down on the ground. The bayonet tumbled from his grasp.

"You cain't stick an unarmed man," Josh yelled at the fallen form.

Bradwell rose toward him looking for blood. With an animal like scream, he lunged forward and buried his shoulder in Josh's midsection. As Josh collapsed and fell, he separated from

Bradwell, managing to get a hand down to break his fall. Josh rolled to avoid the next blow, but he saw that Ferrall had Bradwell under his grip.

When Josh pulled Bradwell away from the prisoner, Ferrall had pushed the Yankee aside on his way to the struggling men. As Bradwell lunged, he had a clear chance to grab him by the scruff of the neck and halt the fracas. He straightened the angry soldier up and shook him while he calmed, avoiding Bradwell's flailing arms.

"You'll be actin' like a soldier, man," the Sergeant commanded loudly, trying to bring the malicious Bradwell to his senses as the others crowded around. Finally, the wildness spent itself and Bradwell stopped his flailing.

Ferrall released his grip and Bradwell stumbled outside the ring of soldiers. Riley helped Josh to his feet and grabbed his hat and rifle for him. Josh was dusting himself off when the men turned to the sound of shouting behind them.

"Y'all got to come back, Cap'n's orders," the man yelled. It was a Ranger Josh knew slightly, who had been with Captain Franklin's group when they split. Once he had delivered his message, the man turned around and trotted back down the road without waiting.

"Form up, lads, there'll be no more fight this day," Sergeant Ferrall told them. "Osborne, Williams, take the prisoner with you. The rest of you grab yer rifles and fall in behind."

The men started off at a trot, Riley and Davy grabbing either arm of the prisoner who offered no resistance. They had run only a short way when they encountered Lieutenant Abernathy and other Rangers.

"We caught us a man claims to be a Yankee Congressman, sir," Ferrall reported to the Lieutenant.

Abernathy stepped close to inspect the man. "Where do you come from," the Lieutenant asked.

"Massachusetts, sir," Hawthorne declared. He could see the Lieutenant's bars and hoped this man had some authority.

"We'll take him along to the Captain, sergeant," Abernathy said. "We have been ordered to return to the Ford."

The Lieutenant turned and set off down the road, but at a restricted pace. Tired soldiers followed in ragged order. There was little light left in the sky and it was hard to see ten yards ahead. The men needed no reminder to keep together.

Josh walked with an eye to his back. He was aware that Bradwell might try to finish the fight in the dark, but he caught no glimpse of him in the men nearest. Josh did not relax his vigil and made sure to walk between Hugh and Charlie.

Josh had not been aware he was close to the prisoner until the man spoke.

"I must thank you Private, for throttling that ruffian," Hawthorne said as he recognized the young soldier who now appeared beside him in the dark. "Your honor does you credit."

Josh was surprised by the man's remarks and noticed the strange accent of his words for the first time.

"Mister, he'uz fixin' to back stab you, and that ain't a fair fight," Josh replied. "This war ain't 'bout killin' unarmed civilians."

Hawthorne was intrigued by this comment. Through his weariness, he struggled to find a kind way to put his question. "I would like to hear you say what this war is about, young man."

Josh was too tired to argue politics and thought to keep his reply brief. "It's 'bout you Yankees tryin' to tell us Southerners how to live." He braced himself for the Northerner's expected preachy rejoinder.

Hawthorne let the smile play across his face, sure that the young soldier could not see him clearly in the dark. How naïve this young man was, he thought, unable to understand the deeper issues of slavery and need for union. Could all these rebels be so ignorant and misguided.

Josh Campbell turned his face slightly away, assuming the Northerner could see his skeptical expression. Josh thought here was a man from far north coming down to Virginia most probably expecting to see his Yankee soldiers whip the rebels. But he had his comeuppance when the Federals ran like rabbits and then he'd got his own self captured. And now he wanted to lecture Josh on why he was fighting.

"There are many issues to be decided in this war," Elihu Hawthorne began to explain. Then he checked himself. "Perhaps we can not agree on the cause of this war," Hawthorne remarked humbly, realizing this was not the time nor place to dispute his rescuer's understanding of the conflict.

Northerner and Southerner said no more as they rejoined the remainder of the company and Captain Franklin. Franklin was informed of the prisoner and spoke briefly with him. Then he spoke to the company.

"Men, the battle has ended today and we are to return to the Ford. We can continue on this road. The Regiment has already returned to camp."

Franklin allowed this news to sink in, then continued, "Our march will take us through General Longstreets Brigade at Blackburn's Ford. They are expecting us. We have some distance to travel before we retire this night, and you must keep together."

The Captain started ahead as the men were formed in column of twos by the sergeants. They shouldered their rifles and set off down the road toward campfires glowing some distance away. There was little conversation as the company crossed Bull Run at Blackburn's Ford.

Numbing weariness seemed to descend on Josh all at once, just after crossing the Run. His gear seemed too heavy and he had to concentrate on marching to will his feet to obey. He longed to lay down and let the day slip away.

Campfires and men with torches lit their way for some distance as they passed through Longstreet's Brigade. Josh snapped out of his trance when the company halted at the McLean house. There, the prisoner was placed in the custody of soldiers on General Beauregard's staff. The man from Massachusetts must have been satisfied with the change since he lodged no protest. Then the Rangers continued on their way, turning to the McLean Ford road for the final leg of their journey.

It was after midnight when the company finally straggled in. Few in the 17th Regiment took notice of their arrival. Every one of the Rangers stacked rifles and instantly plunged toward bedrolls. Within moments of their arrival, most were sound asleep.

Josh found a place to stretch out under the sky and removed his gear. He delayed his rest to remove shoes and rub complaining feet, the cool night air feeling good on bare skin. Josh unrolled his blanket and readied himself for a sleep he knew would come quickly.

He reviewed the day's events with satisfaction. He had seen the enemy and served in battle. Federal cannon had scared him, but he had advanced when ordered and remembered to fire as they had been trained. Surely others had fought more valiantly this day and would be reckoned heroes. But Joshua Campbell had survived the battle and he was truly glad for that alone.

10

The next morning dawned with a cool dampness coating everything and everyone. It might have rained during the night, but Josh was not aware of when. He had plunged into a deep sleep of pure exhaustion, to be awaken only when he felt a call of nature.

He looked about the stirring camp. On first glance, nothing unusual indicated the men around him had been involved in any type of fight, that men had bled and died. Instead, the morning appeared little different than those that had preceded it. Men huddled about campfires, talking and eating. Arms were stacked, officers and enlisted roamed about the camp on various duties. Men fell in for a roll call later than usual, were informed there would be no drills this day, and returned to individual pursuits under a gray sky that threatened day long rain.

Riley had the campfire going and worked on something for breakfast. Josh moved toward the fire, joining the Tucker boys there.

"Ya want a cup o' coffee, Josh," Riley asked as Josh approached the fire.

"I need somethin' to open mah eyes," Josh mumbled, filling his tin cup with hot liquid. "Any word on what we doin' today?" he asked.

"I seen some o' the Carolina boys march across the Bull

Run early, an' a company from the 17th jes marched back to'rd the crossroads," Riley told him. "But ain't no one bin by with orders fer us."

"I seen a courier ridin' thru camp before roll," Will Tucker chimed in.

Walter perked up. "Ain't heard no rumblin' like yesterday, so it don' seem like thars no fightin'."

"I reckon we might git a little break since we wuz last in to camp," Josh speculated. "Y'all hear any 'bout the battle," he asked.

"Most o' the boys figger the Yanks bin beat an' headed back north to Washington City, but ain't no one has the particulars," Riley commented.

"That bunch we follered las night was hell fer leather goin' north," Hugh Driscoll declared, joining the campfire.

"I guess Davy'll have the whole story 'fore too long," Riley noted. "He lit out early 'fore y'all was up," he added, tending to the frying pan.

Josh smiled knowing their part of the 'grapevine' was sure to have some version of the battle, though Davy Williams was prone to add a little icing to the cake now and then.

Charlie filed in to get some food and settled down beside Hugh. With Davy on a ramble and Zeke in hospital, the mess was all up and accounted for this morning.

Josh took stock of his friends. They seemed in good spirits, none the worse for having confronted the Yankees and pursued a beaten foe. Josh shared these feelings.

He finished his coffee and chewed some bacon. Thinking to speak with Ferrall, he left the others to find the First Sergeant. He walked only a little ways when he spotted Lemuel Morse and went over to speak to him. They traded hellos from a few feet away. Morse spoke as Josh got closer, grinning in welcome.

"Heard y'all grabbed a Yank las' night," he said, putting his rifle and cleaning rag aside.

"He wuz on tha Centreville road at dark," Josh informed

his friend, settling down on his heels for a talk. "It weren't no soldier, tho, jes a Yank Congressman from Massachusetts.

"What happent to y'all after we took off," Josh asked his friend. "We didn't see the boys till we got back here las' night."

Morse's smile faded. "Colonel reined us in when we got to the Yankee works. Some of the boys tried to keep on goin', but Featherston had orders from Gen'ral Jones to fall back."

"Them Yanks was on the move an' we never did git close to any," Josh advised him. "I reckon wasn't nothin' y'all coulda done noways, 'cept wear out more shoe leather. You hear 'bout our casualties," Josh asked.

"17th had two kilt and a handful was wounded," Lem told him. "I hear the 18th got shot up perty bad, though. Lost eight or nine kilt and 'bout 20 wounded."

Josh thought the Regiment's casualties were slight, but he was surprised at the numbers for the 18th. He had not seen them engage the enemy so hotly, but then he had been well occupied during the brief fight.

"How'd they come to lose so many," he asked his friend.

"Them boys charged right in the teeth o' them Yank cannons," Morse related. "Federals was usin' rounds loaded with musket balls an' shot the front rank o' the 18th to pieces."

"How bout the Carolina boys," Josh said, "I never did see them once the shootin' started."

"They come through alright," Lem told him. "Lost a few kilt an' wounded, but I hear they never got out o' the woods to git a clear shot at the Yanks."

"Some are sayin' the 18th fired on them South Carolina boys," Morse remarked with a shrug. Everyone knew proving fire by friends was hard and no soldier would admit to doing such a thing.

Morse had something else on his mind. He looked straight at Josh as he framed his question.

"Heard you an' Bradwell had a go round las' night. Some o' the boys're sayin' you wuz fightin' over that Yankee y'all captured."

Josh was caught off guard by the question as he absorbed the casualties to the other regiments. He hadn't thought about the altercation with Bradwell this morning, but it was now clear others had.

"Lem, Bradwell was gonna stick that Yank with his bayonet, an I jes stopped him from doin' it," Josh explained. "Bradwell'd bin actin' strange since his friends got hit durin' tha battle. I know he wuz lookin' to git even with the Fed'rals, but the man we caught wasn't armed."

Josh stood to leave, not wanting to talk about the Bradwell episode in any more detail. "Lucius probly cooled down this mornin' an' I'll talk to him later," Josh said, dismissing the matter.

Morse stood with him, and put a friendly hand on his shoulder. "You bes keep yer eyes open, Josh. Lucius Bradwell ain't the forgivin' or forgettin' type. I'd be stayin' well clear o' him fer awhile."

Josh assured his friend he'd be careful and left to continue his search for Ferrall. He spoke about the battle with other soldiers he encountered, but they had little to add to the account Lem Morse had relayed. Some of the men felt they had been prevented from chasing the Yankees without good reason. Though no one held against Colonel Featherston, there was much criticism of the Brigade commander, General Jones. He returned to his mess without spotting the Sergeant.

Josh spent the rest of the day in camp, dodging an occasional rain, cleaning his rifle and taking care of other chores. He scratched out a letter home to tell his folks he had survived the battle and was doing well. He put in a few words about the brief engagement with the Yankees, and related the capture of the Northern Congressman. But he avoided details about casualties so as not to worry his mother. He wrote a line about the others in the mess and that Zeke had missed the fight with measles. Josh closed the letter in one page, thinking he should write more, and stuffed the letter in his pocket to post later.

Davy Williams returned as they gathered for evening meal, full of information and carrying a sack of hen's eggs. Riley fried an egg for each of them and Davy refused to talk until he'd finished his meal. He had nothing to add on the Regiment's part, so he went on quickly to the larger battle.

"Most of the fight was on the left, west o' here 'bout 5 or 6 miles," Williams told them. "The Fed'rals surprised our boys in the mornin' an scattered 'em. Yanks was fixin' to turn the flank good when they slowed their attack."

"We heard that firin' early, then it did stop fer awhile," Will Tucker put in as if he was confirming the report.

Davy shot him a glance, clearly disliking the interruption, then continued on as if Will had not spoken.

"Genr'l Johnston had his boys comin' in from the west and helped stop the Yanks fer a time," Davy said. "When tha Yanks started up agin, we wuz ready fer 'em.

"The big fight came 'round a place called Henry Hill," Davy told them. "I heard 'bout a gen'ral from Virginia named Jackson that ever' one is callin' Stonewall 'cause he held his line against the Yanks.

"Then we attacked an run 'em off Henry Hill back to the Warrenton Road. The Yanks jes broke an run an kept on runnin' past Centreville all through the night."

"I guess Bo-re-gard's a big hero now," Charlie speculated.

"Prob'ly so," Davy replied, "but I reckon Gen'ral Johnston'll git some credit and that Stonewall feller. I heard Jeff Davis hisself was here to'rds the end."

"How come we ain't follerin after them Yanks to finish 'em off," Hugh asked.

"I ain't heard nothin' bout that," Davy said. "I did hear we lost a good many men. Those who seen it say the field's covered wi' dead, an some o' the wounded is there at McLean's house."

"If we whupped 'em good, maybe they'll quit the fight an we kin all go home," Will declared hopefully. The others turned toward him, pondering this thought for a moment.

Davy spoke up to regain command of the conversation. "Them Yanks we faced cut an run after firin' a few rounds, so they ain't got much fight in 'em. Them boys'll think twice fore comin' this way agin," he added with authority.

"How bout that Yank we took prisoner. You hear what happened to him," Josh asked.

"They took prisoners off to Richmond, ain't none still at McLean's," Davy explained.

Dutchie and some of the other Rangers stopped by to talk with Davy and Josh slipped off. He knew that Davy would just repeat what he had already said, adding a little something each time so that by the end of the night he'd be on a first name basis with generals. He thought he might catch Ferrall now that darkness had fallen.

As he walked through the camp, he noticed there was little commotion this evening. Most men were huddled about campfires, some picking at slow tunes on fiddles or mouth organs. After the excitement of the day before, a full day in camp brought a welcome calm.

He walked past a campfire, his attention drawn by some men playing cards, when he abruptly came face to face with Lucius Bradwell. Bradwell had not noticed him until that moment, but as recognition dawned, the barrel chested man cried out his name.

"Campbell! I bin lookin' fer you."

Josh could not see Bradwell's arms and hands clearly in the dark, and he eased away from him slightly. "Lucius, I ain't lookin' fer no fight with you. We all done things yesterday we ain't done before, an' maybe best fergot," Josh said quickly, hoping to convince Bradwell there could be peace between them.

"You ain't so big wit'out Ferrall to back ya," Bradwell growled, moving to shorten the distance between them.

Josh looked hard to see if Bradwell had anything in his hands, though his fists could do enough damage. He desperately wanted to avoid a fight when he could not see clearly and edged back gingerly toward the campfire he had passed.

"You runnin' Campbell," Bradwell challenged as they weaved back the path Josh had taken. But now light began to reflect on the burly man and Josh could see he held nothing in his clenched fists. They were far enough apart that Bradwell could not swing and connect. Josh turned sideways and stepped over to the campfire, the card players looking up at the intruders.

He tried to reason with the still angry man. "Lucius, we on the same side out here," Josh said. "Whilst the Yanks are tryin' to whup us, you an me got enuf to occupy us without scrappin' our own selves."

Josh was not sure he was getting through, but he saw Bradwell relax his hands. Some of the tension seemed to subside in that instant. It occurred to Josh that Bradwell was less fearsome when he was not shaded by the dark.

"Don' ever stop me from killin' a Yankee bastard," Bradwell hissed. "You git in mah way agin, it'll be tha las' time." He glared at Josh for extra measure, then turned and walked off.

Josh took a minute to settle his nerves. Bradwell's warning chilled him, but at least they had not come to blows. After a moment, Josh walked back to his campfire, alert to anyone slipping up behind him. There was still a group chatting around the fire, but he bypassed them for his blanket.

Morning dawned bright and clear and Sergeant Ferrall arrived as the coffee came to a boil. All of the mess group had awaken and Ferrall took the moment to advise them of some changes, amid faces eager for information that might affect them.

"You'll be after knowin' the officers believe the Federals are gone fer now, so there'll be no resumption of hostilities to spoil yer day," the First Sergeant related.

Davy broke the bashful silence that greeted Ferrall's news. "We wuz hopin' to git another crack at them Yanks," he said boldly.

Ferrall turned to look at Williams directly, "You've not had yer fill of smoke and powder?" he questioned, a wry smile on his face. He glanced about at all of them, but no one seconded Davy's words.

"You handled yerselves well enough in that little dust up t'other day, lads," their First Sergeant remarked. "But don't be foolin' yerselves, you'll be seein' much worse before your time is done." He paused before continuing, to give his words their proper force.

"Colonel says the Rangers did the Regiment proud, lads, and you'll be knowin' the Colonel is not one to give his favor lightly," he confided. This information brought grateful smiles all around.

"The officers decided to make some changes to the Company whilst they can," he continued. "We lost two lads after the skirmish, tho' we've lost a many more to sickness.

"So you'll be joined by a few more souls in yer mess, lads," Ferrall told them, and he had their undivided attention. "I've told Dutchie, Crawford and Cummins to make their meals with you. Their mess has been disrupted by sickness."

The Irishman paused to sip his coffee, awaiting a response to this information, though none was invited. Josh had mixed feelings about increasing the size of the mess. He liked Dutchie well enough and tolerated the bookish Miller Cummins. But Joe Crawford had grown slovenly since departing Holly Springs and most of the boys avoided his company.

"We'll be movin' camp to the McLean house at the crossroads and our tents and baggage are to be brought up," Ferrall informed them. "The 18th is to remain here at the Ford. The South Carolina Regiment has been ordered to Centreville," he noted, anticipating their questions.

The Sergeant took a last pull on his cup and tossed the leavings aside. "We'll move in an hour," he said and left the men clustered around the fire.

"Y'all best finish the grits an coffee 'fore I douse this fire," Riley told them and a few refilled their cups and plates. Josh passed on both and moved off to strike his gear and prepare for the move.

There was not much to do to ready for the brief march and men seemed eager for a change of scenery. The Regiment was formed and on the move at the designated hour.

The walk to McLean's was short and more time was consumed in pitching camp. Josh and the others claimed their possessions left behind more than a week ago and tents sprouted like mushrooms.

Lieutenant Abernathy came by with a roster for guard duty and Josh was assigned to an early evening shift. With nothing to do until then, he busied himself with personal chores to pass the time. As dinner time approached, he caught up with Riley to help fix the meal.

The now larger group congregated to eat their dinner and the newcomers were easily absorbed into the group. But it soon became evident that Joe Crawford would bring a sour note to the gatherings.

"I'm 'bout through wi' salt beef," he declared in a voice that tolerated no dispute. "Tuf as ol' shoes an' tastes 'bout the same."

"Josef, he complains about der food," Dutchie interjected by way of explanation. But Crawford had more to say.

"We ain't had fresh beef fer more'n a week," he continued as if Dutchie had not spoken. "All we git regular is grits an' hardtack. Them officers eat good ever meal whilst we have to git by on slop that ain't fit fer fightin' men."

He paused to take some bites off his cooling plate. Josh noticed that Crawford's grumbling did not affect his appetite. As Crawford ate, Davy Williams took the chance to relay some gossip he'd heard about a woman fighting in a Virginia regiment and the conversation passed on to other matters.

Josh finished his meal and grabbed his rifle for guard duty. The Tuckers were on duty with him as was Miller Cummins, so they made their way to Sergeant of the Guard posted near the main road. The Sergeant took each man to his assigned post. Josh drew a spot near the main house for his shift. The sun was setting on the late July day and Josh knew he would struggle to stay alert.

He was well into his shift when he heard footsteps on the path from the house. He first thought the Sergeant was making his rounds, so he straightened and made ready to challenge the approach. The smell of pipe tobacco preceded a portly civilian man who came into view.

The middle aged man wore a fringe of whiskers on chin and cheeks and seemed oblivious to Josh's presence. Then he fixed a stare on the solitary soldier from a few feet away and introduced himself.

"I am Wilmer McLean, owner of the land on which you stand," he remarked in a plain but pointed manner.

"Pleased to meet you," Josh replied with some formality. "I'm Joshua Campbell of the 17th Mississippi."

"Y'all a long ways from home," McLean said, sucking on his pipe. "Y'all see any action durin' the battle."

"We had a little set to wi' the Yanks, but they run off 'fore we could do much," Josh told him. "We lost a few kilt an wounded."

"Beauregard and Johnston had their headquarters in my home mawnin' of the battle," McLean said evenly, conveying a sense their presence was more vexing than exciting. "The Federal troops put a cannon ball through my kitchen, but no one got hurt.

"I have had enough of this war, young man, and I mean to move far away from any other battles," McLean declared firmly.

"Well, might be there's no more fight if the Yanks had enuf in this one," Josh said trying to find some common ground with the gruff Wilmer McLean.

"There will be more, I fear young man, so I will take family and stock south, to my place in Appomattox," McLean told him. "And I will pray that I'll not be disturbed for the rest of my days."

Josh sympathized with his dream, but did not believe the war would last much longer. It had occurred to Josh that the next battle, if there was one, would be to the north since the Yankees had fled in that direction. Josh was about to voice this thought when McLean walked away abruptly, as if he could not spare the words "good bye". McLean struck Josh as rude and haughty, but then, he'd had to put up with an army and a battle in his front yard.

The rest of his duty was unremarkable and he was relieved on schedule. Josh trudged back to his campsite and fell asleep immediately.

Drills and marching resumed to occupy the Regiment's daylight hours and the men now stepped smartly with experience from their first skirmish. They marched to Henry Hill on a rainy day a week after the battle, but there was little to see except the ruined house and ground plowed by cannon balls. A number of civilians roamed the field, securing bits and scraps of the suddenly popular battle ground. The men were allowed to fall out and look around themselves. Hugh found a brass Federal buckle, but there was little else to be had on ground picked clean. Wet weather dampened everyone's curiosity and the Regiment returned to camp after the brief respite. Josh thought the lonely hilltop depressing, though the miserable weather hardly brightened the visit.

With the resumption of tedious drill, a restless eagerness arose to engage the Yankees. Rumors circulated they would march north after the Federals, but the Regiment stayed rooted to its place. All too often, the mood was expended in grumbling and Joe Crawford could be counted to provide more than his share.

On the first day of August, the mess returned from drill midday to grab a bit to eat. As they trudged into camp, they were met by a sight that immediately revived tired bodies and spirits. Zeke Owens had returned.

Zeke's back was slapped and hand shaken so many times that he spun like a rag doll. He appeared thinner and pale. He returned greetings enthusiastically, but had to sit down after only a short spell. Everyone wanted to talk with him and he was eager to find out what he had missed.

"Y'all goin ter have me along next time," Zeke declared after hearing about the fight with the Yankees and the evening chase. "I ain't goin' back to that hospital if'n I kin help it."

He grinned with that comment, but Josh could see his friend was still not fully recovered.

"Aw, you ain't had nothin' to do but lie 'bout all day," Hugh said to tease him. "I bet they had to throw you out to git rid o' you."

"Boys, all I kin say is that it's a damn sight better amongst you polecats than it is in that hospital," Zeke replied with a smirk.

After they finished a cold meal, most stretched out for a few moments before afternoon drill was called. Josh took the opportunity to talk with Zeke privately, though Zeke's fatigue forced him to recline during their conversation.

"It's good to see ya, pard," Josh told him. "I missed you some these last few days."

"I missed you, too," Zeke said, his voice cracking slightly. "Wasn't a day go by I didn't think 'bout you and what y'all was doin'."

Josh tried to reassure his friend. "You shur didn't miss much o' that little fight we got into. Don' go believin' all the boys say 'bout it. Were'nt much to it but a few shots bein' fired. Then we took off after the Yanks and never did catch up to 'em."

"Jes tha same, I wisht I was thar, Josh. I signed on to fight Yanks, an' I missed the whole show bein' sick," Zeke said in disgust.

"Ferrall says we got more ahead o' us," Josh remarked. "So you'll likely git to shoot at a Yankee sometime.

"You still look poorly," Josh added to change the subject. "You got some healin' to do 'fore you git back to drillin' an' marchin'."

"I do feel a might run down," Zeke muttered, his eyes half closed. "Sawbones sent me back soon's I could stand 'cause o' all the wounded they got to tend to.

"I'll git mah strength back an' be out there with y'all

directly," he added weakly.

Josh glanced at him, but Zeke's eyes had fully closed. Silently, Josh slipped away to allow his friend to rest.

August brought a brutal daytime heat to camp, though some argued Mississippi was hotter this time of year. Showers cooled some days, though rainy nights made sleep difficult. Worn, tired soldiers settled for meals that varied little day to day. Salt beef or pork was tasteless and stringy. Cornmeal and flour was apt to be moldy or infested by bugs. Potatoes and onions were available on occasion, but other vegetables had disappeared. Soldiers griped about the food, but lately had turned to morbid jokes. They could not understand why the army was unable to provide better fare and widely speculated the Federal army ate much better.

Josh was frustrated with poor rations, but weary of grumbling. His dissatisfaction led to anger as he watched Zeke struggle to regain his strength on inadequate provisions. He spoke to the others one night with a sense of desperation.

"Boys, we got to improve our mess or we gonna suffer fer lack o' good food," he declared one night as they finished a bland meal.

"Ain't nobody opposed to that, but how we gonna do it," Riley challenged. The others looked to Josh for his answer.

"I bin thinkin' on it some, an we ain't gonna git no better than this from the commissary," Josh began. "What we gotta do is git more our own selves.

"If each of us throw a little money in, we could use that to git some fruit and vegetables from sutlers," he added. A few nodded their heads to agree. "We kin scrounge some other things as we find 'em."

"I kin git us some eggs ever now an then from the place down the road," Davy put in. "Old man's got some settin' hens an he's willin' to trade fer good tobacco."

"I come across some greens growing wild in a ol' field not far from here," Charlie added.

"Me an Will found a berry patch up near the creek t'other day," Walter Tucker said excitedly. "We kin fill a haversack fer some cobbler."

"This here's what I'm talkin' bout," Josh said. "We put our heads together an we kin do a damn sight better than what the army provides."

"I reckon I could disappear an ol' hen from McLean's place," Joe Crawford cracked with a smirk.

"I ain't particular 'bout who my food starts out with," Hugh said. "But we got to keep the thievin' down cause the whole Regiment is doin' it. McLean's complained to the Colonel often 'bout what he's lost and the Provost is lookin' hard fer anyone has somethin' don' belong to him."

"Who'll be in charge o' the money we put up," Miller Cummins questioned, and looked squarely at Josh.

Before Josh could speak, Dutchie cut in. "Josh has a goot idea and ve can trust him mit der money."

"I think y'all'd agree that Josh is best man fer the job," Zeke said. He glared at Cummins in a none too subtle warning that disagreement would be out of line. There was no vote taken, but Josh was selected to collect money and procure what was needed from sutlers.

That evening settled the task of finding better provisions and their fare improved from various sources in coming days. Spirits brightened further on word the Regiment would move north, brought first by Davy Williams and confirmed by Dutchie and many others. The exact destination remained a mystery until Lieutenant Abernathy wandered through camp one evening.

He was not a frequent campfire visitor though he was respected and well liked by all. On this evening in the middle of August, he made his way through the company grounds. Abernathy accepted a cup of coffee from Riley after calling the mess together.

"Boys, looks like we'll be leaving our camp here," the Lieutenant began. "Our Regiment has been ordered to march on the morrow."

He paused to be sure every one was listening. They were so keen to hear what he would say that no one fussed about the smell of Joe Crawford in tight quarters.

"Y'all have a good day's march, maybe more, to the Loudoun and Alexandria Railroad line. Once we strike the railroad, we'll take the cars for the remainder of our journey." Abernathy wearily tilted his sweat stained hat farther back on his head. "All the Yankees have gone back to Washington City, so there should be none to trouble your passage," he noted with a slight grin.

"Goin' to a town called Leesburg," he replied to the unasked question. "The 18th will join us there. Our Regiment'll be in brigade with the 8th Virginia Regiment, already in the area," the First Lieutenant explained.

"Y'all be a lot farther north than you've ever bin, near to the Potomac River," he informed them.

He paused as if to accept questions, glancing at the faces before him. Charlie thanked him for coming by and he walked off to the next group. A moment passed wordlessly as they each exchanged looks. They had now been soldiers long enough to simply accept their lot and comments or complaints would not alter the march ahead. They simply separated for personal preparations.

"Ain't Leesburg whar that Anne Marlow lives," Zeke asked Josh excitedly in a low voice.

Josh remembered the auburn haired beauty at the mention of her name. "I reckon that was the town she named," he replied with some effort so as not to betray his easy recollection.

Zeke had no trouble with his memory on the subject. "She said her daddy's place was called 'Mountain View'. We ought ter be able to find it by askin' folks when we git there."

"We'll find her, pard, see if we kin git yer canteen back," Josh remarked, smiling as he recalled to Zeke the purpose for a visit.

11

The 17th Regiment required two full days to cover the thirty miles of dusty, rutted roads between Manassas and Leesburg, under an unforgiving August sun. Complaints from the ranks were relentless, and straggling increased with every mile. They bore a light load of rifles, blankets and canteens, but foot troubles began in the first mile. Shoe leather had worn thin in recent months and been subject to frequent dousing in Bull Run. Once stiff brogan shoes had stretched, then busted through in soles and seams. Repairs eventually gave way. Men fell out, and fell behind, to patch their shoes. A few simply shed footwear and walked barefoot. Officers were powerless to quicken the march. Lieutenants and Captains on foot shared the misery of the rank and file.

At the end of the first day, the Regiment had reached the Loudoun rail line. Men simply fell out in a pasture beside the rails and slept where they lay, without benefit of food or coffee. Soldiers continued to file in during the night as they caught up to the Regiment, grabbing what little rest they could.

Reveille sounded early next morning and the men awoke expecting to find rail cars ready to transport them. But the cars did not arrive as the morning waned. Stale hardtack crackers were issued by company for breakfast, supplemented by water from a nearby spring. The men dawdled without orders to march, though they were not allowed to stray far from the railroad.

Just before noon the order was issued to continue the march on foot, Colonel Featherston somehow having determined rail transport would not be available. The Regiment formed in a long column of twos to begin the second days march beside the rails. A train appeared coming from Leesburg an hour into their march and it was waylaid with a message to send cars back. But no train returned and the men resigned themselves to complete the journey on foot.

The men from Mississippi reached the outskirts of Leesburg late on a hot afternoon and filed into their new campground. As happened the day before, stragglers continued to arrive well into the night. Josh had kept with the main body, carrying Zeke's rifle and blanket when he began to wilt under the heat. Most of his mess stayed with the Regiment, though the Tuckers stumbled in an hour late, and Joe Crawford, complaining every step of the way, finally arrived at dark.

Davy Williams brought word there would be no rations issued. Hugh and Charlie remembered passing a corn field nearby and volunteered to secure some roasting ears. Miller Cummins went in search of apples or pears, while the rest scrounged firewood and cooked coffee that Riley had brought with him. Zeke was worn out by the exertion and could not assist with dinner.

The foragers returned with green corn and small, nearly ripe apples. The corn was roasted and each had an ear. Riley cut up the apples, mixed in some water and hardtack crackers and cooked the mixture in a skillet he somehow produced. No one mistook the treat for home cooking, but the fixings met with hearty approval.

Welburn appeared before them and grabbed Josh, Riley and Davy to dig latrines. They were too tired to complain and followed the smirking Lieutenant to a pine glade where they were issued shovels and a pick. They joined some men from other companies, scratching long slits in the earth for over an hour, under Welburn's watchful gaze. Lieutenant Colonel McGuirk arrived to approve the work and they stumbled back to the mess more asleep than awake.

Josh woke for morning roll call, but did not return to his blanket when dismissed. They had no orders for drill that morning, so he found a creek near the camp to wash off some of the grime from two days of marching. The cool, clean water revived him. He used a piece of mirror he'd carried to razor off a stubborn growth and comb his hair.

When he finished he took stock of himself. His cheeks and face were drawn and leathery. He had not succumbed to wearing a beard, though his hair was longer than usual. Stripped to his waist to wash, he saw a lean but hard muscled body from a barely adequate diet and constant drill. He had suffered no serious ailments nor injuries and he concluded that army life had been tolerable during his nearly three months of service.

Refreshed by his wash and shave, he began to take in his surroundings. The camp of the 17th was in a cleared field on the main road to Leesburg, though he could not see the town. Tree topped hills rose around the area, and higher mountains could be seen at some distance. This country had a different feel than the flat land of northern Mississippi.

Planted fields, an orchard and open pasture marked one side of the camp, a sprawling woodland the other. The land seemed bountiful and thriving, a deep, rich color to the pasture and plants. Tall broad limbed trees, thick with leaves marked the woods, making the thin pine trees of home seem scraggly by comparison. This land promised more comforts than the camps around Manassas, and Josh was relieved by the thought. He gave voice to his impression as he returned to the mess campfire where Riley fussed about with no food to prepare.

"This place'll do fer a while, oncet we git some regular rations," Josh said in greeting.

"I'm shur glad fer the change from Manassas, place was gettin' played out with all them soljers 'round" Riley responded.

Josh stowed his kit, noticed that Zeke's blanket was rolled

and returned to sit with Riley. The rest of the mess slowly gathered about the fire, disappointed there was no food or coffee. All except Zeke were there when Davy joined them with some sad news.

"Jes heard Johnny Meadows died early this mornin'," he announced as he joined the group. Riley asked him what happened.

"He 'uz doin' poorly 'fore the march, but refused to go sick call," Davy responded. "Boys in his mess said he seemed fine till the second day. Fell out with a fever an they had to leave him with a medical orderly. Abernathy told 'em this mornin' he passed durin' the night."

Josh knew the news would hit hard. Meadows was a likeable fellow, maybe twenty or twenty one. He seemed a good soldier and had fought in the skirmish with the Yankees. Meadows was the first man of the company to die, and he had been denied the hero's death in battle. Two in the company had been wounded and some few had returned home through sickness, but there had been no deaths till now.

"This here's a fine mawnin' to be alive," Zeke declared as he joined the solemn group. Josh steered him away from the fire and delivered the news about Meadows. Zeke's happy countenance faded as he absorbed this information, but returned after a moment and Josh could see his friend was in good spirits.

Zeke had somehow recovered much of his strength since his return from the sick tents and he was none the worse for their long march. His contented outlook on life seemed to have returned. Josh felt his own spirits lift in Zeke's presence.

"What's got you feelin' so lively," Josh asked. "Looks like you could walk 'nother twenty miles today. Yer shoes ain't even wore out," Josh teased.

"I might could go some distance today," Zeke said with a wink.

The cheerful boast brought a grin to Josh's face.

"I reckon we ought ter look up Miss Anne Marlowe and

pay our respects, now we in Leesburg," Zeke said.

"You ain't thought o' nothin' else since we left the Bull Run, and hard marchin' ain't dulled yer mind none," Josh complained. "She likely forgot we 'uz even alive an we probly won' git past the front door," he taunted.

"I kin shur remind her right fast if'n we git to say hi," Zeke said in a serious tone.

"How you figger to find her anyway, we'll be confined to camp fer awhile," Josh asked him.

"Don' sell yer ol' pard short," Zeke replied with a wink. "Thar's a detail leavin' fer town in the hour to round up some fodder fer the animals, an' Ferrall is savin' a place fer me. Jes come back to see you want to join in."

Soldiers did not generally volunteer for work and Josh was not so intent on finding Anne Marlowe that he would break this rule, so he declined the invitation. But Zeke would not rest until he located the Southern maiden.

Josh walked back to the campfire. The others were still clustered about the fire.

"Ain't nothin' in the pantry," Riley commented. "Hear we'll draw some rations today, but we could shur use somethin' fresh, Josh."

"I reckon the sutlers'll find us today. Maybe they'll have what we need," he replied.

"Ought ter be some money to buy with, since ever one put in," Charlie noted.

"Yeah, all 'cept one an he's good fer it," Josh said evenly. It was common knowledge that Joe Crawford had no money, but Josh accepted his promise to contribute after next pay.

Talk turned to other matters, like who had the sorest feet and Josh wandered off to explore a little. He took a turn about the camp area, greeting friends in the company. Meadow's death dominated conversation, though the previous days march was still on many minds. Josh learned there were no drills scheduled and the day would be spent preparing the camp for a long stay.

With the Yankees miles away on the other side of the Potomac River, anxiety that had percolated all summer was replaced by complacency and the men could relax in their new surroundings.

About midday, he noticed a crowd of men around some wagons on the road. He guessed the sutlers had found the Regiment and wandered over to make some purchases. Josh had become a wary buyer of sutler goods. As a group they would cheat you soon as look at you with rotten fruit and poor quality goods at high prices. They knew the men could not leave camp freely to buy elsewhere. The worst offenders sold hard liquor that they mixed with all sorts of things to color the liquid or give it taste. Josh bypassed the persistent hawkers and made for an open wagon with fresh looking vegetables.

He spotted the vegetables he wanted and noticed some berries and fruits on the wagon. A young boy in rough clothes stood near the front, but a crouching figure in the bed of the wagon was taking the money. Josh made his way toward the rear of the wagon and saw to his surprise that the person in charge was a young woman.

A bright face fringed in a tangle of blond hair greeted him. She was a little younger than he and wore a plain print dress cinched at the waist. She stared at him a moment before speaking.

"Yer a looker," she declared and Josh felt his cheeks color. "Mus' be somethin' here you'd want," she said with a wink and hopped off the wagon to stand in front of him. Josh had to retreat a little to open a respectful space.

"Like to see sum o' those pole beans an turnips," Josh told her, surprised to encounter such a brazen girl.

"Anythin' you want, darlin'," she replied, grabbing a handful of stringy beans and the smallish turnips. She presented these to Josh for his inspection.

"How much kin I git fer four bits," he asked.

"Nuf to keep you fer a few days," she said. "But I don' take no scrip, jes hard coin." She packaged some turnips and beans in brown paper.

145

"You need anythin' else, got some nice apples an peaches," she told him. Josh could see the peaches were bruised and the apples still partly green, but fruit would be a welcome addition.

"I'll take a han'ful o' both fer two bits each," he suggested.

She offered a smile and placed the fruit in another paper wrapper.

"I'll jes' give you a hand with these, darlin', " she said.

"I reckon I kin manage alright," Josh told her sternly, but she was not about to give up the fruit he bought.

"Luke, see to tha wagon whilst I help this here sojer with his goods," she said to the young boy and started off without waiting for a reply toward the middle of the camp.

"Pa said we's to stay close, May," the boy complained after her, but she continued walking.

"You best stay with yer brother," Josh cautioned.

Ignoring his warning, she said, "What's yer name and whar you from. And whar'd you git them perty blue eyes," she added slyly.

"Name's Josh Campbell from Holly Springs, Mississippi. Ain't likely you ever bin thar," he challenged, declining to answer the last question.

"I'm May Turner from up on the Blue Ridge," she told him, pointing toward the mountains some distance away. Josh glanced in that direction and she appeared to accept this gesture as an invitation to continue talking.

"They's four boys and three girls in mah family," she continued. "Matthew, Mark, Luke and John. The two oldest boys is with tha 23rd Virginia near Romney. Besides me, tha girls are April an' June, tho' April's married.

"Ma's dead, but pa's still kickin'. Me an' Luke do tha sellin' an we'll be down this way mos' days."

Josh turned toward her to see if she was going to draw a breath. She fluttered her eyes at him and smiled. He just glared at her, trying to discourage any more chattering.

They were now among the Regiment and some of the men

were calling out to the young woman suddenly in their midst. Josh grew uncomfortable with the girl beside him and feared she might see some things a woman should not see.

"You bes' git back, miss, a soljer's camp ain't no place fer a young girl," he said in warning, hoping she would turn around.

"Sojers is a randy bunch, but I ain't gonna see nothin' I ain't seen with four brothers. An I ain't gonna hear nothin' I ain't heard afore neither," she declared with a determined face.

Josh stopped in his tracks to keep the bold girl from going any further and took the sack of fruit from her. "Miss Turner, this is far enuf. Civilians ain't sposed to be in camp without a pass. You git back to yer wagon."

"Josh from Mississippi, I like you. You better come see me or I'll come lookin' fer you." She reached up and pinched his cheek, then she turned and walked back the way they came, a little sashay in her stride. Josh felt an unbidden tingle come over him and held his stare on her until she passed out of sight.

"An sure I am that girl has her cap set fer you, lad," Ferrall said from behind, rousing him from his trance.

Josh felt his cheeks color again and cleared his throat to speak, but thought better of it and walked back to his mess area.

The vegetables Josh procured made a fine meal with the fresh beef issued in their ration. When dinner meal was finished, not a morsel of food remained. Crawford complimented the meal by failing to grumble about the fare.

Zeke had returned from the detail with the information he sought. He learned the Marlowe home was about three miles from camp on a bluff near the Potomac River. Zeke determined to visit the home as soon as possible and he made clear that he expected Josh to accompany him in spite of any objection he might have.

Josh settled down for a proper sleep that night, a full belly and distracting thoughts of May Turner on his mind. For once, his dreams concerned something other than the next drill, the next meal, or the next battle.

$\times \times \times \times \times$

The day had turned to a miserable, steady rain. Josh and Zeke stumbled in to camp soaked through and too tired to pick at each other. But Josh resolved not to let Zeke disremember this day.

The day started bright enough, a Sunday in September when they had been granted a day's leave from camp. Zeke had persisted with his desire to visit Anne Marlowe and Josh had grown comfortable with the idea after two weeks in camp, welcoming a chance to see the countryside.

They had cleaned their uniforms and put on a fresh shirt. A bath with soap the day before provoked some wayward comments at dinner. Josh thought they looked quite presentable.

Even the prospect of a three mile hike could not dampen their spirits as they departed that morning, hastening from an early prayer meeting. Fortune smiled when a friendly farmer offered a ride on his hay wagon and he carried them most of the way. The friendly fellow deposited them at the driveway to walk the last few yards.

The house was not visible from the road and they walked some distance before the drive opened to reveal a four columned mansion. Josh had some foreboding then that they were out of place, but Zeke seemed more excited as he got closer.

Their knock was answered by a small, middle aged, black woman in apron and headscarf. Without a word, she looked them over in a way that made Josh button his open uniform jacket.

"We from the 17th Mississippi Regiment camped near town and come to see Miz Anne Marlowe," Zeke had announced with a friendly smile. The woman curled an eyebrow in some surprise and Zeke added quickly, "Is Miz Marlowe to home?"

Breaking her silence, she asked "Miz Marlowe expectin' y'all," clearly skeptical of their response.

"We met Miss Marlowe a while back in Manassas," Zeke

said earnestly, trying to convince her that he knew Anne. The information had no appreciable affect on her.

Her attitude made it clear that two boys from Mississippi would not enter without further approval and she hesitated before leaving them at the doorstep, saying, "Please wait while I see if Miz Marlowe is to home."

Josh had pulled the hat from his head and nudged Zeke to do likewise. Through the door they could glimpse an extensive entry crowned by an impressive chandelier. They had been caught looking up when Anne Marlowe swept into the hall before them.

They recognized her immediately and her welcoming smile did much to calm Josh's uncertainty.

"Mah brave friends from Mississippi, ah am so glad y'all have come," she greeted them, beckoning them in and bowing gracefully.

Josh had been overwhelmed again by her stunning natural beauty and swallowed to chase the dryness before he tried to speak. Zeke had more than two months to consider a greeting, but stood mute and grinning like a child.

"Ah can return the kindness you showed to me that hot day in Manassas," she had declared, slipping between them, taking each by an arm and gently guiding them through the hallway toward a side door. "Y'all must tell me of your adventures in the recent battle."

Josh had eased a little with her warm greeting, though he tensed slightly to her touch on his arm.

They were shown to a wide, shaded porch with a view of mountains in the distance. Anne had whisked away to order a cool drink for them and returned with an older man that she introduced as her father. Zeke and Josh formally shook hands with the man, who identified himself as Randolph Marlowe. The two soldiers remembered their manners, waiting for Anne and her father to take a seat before seating themselves.

Anne proceeded to introduce the uniformed guests.

"These are the gallant men ah told you about, papa, who came to mah aid when ah was overcome by heat at the parade in July."

The elder Marlowe exhibited what Josh took for a smile, though it seemed more of a grimace. "I'm most grateful for the kindness you exhibited to my daughter," dismissing their memorable moment with Anne easily. "Y'all camped near Leesburg," he inquired with strained politeness.

When Zeke nodded, Marlowe continued before Zeke could speak, saying, "Your presence will do much to deter the Yankees." Josh was not sure from his tone if he was not also dismissing their military presence.

Conversation paused when the older man ceased speaking. Josh sensed he and Zeke were being apprised by both of the Marlowes.

"This here's a right nice home y'all have," Josh had interjected, and Zeke muttered his agreement. The compliment failed to prod a response from either Marlowe. Josh had strained for something else to say as Zeke remained silent, wondering why Anne did not speak.

She rescued them with a question about their part in the battle at Manassas. Zeke colored and Josh launched into a brief explanation of their contact with the Yankees and subsequent chase. Zeke did not volunteer information about his sickness, and Josh ignored any implication that Zeke was not with the Regiment.

Mr. Marlowe's sour mood was forgotten when Anne's younger sister Mary joined them. Full of youthful wonder and happiness, she had immediately bombarded the two soldiers with probing questions of battle and camp life. Though Zeke grew impatient with the imposition and cut young Mary off twice, Josh had brightened with the chatty interlude. Anne seemed to enjoy her self imposed reserve and allowed Mary to commandeer the conversation.

They had been there less than half an hour when some commotion arose in the hallway and Mary rushed off to see what it was. She returned immediately to announce that 'Rance' had arrived. Anne Marlowe brightened visibly at the news and stood to greet her visitor. The elder Marlowe rose with her, straightening his clothes and wearing a more pleasant look on his face. Josh caught Zeke's worried expression when the two soldiers had been instantly ignored.

A tall, sandy haired young man strode through the door with a welcoming smile from Anne Marlowe. He wore the yellow facings of the cavalry on a gray uniform that looked newly cleaned and pressed. Though the man could not have been more than a few years older, Josh noticed the Captain's bars on his shoulder. He proceeded directly to Anne and took her hand with a slight bow. She blushed visibly and cleared her throat to make introductions.

"May ah present mah dear friend, Captain Rance Marston of the 1st Virginia Cavalry," she said. Marston had barely acknowledged their presence, never removing his eyes fully from Anne.

Josh was uncertain whether to salute the officer and only stood to greet him. Zeke looked grim at the intrusion but stood also. Anne continued her introductions.

"These are Privates Campbell and Owens from Mississippi," she said, gesturing to each in turn, though Josh thought she emphasized the rank too much. "Ah had the opportunity to make their acquaintance on mah journey to Manassas in July," she had added by way of explanation that reduced them to a level just above stranger.

Marston turned to them with an expression he might have used for a bothersome bug. "What regiment y'all with," he had asked, with an implication of forced courtesy.

Josh had already sized up the man as a pompous bastard, but he would not give him the satisfaction of cowering. He and Zeke might be in an awkward situation, but he was not going to beat a hasty retreat.

"17th Mississippi, sir, we wuz on the right durin' the late

battle," Josh said, hoping that Marston might have somehow missed the fight.

"Y'all some o' Featherstone's boys," the Captain said, as if he knew the Colonel personally despite the mispronunciation of his name. "Didn't see much action on that wing," he commented dryly.

Zeke started to say something, but the Captain continued on. "Ah rode with Stuart that day and we gave some red legged Yankee scoundrels quite a licking."

He turned toward Anne, took her hand in his and spoke in a formal tone. "Ah shall not rest as long as those Northern scum threaten our homes and loved ones."

She blushed at the declaration and Marston concluded with a slight bow. Anne's father had shed his earlier discomfort and looked serenely pleased.

Zeke looked ready to explode from anger and embarrassment, so Josh stepped nearer to his friend and spoke before Zeke said something they might both regret.

"We bes be gittin' back to our camp, Miz Marlowe,' Josh said. "We don' want to take no more o' yer time, do we Zeke," he added, commanding his friend to be polite.

"Yes, ma'am," Zeke had agreed resignedly, "it was shur good to see you again."

Josh thanked Mr. Marlowe for his hospitality, though the man barely acknowledged the courtesy, and turned to the horse soldier.

"Pleased to have met you, sir," Josh said, stepping toward the resplendent cavalryman and offering a half hearted salute. "We'll be lookin' fer ya on the battlefield."

The officer swelled a little, ignoring the implied challenge. Josh had nudged Zeke toward the door and followed him into the hall, as Anne bid them goodbye with a word to the servant to show them out. Zeke pulled is hat down on top of his head and they strode out of the house in silence under the watchful glare of the house maid.

Zeke had fumed a little before he could speak. Neither man said anything until they were well away from the house.

"Damn all cavalry," Zeke had bellowed. Josh looked at him, noticed the angry look on his face, and bust out laughing.

Zeke shot a hard look at him. Then his face softened and he finally cracked a smile. Josh was chuckling to himself as the tension eased

"I don' know what you think's so funny, Josh," Zeke said. "Anne and her daddy think we a couple o' hayseeds."

"Next to that popinjay cavalry officer, we don' even look fit to speak to a lady," he added sadly.

"Pard, if you got to be an officer to 'tract her 'tenshun, then she ain't worth the trouble," Josh said in a serious tone. "An if you thought she wuz gonna swoon at the sight o' you, then you ain't thinkin' right.

"Folks like the Marlowe's look down on the likes o' us," Josh continued. "An the fancy Cavalry boys gonna git all the glory from the battles. We jes gonna do the fightin'."

At that point, the sky had flashed, a loud bang following. They instantly realized a storm was coming. The two men started to trot, trying to beat the rain, but it had caught them before they traveled a quarter mile. Rain dogged them all the way back, thoroughly soaking every stitch of clothing they wore.

As they neared the camp, Josh no longer felt anything but wet and tired. He had regretted going on the trip, though neither man could have expected the drenching rain. With their cool reception, Josh vowed a long time would pass before he graced the Marlowe doorstep again.

He had to feel a little sorry for Zeke with his high hopes, but Zeke would surely get past this quickly. As for Josh, May Turner's face had begun to fill his mind in unguarded moments, and she had been more welcoming than all the Marlowes put together.

Cooler weather and better food could not entirely dissipate the restlessness of the Regiment as summer waned that September of 1861. The lack of any enemy activity combined with endless drill to frustrate men. Yankee artillery had fired almost daily, but the Northerners seemed content to stay on their side of the Potomac. Homesickness spread during this period of inactivity, evidenced by increasing numbers of requests for furloughs or discharges.

The mood changed quickly with the first pay. Each of the enlisted men received two month's wages. A clothing allowance was also issued, but set aside for new uniforms. However, the pay worked major changes in camp. Liquor appeared in abundance and men gambled every night. These vices swelled the roster for punishment duty. When extra guard or camp duty failed to deter excesses, other punishments were employed. Stocks were built for serious offenders and some were made to wear a tight barrel through the day. But the soldiers simply became more secretive in their habits.

Josh avoided these temptations, as did most of his mess. Davy and Joe Crawford were the exceptions and soon out of funds. Josh did appreciate one effect of the Regiment's pay issue, the sutlers returned to ply their wares. He had a chance to see May a bit more, though she was always obligated to sell all her goods before she could spend any time with him. The encounters were brief, but he looked forward to seeing her. They walked and talked and he had held her hand on one occasion.

Mail finally caught up with the Regiment during this time. Letters and packages from home were savored and treasured. Some of the married men grew melancholy on word from their family, yet all were grateful for news of home no matter how outdated.

Josh drew a letter from his sister who acknowledged his last letter, thanking him for letting them know he survived the battle. Sarah was four years his junior and serious about her writing. In a long letter with careful script she reported on his mother and father, conveying their good wishes, and the doings of neighbors and friends. Josh consumed the carefully crafted words as a thirsty man drank water.

One piece of news troubled him in a surprising way. Sarah reported that Rebecca Tolliver and her family had left Holly Springs for relatives in New Orleans just after news of Manassas reached town. Josh had wondered at the absence of letters from Rebecca who had promised to write faithfully. He was surprised she had not written of her departure, nor communicated a new address at her destination. He had simply assumed she would be there when he returned. That wistful hope was dashed and he felt some regret in passing. A tie that bound him to home was cut.

As a colorful Virginia fall began and the heat of summer finally abated, Confederate and Federal inactivity reassured many that the War might soon be over and the soldiers could go home. The generals and politicians on both sides of the Potomac had far different ideas that would soon extend the fight.

12

A special train rumbled out of Richmond to begin the long journey north. Its military cargo was not unusual, officers and enlisted men of various ranks and at least one important civilian. That the soldiers were Federal was unique, though, unarmed and being exchanged to perhaps take part in the war again.

The lone civilian passenger was Congressman Elihu Hawthorne. Being neither in the military nor a combatant, he had enjoyed a special status with his captors. Hawthorne had been treated more as a guest of the Richmond military authorities with a limited ability to move about the city. The intercession of a friend and former Congressman from Virginia had procured him a spot in the first exchange.

Privately, Hawthorne had to concede that his treatment was more than fair at the hands of the rebels. He had been well fed and housed, and allowed to renew acquaintance with many of the new Confederacy's politicians, men he had known before the war. He had simmered in embarrassment at the haughty tone of these men. Everyone he met believed the war would end quickly with Southern independence. The feeling was widespread that the North had been whipped at Manassas and would not seek battle again. He had grown tired of the boast that one rebel was worth ten Yankees. The accepted wisdom of Southern military superiority was coupled with an intense disdain for Lincoln and his administration.

Hawthorne lunched or supped almost daily with politicians from across the South. They seemed eager to convert his view of their Confederacy so that he might inform others upon his return. After a month in the new nation, he could not deny the affect his stay had upon his thinking.

He had convinced himself the rebellion was a paper tiger, built upon the despicable and decrepit foundation of slavery. But his meetings and discussions in Richmond revealed a long list of rebel grievances emanating from perceived Northern interference in Southern lives. Southerners consistently decried the tyranny of abolitionists demanding they change their way of life. They voiced the simplistic proposition that they should be allowed to leave the Union if they derived no benefit from it. In this desire, they fixed their hatred upon Lincoln, who was cast as the principal obstacle to peaceful separation.

Whether by the force of their argument or simple weariness, Hawthorne had to concede a rationale for the rebellion. Their position had a certain logic, but it led to an abhorrent conclusion. He could not agree to dissolve the 'united' states. The country could not achieve greatness and a place among world powers if it were divided in two. In this he agreed with Lincoln and silently wondered at the Southerners' narrow and parochial view.

Support for slavery also disturbed him. There was simply no place for human enslavement among civilized nations. He had argued the point repeatedly and insistently with his hosts. They countered with a number of arguments, and a few even voiced the belief that slavery would soon be eliminated in the Confederacy. However, the secessionists never seemed to confront the issue directly and always retaliated that it was a right among Southerners to own slaves, a right with which the Federals could not lawfully interfere.

Now, as the train he occupied made its way north, a mixture of thoughts tumbled about his mind. His stay in Richmond had opened his eyes to many things. The journey back to the Federal Capital mirrored a journey in his thoughts and, as if a fog were lifting, he began to develop a plan for the future.

Hawthorne was now certain rebellion could not be crushed by a single battlefield victory. In the aftermath of Bull Run, Southerners had glorified their military leaders and fighting men. Hawthorne realized that the North must prepare for a long fight, for victory would not be quick. The Union must have the same confidence in its military that the rebels had in theirs. The North had more manpower and material resources than the South. If the soldiers were ably led, their cause could not be denied eventual victory.

He also concluded the primary aim of the war must be the complete eradication of slavery. Hawthorne had not heretofore allied himself with abolitionists for they had seemed too righteous and inflexible. But he could not deny the justice of their goal nor the will they brought to achieve it. Their zeal could serve as the foundation to support the Union during a long and costly war and prevent any termination of the conflict that would allow the South to retain slavery.

Having resolved this much, he now had to formulate a plan of action. Hawthorne knew that those men in Congress branded 'radical' Republicans were of the same mind to prosecute the war to end slavery. He must join their ranks, and of necessity denounce those 'Copperheads' who wished to placate or mollify the South. He would add his voice to pressure the Lincoln administration to stay the course for total victory and actively oppose any effort to negotiate a peace.

Northern victory could only be achieved by military means. Therefore, the Union must have a better military force than the rebels. Federal forces must be larger in number, better equipped and better led. He had seen enough of mismanagement at Bull Run to convince him the military could not be left to its own devices. The President deferred to his military advisers and was inadequate to the task of command. Congress would have to oversee the army and navy in their prosecution of the war and, if necessary, forcibly stiffen military resolve.

Hawthorne would propose the formation of a Congressional committee to supervise the military. Committees were a traditional weapon, unsheathed by Congress to impose its will upon those who might otherwise resist. In this manner, the elected representatives of the people would take an active part in the handling of the war. He envisioned a joint committee of men from both House and Senate. Of course, the 'radicals' should be in the majority.

Hawthorne saw himself at the forefront of such a committee, leading it, shaping it and bending it to his will. Such a committee could be more powerful than the President and those who dominated the committee would share in this power.

The Congressman was roused from his dreams as the train slowed in northern Virginia. They had been informed the train would take them to the last stop in rebel control and they would be marched across the lines to Federal hands.

Hawthorne joined the throng of anxious men descending the cars and walking northward. Their release coincided with the release of rebel soldiers and he could see a gray clad group moving in the opposite direction, along the other side of the unused rail line.

The Congressman felt a surge of relief as his ordeal ended and he returned to Federal protection. He was greeted by an army captain who asked his name, and Hawthorne explained who he was. The captain consulted a list, nodded when he found the name and waved him on. Puzzled that no one was there to welcome him, he procured a waiting cab and boarded for the ride to his lodgings.

As the buggy made its way through the Capital streets, he noticed that little had changed during his time away. The most notable difference was the presence of many more uniformed troops, a comfort to one recently among the enemy. Since Congress was not in session, the city lacked some of the usual bustle. Many of the members would have returned home to attend to local matters.

He longed for the familiar surroundings of his apartment, together with a hot bath and comfortable clothing. As the cab neared its destination, he resolved to rest and renew this day and to embark on his crusade at first light on the morrow.

Mississippi soldiers settled into the shorter days and cool nights of a Virginia October. Trees shed their leaves to blow upon the ground. Chill winds penetrated worn uniforms and men began to add layers of clothing brought from home or purchased from sutlers. Men gathered planks to place on the floor of their tents and made provisions against the weather. The perception grew that the Regiment was in place for the coming winter and those who had predicted an end to the fight by fall were loath to remember such statements in those days.

A new song made the rounds that fall to lift sagging spirits. It was called 'The Bonnie Blue Flag' and the lyrics inspired pride and a general feeling of comraderie. Starting with the words 'We are a band of brothers . . .' the chorus echoed with 'Hurrah for the Bonnie Blue Flag that bears a single star.' The song immediately became a marching favorite and was often heard in the evening, loud 'Hurrahs' punctuating the night.

The Yankees seemed content to stay on their side of the river and no crossings had been reported since the 17th had arrived near Leesburg. The Northerners fired their artillery almost daily without hitting anything of importance. Guard duty and patrols on the Potomac were among the more pleasant duties for the soldiers of the 17th. Federals and Confederates traded shouts, taunts and news across the River. But the Northerners were easier heard than seen and indicated no desire for a fight.

Josh felt the change of season as much as witnessed it and his thoughts were drawn to the contrast with home. He noticed the large number of leaves falling and blowing about the land.

The tall, scraggly pines of Mississippi bore needles only and other leafy trees were few in number. The abundant colors of the leaves also served to remind him of the difference in his new home. A strong woodsy smell marked the season in Virginia. With the harvest completed, farms lay fallow and the land around him seemed to be dying. Josh thought wistfully of home and recalled the promises of those who thought the Confederacy would be free by now.

Drill was infrequent and some days the men were called for roll and released for the day. Once living quarters were improved and food secured, most had little to do. While men idled the days away, Josh noticed that Miller Cummins rarely wasted his free time. The inquisitive soldier seemed to have a book or newspaper ready to hand and never complained of his free time.

Josh had known little of Cummins before he joined the mess. Cummins was small and slender of stature and Hugh teased that he'd blow away in a strong wind. He needed his spectacles to read, but not march or drill. Having attended the College in Clinton, Mississippi for two years, Cummins had more education than most. While he didn't flaunt his learning, Josh could see he thought and acted different from the others and put this down to education.

Cummins was not given to bragging or idle talk, though he did join in on campfire conversations. Josh noticed he spoke in the rounded tones and full words of the educated man. He found Cummins' opinions knowledgeable and paid particular attention on those rare occasions when Miller had something to say.

One evening in October, the mess gathered after dinner with Davy Williams imparting his knowledge of Regimental affairs.

"Colonel figures we here fer the winter and the Yankees ain't gonna bother us none," Davy said with his customary air of authority, as if he'd spoken to Featherston directly.

"Colonel likely has some information we don' have, but I

do believe the Federals will make a move before too long," Cummins remarked to everyone's surprise.

"What makes you think thataway, Miller," Riley asked, and they all turned their attention to the usually quiet man.

"Richmond paper reported George McClellan has taken command of the Federal army," he continued. "Lincoln and the Northern politicians will agitate for action before winter, and a new General will have to oblige."

"Yanks're mostly on t'other side o' tha river," Zeke pointed out. "If they try to cross over, we'd stop 'em fore they'd git a foothold."

"There's a lot of river to cover, Zeke," Miller reasoned. "I expect they might find a place we don't watch too closely."

"You reckon they'll try soon," Charlie inquired.

"Fall is tolerable weather in this country," Miller speculated. "I'd figure they'll come before end of the month."

"Well, the officers shur don' think yer way," Davy challenged. "An I reckon they knows a lot more bout the Yanks'n you do."

"I hope they're right, Davy," the thoughtful Cummins replied, "but the Federals ain't likely to tell us their plans." Heads nodded in the face of Miller's logic, though Davy grumbled that Miller wasn't so smart.

Dutchie broke in to tell them about a detail forming in the morning to obtain supplies and the men turned to other subjects. Miller took his leave from the campfire and Josh decided to follow.

He caught up to Miller as he wandered toward the front of camp. "You headin' off ta do sum readin'" he asked good naturedly.

With a welcoming smile, Miller said, "I try to read a few pages before I turn in every night, Josh."

"You truly think there's gonna be 'nother fight," Josh questioned.

Miller halted and turned to him. "You can be sure of

another fight and more after that," Miller declared firmly.

"It'll take more than one battle to win this war. The Federals have to attack and they will."

"What makes you so shur," Josh asked.

"I met Northerners in the college, Josh, and before hostilities started, I read their papers regularly," Miller informed him. "They have the will, and the resources, to win this war and they'll not give up."

The conviction in Cummins' tone chilled Josh. He respected the educated man too much to dismiss his opinion and could think of nothing to dispute the claim.

Josh bid the scholarly Private good night and drifted off to his tent. Zeke found him and they went to visit some of their friends in the company. But Miller's prediction haunted him all night. Josh could not shake the nagging thought that the Regiment's next clash with the Yankees might be far more contentious than their first encounter.

>< >< >< >< ><

Federal troops were not idle on this chilly, late October night. Leesburg lay nearly a mile from the Potomac and nearby in both directions along the River stood two ferry operations, stilled by war. Conrad's Ferry lay in the northerly direction while Edward's Ferry crossed the river a few miles downstream. Federal and Confederate forces picketed their respective sides at each ferry, but the wooded, steep banked area between was only lightly patrolled. Directly east of the town the river widened enough to contain a slip of land called Harrison's Island. As clouds brushed a harvest moon in the very early hours of October 21st, blueclad soldiers began to congregate on the Maryland side, awaiting their turn to cross.

A small patrol had crossed by boat near midnight to reconnoiter the Virginia side. They returned quickly with news that no rebels awaited them and the way was clear for a foray inland. Impulsive commanders ordered a larger body of Massachusetts men forward. The anxious men were conveyed by boat first to the island, then marched across the short width before boarding another boat to take them to the enemy shore. The steep rise that bordered the River at this point made landing difficult and required the invaders to immediately climb upwards along a narrow path through trees and scrub brush. Officers unused to large troop movement failed to foresee the military defect in this time consuming operation. Impatient for an attack upon a foe ignorant of their presence, they did not perceive the catastrophe retreating men would face awaiting too few boats to carry such large numbers, beneath an enemy occupying the high ground.

The Massachusetts men climbed the wooded bluff beneath bright, but steadily waning, moonlight. Trees crowned the heights and those first to the top sought the welcome cover. Nerves tensed, ready for the shout or shot that would rouse the rebels. To the relief of these eager Bay Staters, no warning sounded while their numbers increased.

As the Federals reached the top, ranks formed and scouts crept cautiously forward. Their first reports confirmed information supplied by the patrol, no rebels nearby! Officers issued orders in whispers and the Massachusetts men marched inland under the lighter sky of dawn. Soldiers from Pennsylvania and New York began the slow process of crossing behind them, bringing artillery for support.

Some distance away, a sleepy Southern picket at his isolated outpost glanced at the graying sky and knew his duty was near an end. His nighttime fire had burned out and he trembled a little in the damp chill. Feeling the call of nature, he slipped deeper into the brush for relief. The woods about him were alive with sounds unnatural for early morning. He walked back toward his post, but remained within the brush and beheld a stunning sight. Armed, blueclad soldiers moved in force toward an unsuspecting Confederate camp. The sentry immediately took off through the brush to sound the alarm, abandoning the rifle he had clutched throughout his night's duty. Within moments, the Northern vanguard's approach was no longer secret.

13

"Josh und Zik, up mit you," Dutchie said and moved off to rouse others. Josh started from a deep sleep, opening his eyes to gray light and heard the drumming of assembly. Zeke stretched beside him as they struggled in to shoes and jackets and put on their kit.

"What's the fuss about," Zeke said to Charlie Akins as he grabbed his rifle.

"Yankees landed on the Virginy side an we gon' off to find 'em," Charlie told him.

Ferrall's voice soared above the chaos, "Form up by the road, lads. You'll be sure to fill yer cartridge pouch."

Josh joined the others shuffling toward regimental formation. He fell in with his company as Lieutenant Abernathy called roll. Ferrall and Haskins moved amongst the men, checking they carried the necessary gear. In the excited rush to fall in, soldiers had failed to grab some of their equipment. Josh heard Ferrall ask several if they had their bayonets.

The Regiment formed quickly in column of fours and just minutes out of their blankets, soldiers stepped off smartly. Officers maintained a brisk pace, sergeants quieting chatter in the ranks. Someone started off with 'Dixie', followed by 'The Bonnie Blue Flag', and the whole Regiment was abruptly singing. The songs did much to calm anxious nerves.

They marched more than a mile before turning on the road

to Edward's Ferry. Warming sunshine flooded the Ferry crossing as they halted near the river. By companies, the Regiment fanned out on either side of the road and a patrol was sent forward to the bank of the Potomac. Although a few Yankees appeared on the Maryland side, no Federals were sighted on the rebel side of the river.

With the column halted, Josh could hear no sound of musket fire in any direction. He began to relax a little as the sun climbed in the sky. Somebody down the line said the Yanks had gone home. Men were permitted to boil coffee and hard crackers were issued for breakfast.

Word circulated the 13th Mississippi Regiment was nearby and the vanguard arrived as the 17th settled into position. The 13th secured an area to the rear of the 17th, where the road turned east. As their compatriots did, the 13th broke from columns and began to stand down.

The morning wore on without action on their front, though distant rifle fire could be heard occasionally. Men who had been present for the battle at Manassas reminded those who would listen of wasted marches and false alarms, and of Federals that retreated after first contact. Josh remembered that day, the exhausting march and counter march, then the heart pounding excitement of the skirmish and chase. Still, this time seemed different to him in some inexplicable way.

Just before noon, a party from the 13th Regiment passed the Rangers on their way to fill canteens. An unkempt private shouted hello and strayed over with another man in tow, just as poorly uniformed, to where Josh and his friends rested.

"Looks like 'nuf o' us mud heads to stop the whole Fed'ral army from crossin' here," the private said in a friendly tone. "Whar y'all from," he asked.

"Marshall County," Zeke replied. "Where you boys call home?"

"Me an Henry from down Vicksburg way," the man said. His friend nodded toward the group as the fellow introduced himself. "Caleb's my name, boys."

Josh, Zeke, Davy, Charlie, Hugh and Riley took turns naming themselves. Will Tucker introduced himself and his brother. Miller spoke his name, but Joe Crawford had his eyes closed and said nothing.

Caleb and Henry squatted in their midst. "Heard y'all already had a set to with the Yanks," the talkative Caleb said.

"We run 'em and chased 'em at Manassas," Davy confirmed for their visitor. "They ain't much for stayin' when the lead flies," he added.

"We restless fer a little action," Caleb declared. "Ain't done nothin' since we got here but march all over this damn state."

Silent Henry just nodded with his friend.

"Got us a hell for leather Colonel, ol' Congressman Barksdale," Caleb told them proudly. "All he talks 'bout is killin' Yankees," the man from the 13th added.

"We got us a right smart Colonel you might heard of, name o' Featherston," Charlie said sternly, letting the visitor know by his tone the 17th was proud of its leader.

Caleb seemed to sense further comment on Barksdale would be unwelcome and stood to leave. The mute Henry stood also.

"You boys keep yer heads down, an shoot straight," Caleb said with a grin. He waved in parting, accepting friendly good byes in return, and the two men returned to the watering party.

"Damned latecomer thinks he's got the only Colonel kin fight," Charlie grumbled, raising a laugh from the others. "I see that Barksdale takin' enemy fire, then he might have somethin' to talk about." Charlie simmered quietly as his friends returned to reclining positions.

In late morning, a company was detached and sent north toward the sound of firing. The Samuel Benton Rifles marched off amid envious looks from the remainder of the 17th. Just after noon the sounds of distant battle became more constant. A sporadic booming report of artillery mixed with the rattle of rifle fire. It was difficult to tell the size of forces engaged. The sounds persisted during early afternoon as the officers trained their attention in that direction. Couriers raced by and rumors circulated of a pitched battle to the north near Leesburg.

Finally, orders were passed to form ranks for marching. Formerly relaxed men hustled to formation and prepared to shoulder rifles. Once formed, the Regiment was turned to face a gathering of mounted officers. They were called to attention and Colonel Featherston addressed them astride his horse.

"Men, we have been ordered to assist our gallant friends from Virginia at a place on the River where the Yankees have crossed in force."

The Colonel paused amid complete silence. "We must hasten forward and cannot tarry on the way. Forward men."

Featherston motioned toward the color bearer in front and commands were issued to march. As the ranks stepped off, the men marched in regular time. Once the whole Regiment was on the move, orders were passed to quick time.

They started in the direction back to Leesburg, but veered onto a smaller road bearing north before they reached the town. Still on quick time, they trotted through woods and past cornfields lying fallow after harvest. Sounds of battle grew more distinct, the crackling sound of rifle fire reaching them in waves. A sharp sound indicated that artillery was still active.

The Regiment was ordered off the wagon track into a grassy area and continued over a low rise in the ground. As they crested the rise and spread along its height, the field of battle lay before them. They formed in two ranks and men strained for a good look over the objections of their sergeants.

Josh had a good view of proceedings from the second rank and felt a tingle of excitement. Though shrouded in the smoke of battle, Federal and Confederate lines were visible. He could make out the flag of the 18th Mississippi in one area. Then, at some distance from the 18th, stood the men of the 8th Virginia. Wounded men staggered away from the ragged firing lines of both Regiments.

There was little order to the Federal line formed near a woods on the other side of a field, about two hundred yards from where the 17th stood. Smoke gathered in pockets to mark where men fired in small groups. The Yankees lacked coordination and dead lay scattered between the lines. Josh could see two cannon within the Federal line, but the gunners were not then serving either piece.

Behind the 18th, Josh noticed a group of officers attending to someone laying upon the ground. One of the men broke away and ran toward the 17th. Colonel Featherston received his report, saluted and turned to his company officers clustered about him. After a moment, the officers trotted back to their commands.

"You'll be tastin' the powder now, lads," Ferrall declared. "See to your rifles."

Josh felt the familiar twinge in his gut and his throat was awkwardly dry. He glanced at Zeke, and his friend nodded back in grim readiness. Josh checked his pocket and fingered the eagle talon as a chill crawled up his back.

Around him, others faced front with determination and tension etched on their faces. Officers unsheathed swords and paced about. Charlie spoke a not so quiet prayer and several men joined him to say 'Amen'. Finally, the drummers beat the long roll and the Regiment stepped off.

They made for the gap between the Virginia and Mississippi Regiments in good order. Federal cannon sent two rounds their way. Men paused and ducked, but the shot sailed overhead and harmlessly behind, and shirkers rejoined the formation. They formed rank and file facing the Federals as if on drill and without drawing significant rifle fire. Orders were shouted to load and the clink of ramrods echoed through the Regiment.

Josh focused his attention on his weapon. He bit the cartridge and rammed it home, bitter taste of powder on his tongue. Then he raised the rifle and placed a cap, ready for the next command. First rank was ordered to "Ready, aim, fire" and a volley crashed into woods and brush thick with Federals. Smoke billowed, then drifted back on the Regiment so that it was hard to see across the field. Then second rank was ordered to ready and aim and rifles sprouted at shoulder height over a kneeling first rank. Hammers were cocked and triggers pulled on command as the volley spit forth toward the blue coated troops. Again smoke billowed, but Josh had begun to reload and concentrate on his rifle.

A man in the front rank nearby twisted sideways then backwards and on to the ground, his rifle falling away. Another helped him up and they made off to the rear while the ranks closed. The front rank fired again and began to reload. Josh waited for his turn to fire.

Just then, a loud yell went up from their left and the 8th Virginia plunged forward. Josh looked that way and thought he saw some men from the 17th join the charge. The 8th pushed toward the woods, but stopped short of the Federals and delivered a round into the woods. The line wavered as rifles were reloaded, but did not advance and as quick as it started, the charge was spent. Firing sporadically, the 8th began to recede slowly leaving casualties in their wake.

During this time, the 17th had not fired for fear of hitting friends. Now the way was clear and men anxiously anticipated the order to fire. It did not come and Josh turned a little to see behind. Featherston was gesturing to officers from the 17th and some from the 18th, who broke off quickly to join their companies. What was left of the 18th began to form ranks in the space beside the 17th.

A bullet cut the air above his head and Josh turned round to the front, then side to side. Zeke, Riley, Charlie and the Tuckers entered his field of vision, all in good health. He leaned a little forward and glanced to his left, catching sight of Davy and Hugh. Now he was sweating on this cool day and rubbed moisture from his hands. The accumulated heat of late afternoon waned as the sun dipped toward tree tops behind them, lengthening their shadows.

The command was passed to load and fix bayonets. Again the clink and clatter of ramrods passed through the Regiment. The buck and ball cartridge would find many a target at close range. The deadly sword bayonet sprouted along the ranks and the men were ordered to shoulder arms. Hearts beat faster in anticipation of the order to charge.

From behind, Colonel Featherston yelled at the top of his lungs so that his voice would carry. "Charge, Mississippi. Drive them into the Potomac - or into Hell!"

A loud, shrill yell instantly rose from the ranks and the entire Regiment surged forward at the double quick. Josh screamed with the others and nearly ran over Miller Cummins. Spirit soared in his breast and powered his feet forward. Zeke was there beside him, then cut off by a soldier and forced behind. Will Tucker edged up on his right, then stumbled and sprawled forward head first. As Josh risked a look back, he saw the young man prone on the ground reaching for his leg.

Josh could see Federals firing in their direction and bullets sizzled the air about them. A man just behind yelled 'Oh, God' but the sound faded as Josh ran on. He was among the first to a spot marked by several officers with swords held high, among them Lieutenant Abernathy. They were close enough to see Yankee faces bearing a wild look as the stunned Northerners frantically loaded their rifles. The cannoneers scrambled about their guns as if to drag them away. It occurred to Josh that the Federal artillery should be firing.

In a matter of seconds the 17th and 18th formed near the edge of the woods and were commanded to fire. The combined sound of a thousand rifles resembled the crack and thunder of an artillery round as the volley ripped into woods and brush. Blueclad soldiers stumbled and fell, grabbing at shattered limbs. Others broke and ran, some tossing their rifles aside. Without further orders, Southern troops instinctively plunged into the woods after retreating Yankees.

Wounded and unwounded Federals threw up their hands in surrender. Some Rebel soldiers paused to take men prisoner. More than enough ran directly at the artillery to claim these much sought prizes and the pieces were quickly in rebel hands. Most continued on in their excitement.

Josh nearly lost his cap as he ran forward, dodging tree limbs and vaulting small brush. He had no interest in the cannon, but he desperately wanted to capture a Yankee as they scattered through the woods before him. In a small clearing he spotted movement in a fallen blue form and ran toward him.

"Yer captured, Yank," he yelled, to be heard over the chaos around him. Josh leveled his rifle and bayonet at the prostrate, weaponless man.

The Federal sported blood streaming down his pants leg, his clothes disheveled. He raised slowly upon his arms and twisted his face toward Josh. His young face was smudged with dirt and powder, dark hair tussled in the absence of a cap. White teeth showed through a half grin and he seemed ready to speak. Josh looked into his eyes and relaxed a little when he saw the man had no fight in him.

Suddenly, he pitched toward Josh and his head hit the ground with a thud. Josh looked up to see Lucius Bradwell pull his bloody bayonet from the man's back. Josh stared open mouthed, too stunned by the unspeakable cruelty to utter a sound.

"Ya gotta stick 'em Yanks, Campbell, not talk 'em to death," Bradwell said, then let out a big laugh. "You ain't got no stomach fer killin', farm boy," the burly man challenged with a smirk.

Bradwell stood there, his body tensed from the kill. Blood spattered his uniform and even his face. The battle crazed man was poised to meet Josh's response, but when Josh remained still, he turned warily and resumed his chase.

Josh remained motionless for some time, willing the Yankee to rise. Then he shucked his rifle and bent to pick up the Federal. He lifted and turned the man's head and shoulders, but the eyes rolled and his tongue flopped out. Josh knew the man was dead, but part of him refused to admit it. He lay the still warm corpse gently upon the ground.

The fight had moved farther ahead as Josh rose to his feet and he stood alone for a moment. He could not erase Bradwell's despicable act from his mind. He picked up his rifle and started walking to find the renegade soldier, determined to confront the man.

Suddenly, Zeke was beside him, tugging at his arm.

"Josh, you alright," he pleaded. He shook Josh a little until his friend turned to face him. "Whaz the matter, Josh, you hit," he asked anxiously.

Josh glared at Zeke in a trance and some time passed before he recognized his friend. The hard look lifted from Josh as he became aware of his surroundings. Zeke looked him over and seemed satisfied there was no wound.

"Tha Yanks're on the run, les go," he said and tugged Josh forward.

Josh felt his head clear and the sounds of battle returned to his ears. Rifles cracked, men yelled, some screamed and cussed. He realized his first duty was to continue the attack.

He pulled out of Zeke's grasp and said, "Les go, pard." Together, they ran toward the river bluff.

They reached a line of gray soldiers just as the last Federals disappeared over a rim in the woods. In a few steps, they were at the edge and found a space in the line formed there. Josh looked about to see familiar faces and some of the 18th in the crowd.

Instinctively, he began to load his gun and raised the rifle to find a target. Below him, Federals fell and tumbled down the steep slope, grasping at tree trunks and bushes to slow their fall. He saw a bluecoat braced against a tree and fired. The soldier pitched hard against the trunk, his arms flying upward, and then slipped sideways to fall on his face. Josh drew the rifle back and began to load again.

Behind him officers yelled to keep firing. Bullets poured down upon the hapless Federal soldiers fleeing toward the Potomac. Directly below Josh a man uttered a deep throated scream and fell headfirst down the slope, crashing against a rock. At river's edge, men jumped onto the few boats afloat in panic. In the melee boats swamped, sending occupants in to the chilling water. Others simply dove into the churning River. Heads bobbed on the surface and some disappeared forever.

Josh fired again at the scrambling mass of blue, then prepared to reload. Mississippi troops jammed the line and he pulled back a little for space to perform the drill. He heard a man scream "Murder" and turned toward the shout.

Miller Cummins shouted "Murder" again. Then Ferrall was beside him, grabbing his jacket and shaking him roughly.

"Do yer duty, lad," Ferrall screamed at Cummins, but Miller tried to wrest free of him. Josh thought Miller might strike the Sergeant, but the stocky Irishman had a firm grasp.

A soldier spun back from the firing line, grabbing his arm as blood appeared on the sleeve. Ferrall thrust Cummins toward the man and stepped over to inspect the wounded soldier.

"Private, you'll be takin' this man to care," he barked. Miller glared at his Sergeant, then turned and helped the wounded soldier upright. Wrapping an arm around the bleeding man, he grabbed his rifle and staggered off to the rear.

Ferrall looked straight at Josh. "Load and fire, lad. Do yer duty," he commanded and Josh stepped back into line with his rifle raised.

But Miller's charge rang in his head. It was murder. Few Federals returned fire in their panicked dash for safety or shelter. He felt no pride in shooting helpless men. Amidst the firing he could hear shouts of surrender from below. Josh raised his rifle slightly and shot at a tree limb ten feet above the river.

He stepped back again and took his time reloading. He

looked along the line in both directions, peering through the smoke. Men continued to fire at the Federals below and officers paced along the line behind them. Bandsmen and drummer boys scurried about, bringing ammunition and water for parched throats. Josh placed a cap and slowly took a place in the firing line again. Aiming at a wide tree trunk, he pulled the trigger and felt the rifle kick.

Shadows now enveloped the woods and bank as the sun fell below the horizon. Firing slackened without clear targets, but the sounds of desperation continued to rise from below. Josh prolonged his effort to reload, silently pleading for the order to cease fire. As more men fell back exhausted from the firing line, the order was given.

Men relaxed with the command as the frenzy of battle passed, though some scrambled down the slope after the Yankees. A company of the 17th was detached to make their way down to the river bank and round up prisoners from below. Company officers allowed a brief respite and gathered among themselves to decide orders.

Josh surveyed the line, looking for familiar faces. He spotted Zeke at once, staring absently toward the trees, then Riley and Davy close by tending to their weapons. Walter Tucker passed, unscathed but calling for Will. Charlie and Hugh stood well back from the rim, both with their caps off and heads bowed. Dutchie was fussing with Joe Crawford, the foreign words unrecognizable. Josh noticed others from the company and Regiment around him, and it seemed that most had come through the fight without harm.

Zeke wore a puzzled expression when Josh stepped beside him. He realized this was Zeke's first time in the line of fire. "It's over, pard. Them Yanks is gone," Josh said and slapped Zeke's shoulder to reassure his shaken friend.

"See to yer rifles, lads. Clear the chambers," Ferrall reminded, and some of the men fired into the air. He told them to remove bayonets and checked to make sure they followed his instructions.

The First Lieutenant called the Rangers to formation. Josh and the others walked a short distance to the assembly point. Jasper Welburn's tinny voice urged the men to attention, and Josh had no memory of the Third Lieutenant's presence in the charge and chase. Bradwell's burly form was notably absent.

Captain Franklin appeared and instructed them to help gather wounded. Josh and Zeke joined a squad with Ferrall. They were led back toward the clearing where the charge started, inspecting fallen forms for signs of life.

"Nights could git cold, lads," Ferrall reminded the small group in a low voice, "and there are some overcoats about that will do their owners no more good."

As they fanned out the men passed still Federal bodies. Josh noticed the dead were sprawled awkwardly, some forward, some backward, with limbs twisted asunder. They seemed to have been tossed about like raggedy dolls. Even in near darkness, pale gray faces stared unseeing. Blood stained grass and leaves, and uniforms of the dead.

A strange and horrible smell assaulted his senses and Josh nearly gagged in reaction. His mind had no connection with the smell rising from the field, but he could not rid himself of it. Others held cloths or sleeved arms before their mouth and nose.

Josh spotted a Federal sprawled on the ground face down. Zeke followed as he slipped over to the body and prodded the form with the butt of his rifle. There was no response. Laying his rifle aside and fighting an increasingly sick feeling, Josh turned the man over while Zeke kept his rifle leveled at the form. A dirty, lifeless face stared back above a blood stained chest. Josh bent low, but could hear no breath.

"Fine overcoat there," Zeke commented.

Josh noticed the long, caped coat had only a little blood on the lapels. He glanced back at Zeke and his friend shrugged. Josh worked quickly to remove the coat, then folded it and slipped it under his arm. He grabbed his rifle, stood and backed away from the fallen form.

"Them shoes is nearly new," Zeke commented. "Reckon there ain't no harm in takin' 'em."

Zeke cradled his rifle, knelt and removed both shoes, stringing them together and tossing them over his shoulder as he stood.

Josh simply looked at him and they continued walking the field. Discovering no more bodies, they spotted Ferrall and made their way toward him. Others in the squad joined them, sheepishly sporting new apparel, shoes or equipment. But no live Yankee prisoners had been found.

"Well, lads, appears our work's done here," the First Sergeant declared. A drummer began to beat assembly and the Regiment formed ranks. Josh wondered whether they would spend the night at this place or be allowed back to camp.

His question was answered when the order to march was given once the Regiment formed. From the column, Josh could see a large group of Federal prisoners under guard of the 8th Virginia. He also saw a hastily erected tent that served as a field hospital for wounded of both sides. The few Southern dead were laid out neatly nearby.

The march seemed short as the men eased into a repetitive task. Many struggled with plunder from luckless Northerners on the way back, though nothing was abandoned. They were allowed to fall out upon reaching camp and Josh felt weariness engulf him. He stacked his rifle with the rest, dropped his gear and Yankee coat inside his tent. He joined the mess for coffee and helped Zeke start a fire. Physically tired, his mind raced with the memories of battle and Josh now found himself wide eyed and too alert for sleep. The mess apparently shared his feelings and busied themselves with small tasks around the campfire.

As the men gathered near the fire, he suddenly noticed both the Tuckers were missing. Riley seemed to read his mind.

"Will got hit when we charged," he commented to Josh in a matter of fact voice. "Walter found him with the wounded whilst we wuz lookin' fer prisoners an got permission to stay with him at the field." Riley said he didn't know how bad Will was hurt.

As he absorbed this news, Josh watched the others. Joe Crawford was rummaging in a sack for some biscuits, a new Federal pistol wedged in his pants. Riley fussed with the coffee and Dutchie sat by himself, mumbling quietly. Miller was seated too, staring silently into the darkness. Davy wasn't about, but that was hardly surprising.

Hugh and Charlie joined them, Charlie sporting a bandaged right arm and blood on his pant leg.

"How'd you git that," Zeke asked, nodding toward the sleeveless, wrapped arm.

Hugh responded, "Ain't no bullet wound. Charlie went over the hill after them Yanks. Slipt an tore his arm on a rock."

Charlie had a sheepish look. "I jes went down to help some o' them fellers and got my own self hurt."

That brought a chuckle from all of them and they were still teasing him when Davy joined them.

"I got a lot to tell you boys 'bout that scrape with the Federals," he began, refusing a cup of coffee to keep his mouth free. Everyone turned toward him.

"Colonel Burt got kilt in the battle," he said to mild surprise. Josh remembered the fallen form amidst a group of officers behind the 18th when they arrived at the field. The leader of the 18th Mississippi was as popular with his regiment as Featherston was in the 17th. The 18th would be feeling his loss this night.

"That's why the 18th joined our charge," Davy continued, "Featherston wuz in command o' them, too.

"The 18th got hit hard again, lost bout thirty kilt an more'n sixty wounded. Course they wuz at it all day. We only lost one kilt an bout eight or nine wounded.

"They's likely sev'ral hunnert dead Yanks, an we captured 'bout a thousand," Davy said and Zeke whistled at the totals.

"I bin hearin' Gen'ral Evans was drunk an had to be taken off the field," Davy confided. "Seems ol' Featherston saved the day with his charge." Davy wound down and looked for a place to sit.

"I ain't seen Bradwell since we got back," Josh asked cautiously. "You seen him 'round camp, Davy?"

"Naw, last I seen o' Lucius he wuz goin' over the bluff after them Yankee boys," Davy replied.

Conversation sputtered as weariness began to replace the day's excitement. They each recounted tidbits of their individual part in the fight. Davy was the only one to brag about seeing a Yankee get hit when he shot him. Joe Crawford cackled about how scared the Federals were when they rushed them over the rim of the bluff. When he compared shooting them from the bluff to killing chickens, Miller got up and walked away. The rest refused to join in such ridicule and Josh knew they all felt guilty about shooting at the Yankee soldiers in full flight.

Dutchie stifled conversation when he declared, "Ve ist all brave boys ven der Yan-keys run away. Ve see who ist so brave ven der Yan-keys shoot back some time." The usually amiable carpenter walked away without waiting for a reply to his parting words. One by one the rest wandered off to their tents and blankets. Josh found himself the last one at the campfire, enjoying its warmth before going to sleep.

So many thoughts tumbled through his head that he could not rest his mind. The battle came back to him in pieces. The charge had been thrilling, but he could not shake the red tinted image of Bradwell killing the Federal soldier at his feet. He began to worry that they had no word on Will Tucker.

A damp mist gathered on this chill night and closed the world about him. Josh stoked the fire. The night was quiet while the Regiment slept.

Suddenly, Lucius Bradwell loomed before him without making a sound. Josh started in apprehension of what the crazed soldier might do, realizing he had no weapon to hand, then simply watched the man close on the fire. Without a word, without glancing in Josh's direction, Bradwell squatted to warm his hands in front of the fire.

Josh checked his fear as he observed the man reflected in the fire's light. Bradwell's jacket and shirt were askew and spotted with dark stains. His jackets cuffs were stained solid dark with blood and his hands seemed almost black. A bloody bayonet was belted at his side and he carried a haversack bulging with booty.

Josh recovered from his surprise and summoned his anger to confront him. "Lucius, yer a damned killer of men," he said with an edge to his voice as he tensed for the man's reaction.

But Bradwell casually raised his face toward him as if just realizing someone else was present. The campfire lit a vacant stare from half closed eyes. Those eyes seemed lifeless and dead to Josh, set in an expressionless, dirt streaked face.

"Yanks're all dead," he muttered, "all dead. Cain't git me now." His voice was hardly more than a whisper and he spoke without feeling.

Slowly, Bradwell stood, adjusted his haversack, turned and walked into the mist.

Josh was shaken. His heart beat fast and a chill rattled his body. Bradwell had emerged in ghostly form with a face as blank as a dead man. The killing frenzy Josh saw earlier had subsided, replaced by a trance like stare.

Josh trembled a little and stood to gather himself. He had planned to thrash Bradwell when he found him. But as he confronted the man, he could not summon sufficient anger at the head sick human shell. Retaliation would wait until Lucius Bradwell could be brought to understand his criminal act.

Suddenly spent, Josh knelt with an effort to bank the fire. He knew he must end the long night with sleep to renew his body. He walked to his tent and crawled in. Zeke's rhythmic snore seemed a comfort and he lay down beside his friend. Another day, and another battle, had passed without personal harm.

Perhaps his luck might change if the Yankees ever did stand and fight, but for now, he silently thanked God to have survived again, a whole man.

14

Elihu Hawthorne returned to a Capital in which fear of rebel capture had been replaced by confidence as the bastion of union. Soldiers by tens of thousands ringed the Capital with their camps. Most of these men had only just arrived and had no part in the distasteful episode at Bull Run. In swelling numbers, the Union's defenders trained daily as a visible show of readiness. The daily rumble of artillery was oddly reassuring to the populace.

Expecting his fellow politicians to be despondent about the future and receptive to a plan for Congressional oversight, he found instead a rising confidence in the military and the President. The sting of defeat at Bull Run had first been tempered by relief that the rebels did not press their advantage. In time, the rebels remained at a respectful distance on their side of the Potomac while the Federals continued to occupy Arlington Heights. Maryland had been secured to prevent surprise from the north. Through the early fall of 1861, the Capital's citizens and the Union's leaders grew comfortable in their precarious position.

Hawthorne sensed that everyone, even veteran politicians, had swooned over the Army of the Potomac's new commander. George McClellan was the 'Young Napoleon' and he willingly accepted the mantle of savior of the Union bestowed upon him by every Northern newspaper. McClellan had immediately set about organizing city defenses and training troops. He organized and reorganized the army with a tireless spirit. The General was hard at work forging the weapon to smite rebellion forever. Many members of Congress seemed to consider McClellan above reproach and Hawthorne had not detected even a hint of dissonance.

In such a climate, the Congressman expressed his true feelings guardedly, lest he lose all credibility with his fellows. Then, suddenly and rapidly, the political climate changed. In late October, news of the disaster at Balls Bluff hit the Capital like a thunderstorm. First reports hinted at a desperate fight and retreat. Then the full description of events with eyewitness reports began to circulate. Newspapers printed numbers and names of the dead, wounded and captured. In a final, grizzly demonstration of defeat, a few bloated bodies actually floated to Washington's shore.

The White House led the city, and the nation, in grief. A close and dear friend of the President, Colonel Edward Baker, had fallen at Balls Bluff. The Lincolns had named a son after this illustrious political confidant of the President. Lincoln mourned his friend publicly.

Hawthorne had been alarmed at the crushing defeat. Once again, Massachusetts' men had been among those engaged and stampeded in disarray from the field of battle. Though they suffered many of the casualties, skeptical whispers about their courage would again arise. Hawthorne wondered when the state would be allowed a measure of pride in its fighting men.

However, he refused to linger long on personal feelings of disgrace. Instead, Hawthorne immediately realized that McClellan's image had inevitably tarnished and hard questions would be asked about responsibility for this stunning defeat. If others proved timid, he meant to ask those questions. Congress was not that moment in session, so the gentleman from Massachusetts had some time to plan his assault on the military.

He was in a reflective, satisfied mood when he happened upon Ben Wade on a frosty day in early November.

Wade was leaving an eating establishment after the midday meal. Hawthorne raised his hat slightly in greeting and made to continue on. The Ohioan paused a moment to register his face, then, to Hawthorne's surprise, latched on to the Congressman's arm.

"My good man, you are just the person I had hoped to see," the rotund Senator exclaimed and Hawthorne could tell that lunch included a plentiful measure of spirits. Wade's fondness for libation was well known though the Senator never appeared to carry it to excess.

"Though you have not known it, you and I have beaten the same drum of late," Wade began, leaning close in a conspiratorial manner. Hawthorne was surprised indeed for the Senator had actively avoided him in recent weeks, even at one point exiting a side door of the Capitol in haste as the Massachusetts man approached.

"There are many in Congress and the White House who have been beguiled by our military leaders. They have fallen for the charade of fancy parades and bountiful equipment to erase the memory of defeat," Wade confided.   Hawthorne thought it prudent to remain silent until the Senator made his point.

"You and I were not so easily smitten by our charming young officers," the Ohioan crowed. "There is hard work ahead and victory will not be won until the fight is taken into the heart of the rebellion," Wade declared resolutely.

"I am glad to hear you speak so forcibly, Senator," Hawthorne interjected, to remind the man that he was but inches away.

Wade somehow construed the comment to lean closer. "And now we have dramatic proof that our fine young generals are a bumbling lot," he said. "This matter at Balls Bluff is a fiasco. We have lost many fine men and delivered victory to the rebels on a silver platter."

"I have learned of incompetence at the highest levels of the army," Wade affirmed.   "There can be no denials, no sugar coating," he said earnestly.   "I mean to have this matter investigated by Congress."

Hawthorne brightened at this statement. Finally, his plan for Congressional oversight might garner support.   And none other than the powerful Senator from Ohio seemed prepared to deliver this support. Hawthorne might have hugged the man if he were any one other than prickly Ben Wade.

"Senator, I am most gratified to hear you say this. Surely you must lead such an investigation. We need a man of your stature and persistence to conduct an inquiry." Hawthorne was not above carelessly dangling the one carrot any member of Congress would find appealing.

Wade visibly puffed at the compliment, but regained his composure quickly. "When Congress opens in December, I intend to propose a joint committee to review the conduct of this war," Wade said.   "I will need able men and loyal Republicans to undertake this task. I shall count on you to rally support in the House." Wade's tone implied this duty was a command rather than a request.

"I will be honored to assist you in any way possible, Senator," the Congressman rejoined. Membership on a committee with oversight of the military could bring unbounded power and influence.

The debacle at Ball's Bluff might have delivered a golden opportunity to the Massachusetts Congressman. He could be part of the means to expose anyone who hindered the war effort. In the alternative, he would be able to claim some modest measure of contribution to success. Victory has many fathers, Hawthorne remembered, but defeat is a bastard. Sitting in careful judgment of military action, with the incomparable asset of hindsight, invited a bright political future for him.

Hawthorne's introspections had caused him to momentarily ignore the Ohio Senator and he was somewhat surprised when Wade tipped his cap and bid him goodbye, saying he had other business to attend to.   Hawthorne resumed his ruminations, feeling almost lightheaded. He had recriminated himself in recent weeks for taking an unpopular tack. Now, through the mischance of inexperienced officers on a stretch of the Potomac far upstream, his future in the Capital was suddenly brighter. Elihu Hawthorne was a man to be reckoned with and those who passed him on the street, bundled against the early chill, must have wondered what had provoked such a radiant smile.

>< >< >< >< ><

The 17th Mississippi survived the battle called Leesburg by the Confederates with minor casualties and a bounty of glory. Laudatory dispatches from generals and political leaders were read or posted in camp. Colonel W. S. Featherston was widely hailed as the epitome of Southern courage.

Although appreciative of recognition, the 17th seemed a gloomy lot. The Virginia weather turned cold and rainy, affecting the mind as well as the body. For men raised in warmer climes, the chilling weather proved an unrelenting irritant. Food remained uninviting though the Regiment was well provided. Roll was called each morning, but days passed again without regimental or company drill. Despite the decline in forced activity, men were not allowed to stray from camp for fear of another Federal incursion. Soldiers could do little except huddle about campfires, drawing away only when commandeered for guard or special duty. Hard spirits contributed to innumerable squabbles among the men. Around evening campfires, a sad dirge like 'Lorena' was more frequently heard than happier songs.

Josh observed the ominous mood and knew he too was infected. The battle had taken a toll in men's spirits, but they grumbled most about being so far from home. There was no hint of when men from the 17th might be allowed leave. Suspicions were cast on General Evans and Miller Cummins complained the South Carolinian had little concern for troops from Mississippi.

Josh's sleep was often troubled. Vivid dreams of the dead Yankee's face spurting blood recurred nightly. Or he recalled the Northerners' distorted bodies as they crashed against rocks and trees in their efforts to flee. Josh was reluctant to share feelings with his friends, since any sympathy toward the Federals was often ridiculed. And he dare not reveal that he had avoided killing, lest that be interpreted as cowardice. Suspicion that he had shirked his duty at the Bluff began to displace the pride he felt as part of the first line in the Regiment's charge.

Sergeant Ferrall admitted a grudging approval of the company's part in the battle, though he noted the 17th had simply turned a retreat into a rout. Ferrall was too busy for further reflection. Zeke always turned the subject elsewhere when the battle was mentioned, refusing to reveal his private feelings. Even the usually thoughtful Miller Cummins, anger coloring his face, would not speak to Josh about the fight.

Josh resolved to suffer through his troubles in silence, but chanced to find one who admitted to personal feelings when he joined Charlie Akins to get fresh water for the mess.

"I reckon the Yanks'll be lickin' their wounds fer a while after the hurtin' we put on 'em," Josh ventured as they returned to camp burdened by full canteens.

"T'was hard to see so many dead and wounded," Charlie reflected evenly.

The sentiment revealed some concern for their enemy and Josh recalled his friend's religious nature. Perhaps Charlie was also distressed by the bloodshed.

"Weren't easy to shoot them Yanks when they was runnin'," Josh noted cautiously. "Don't seem fair to hit 'em harder once they whupped."

"T'is a Christian feelin', but wasted on a godless foe," Charlie declared, and Josh noted the change in tone. "Northerners have made this war, and they'll know God's vengeance."

Charlie had spoken so forcefully that Josh was wary of a response. They stopped walking to adjust the heavy canteens and

Charlie looked directly at his companion.

"I was troubled after the battle, but I have prayed to ease my mind," the religious man explained. "We are instruments of the Lord, and He guides our hand in battle," Charlie assured him.

"Yer shur God's on our side," Josh wondered aloud.

"I see His hand at work in our cause," Charlie said. "Take comfort that you do His bidding when we fight."

As they neared the campfire and unloaded the canteens, Josh reflected on his older friend's words. Charlie accepted an Almighty that controlled his actions and held him blameless for the bloody result. Josh knew his burden would ease if he agreed to such reasoning, but the God of his mother could not pull the trigger of a rifle. His mind remained unsettled, though he was relieved to know someone else had struggled with the gruesome sights of battle.

Charlie displayed a generous side when he decided to see Will Tucker. Walter had brought word that his brother was in a bad way and asked the others to visit. Charlie organized a trip to the hospital a week after the battle and secured a pass from Captain Franklin. When the day arrived though, enthusiasm had dwindled. Hugh had a sweetheart in town that he slipped away to see, sometimes without permission. Riley, Davy and Miller were assigned guard duty. Dutchie and Joe Crawford begged off for vague reasons. Josh and Zeke kept their commitment, though they had nothing better to do.

They left after noon and walked a mile to the temporary hospital on the edge of town. An empty warehouse had been commandeered for the wounded. The structure appeared secure against the weather, though only a few windows were evident. White uniformed men and orderlies loitered about smoking or taking the air outside. Zeke pointed to a door on the side to gain entry. The stench of unwashed bodies and wounds leaking blood assaulted them and all three reached to cover their mouths. Fresh pine boughs had been laid about to cut the smell, without evident effect. Men were sprawled everywhere, soldiers and some civilians attending to their needs. They had to disturb an orderly to find Will Tucker and were angrily waved toward a corner. The three men picked their way in the gloomy light past bandaged survivors until they spotted the familiar face and knelt at his side.

Will lay on the dusty floor with his eyes closed, a thin blanket covering his body. The three men paused at the sight of the pale, still figure, fearing a fatal discovery. To their great relief he stirred and Charlie bent low to tell him he had visitors. Will strained to look around as Josh and Zeke put their heads nearer.

A half smile creased Will's face. "Shur glad you fellers come by, I git a might lonely jes layin' here all day," he said in a raspy, whispering voice. "Y'all hep me a little ah kin sit up an converse." Charlie found a jacket nearby and folded it behind Will's head to prop it up a bit. Will struggled to rise higher, but his arms were too weak and he settled back after the effort.

"Thought Walter'd be here 'bouts," Josh remarked. The Captain had allowed Walter to stay with his brother most days.

"He wuz here a little bit ago, but I dozed off fer awhile," Will said. "He likely took a stroll to ease his mind. Ain't no good fer him to stay roun here."

"They keepin' you alright," Charlie asked with some concern.

"Orderlies'll fetch fer me when I kin catch 'em," he replied. "Provisions ain't much in here, so Walter brings me some food when he kin."

A guilty pause intruded as each of the three visitors realized they should have brought something for the ailing man.

"I reckon the boys are spoilin' fer another fight wi' tha Yanks," Will remarked to spark some comment from his friends.

"We ain't seen no Yanks on this side an' they ain't likely to come visitin' after that hurtin' we put on 'em," Josh said forcefully.

"You ain't missin' nothin', Will," Zeke added, patting him on the arm. "Jes a lotta marchin' no'eres an standin' guard in tha cold weather."

"You'll be back 'fore the nex' fight, Will," Charlie said cheerfully, and the others nodded their agreement. But Will's face hardened.

"I ain't comin' back boys," he said quietly. "They done took mah right leg." He choked up as he spoke.

The revelation stunned them again to silence, punctuated with forlorn groans of a wounded man nearby. They each avoided Will's glistening eyes, searching for something to say.

Will cleared his throat and went on. "I got hit when we charged the Yanks. Damn ball broke mah leg bone," he related, pointing to his right leg. They looked in turn and saw the right leg, outlined by the blanket, ended short of the left. A dark stain marked the spot.

"They talkin' bout shippin' me off to hospital in Richmond, then on home when I git better," Will informed them. "Y'all gon' have to fight this war without me," he said, mustering a half smile.

Charlie finally found his voice. "You done yer part, Will," he told him solemnly.

"Walter know 'bout you gittin' sent home," Zeke asked.

Will pulled the blanket tighter as a chill shook his body. "He wuz yere when the doc told me, but he ain't said much since on the subject," he told them.

"I bin worried 'bout Walter. Y'all got to promise me to look after him whilst I'm gone," Will pleaded. "He's apt to be lonely an scart without me. Y'all got to make sher he don't do nothin' crazy like desertin'." His voice tailed off with the effort of his plea.

"We'll see he's took care of," Charlie assured him in a thick voice, Josh and Zeke mumbling their agreement.

"Ah'm wore out, boys," Will said faintly, "ain't got much strength." He settled deeper into the rough pallet underneath him. "Shur could use a drop o' water."

Zeke rose quickly and left in search of the drink. Charlie and Josh tried to cheer him with camp news, but nothing they said sparked more than passing interest in the ailing young man. Charlie asked him to join in a prayer that finished as Zeke turned up with a ladle of water. Josh and Charlie propped Will up to drink a few sips, then lay him back when he'd had enough.

"We bes' be gittin' back to camp 'fore Ferrall misses us," Josh said, rising from his crouch with the other two.

"You take care o' yerself, Will," Charlie said. "I'll be prayin' fer ya."

"You be shur to write when you git back home," Zeke added.

"Y'all jes keep an eye on Walter fer me," Will reminded, then raised his right arm slightly to signal good bye.

His visitors said their farewells and slipped out the nearest door. The air was cool and damp, but a welcome change to the stifling hospital. They walked some distance toward camp without a word, occupied by their respective thoughts.

"I don' care to visit no more hospitals," Josh resolved.

Charlie shot him a hard glance. "Long's you kin do it, you got to look after them that's ailin'. The well are obliged to take care o' the sick jes like the livin' are obliged to bury the dead. That's the Lord's way."

Charlie's words humbled his companions. Josh felt chastened and it fell to Zeke to speak a few steps later.

"It's a hard task for a man, but I reckon yer right, Charlie," Zeke said thoughtfully. "We jes ain't had no experience with this here, losin' a friend to gun shot."

"Ain't no more we kin do fer Will now, 'cept take care o' Walter," Josh concluded. They all agreed to enlist the others in this effort.

They walked on without a word. Seeing Will Tucker so pale and feeble forced Josh to think hard about the fight at Ball's Bluff. Unlike Manassas, Yankee bullets had come close this time and hit a friend, a member of the mess. Will had been hit as he ran beside Josh in the charge. If the bullet had cut the air a foot to the side of Will, Josh might be the one with part of him cut off. He shuddered with the thought. He tried to turn his mind away, but the sad sight inside the hospital refused all his efforts and haunted him through the night.

May Turner appeared on the first day of November to finally rescue Josh from his dismal mood. Once the fear of Federal attack had ceased, sutlers had begun to appear regularly, though the Turner wagon was not among them at first. He had awakened on a frosty morning and wandered expectantly to the wagon park after roll call. As he walked among the sutlers hoping to catch a glimpse of her, she suddenly appeared beside him with a smile as warm as sunshine.

"Hey thar, Joshua Campbell, whar you bin keepin' yerself," she said in greeting. He fixed his gaze on her, startled and speechless for the moment as he devoured her friendly face and sparkling eyes. He smiled dumbly in greeting before he found his voice.

"Yer a joy to see, May," he declared emotionally. "I bin hopin' you'd come by," he managed to choke out. Feelings rushed at him and his head began to swim.

She responded with a gentle touch to his hand and looked searchingly at his eyes. "I kin feel yer troubled, Josh." She was close enough that he could smell rosewater scent, see her pained expression and sympathetic eyes. She seemed to lean toward him.

On impulse, Josh wrapped her in his arms and dug his cheek into her hair. He could feel her hesitate, then respond to hold him tightly.

He gathered his feelings with a struggle and parted from her, turning his face from her demanding gaze. "I'm sorry May, fer takin' such liberty with you. I ain't got no right to do that," he mumbled in apology and embarrassment.

She stepped nearer, placing her hands on his arms. "No need to be sorry fer somethin' I wanted," she said softly, then looked to the ground. "I guess I bin a wantin' you to do that since I knowed you."

He lifted her face with the edge of a finger and looked

directly into her eyes. She looked so lovely and alive in the morning light that he was ready to abandon gentlemanly control. The sound of a squad drilling nearby forced him to rein in his emotions.

"We got to git off from camp fer a little privacy," he suggested. "Kin you go with me a ways."

"I kin step off a short while, Josh. I'll jes tell my pa afore I go." She clutched his hand, then turned toward the wagon a few yards away. Josh watched her speak to a tall, lean man beneath a wide brimmed hat. The man stopped a moment and looked in his direction, then simply turned back to his wares. May ran the short distance to him, hooked his arm and in a few moments they had cleared the main part of camp.

"You gon' ta git in trouble fer slippin' off like this," she asked, her face clouding with concern.

"Ain't no worry bout that, May, we done had mornin' roll an' t'ain't no drill til later," Josh assured her.

They walked arm in arm to a field several hundred yards away from camp, and slipped behind a haystack for privacy. The fresh cut hay provided a comfortable resting place.

She removed her coat, spread it on the hay and sat down. She reached for Josh's hand and pulled him down beside her. May nestled close and he put an arm around her, feeling the curves of her body through the thin dress and wool sweater. Instinctively, he pressed his lips to hers and she responded warmly. He pressed his body more forcefully and she lay back, wrapping her arms about him. Josh was overcome with feeling and he moved to cover her body with his. Slowly, she disengaged her lips, lightly pushing him away to check his passion. Josh recovered his control as they settled close beside each other.

"I bin frettin' these past days jes to git a sight o' you," she whispered. "I heard 'bout the battle an come down to camp next day, but yer Sergeant said you wuz on duty. He tol' me y'all come through with nary a scratch."

Josh warmed with May's concern, and grinned at the

thought of a stern Sergeant Ferrall talking with a worried and inquisitive female. Watching his face, she grinned in return, puzzled at his expression.

"Whats so darn funny," she asked. Josh explained what he was thinking about Ferrall and she nodded in understanding.

"May, I bin fightin' that battle fer a week in mah mind, an I'd bin poor comp'ny these past few days," he confided, turning serious. "But settin' here with you is the most comfort I had since then. Yer a tonic for mah soul." She smiled and his emotions surged within.

He pressed against her gently and she lay back invitingly. Her chest rose and fell beneath him and he caressed a breast ever so lightly. She did not recoil from the touch, and looked into his eyes expectantly before he kissed her hungrily again. His body responded naturally in a way that May detected with a shudder.

She pushed back firmly to create some space between them, then rolled him onto his side so that she could rise on one elbow. "Things're movin' a little fast, Josh," she protested. "I don' wanna do somethin' I'll be sorry fer in the mornin'," she added quickly. "Sides, you ain't exactly declared yer intentions fer me."

Josh blushed at his unchecked impulse and sat upright. "I'm sorry, May, fer actin' this away," he apologized. "I cain't seem to get hold o' mah feelin's 'round you.

"You got no cause to doubt mah intentions, May," he continued. "Soon's I git a pass, I kin come a courtin' proper."

She smiled reassuringly and nestled into his arms. "I like you right fair, Josh from Mississippi, but we got to do this thing right."

"May, I don' know if we got time to be proper," Josh cautioned. She turned and cut a hard glance at him, but he continued. "We could git orders to move camp any time, an the Yanks might take a notion to come this way agin."

"Josh, you bes' come meet mah family, 'fore we go any futher." She looked directly at him with a demanding expression.

"I could lose mah head over you, an you be gone next day. This war brung us together an kin take us apart," she said knowingly. "But we least got to try to do what's right."

"These strong feelin's is new to me, May. I'll git time to be respectful." Josh smiled to show his willingness.

She responded with a quick kiss, stood, and picked the hay from her sweater. "I best be gittin' back or Pa'll be lookin' fer his huntin' rifle," she chided.

Josh rose too, then he abruptly embraced her again. She looked into his face expectantly, but he simply kissed her cheek, then released her. She retrieved her coat and they started back to camp. They were nearly at the wagon park before she broke a dreamy silence.

"We ain't comin' to camp ever day, Josh, cause we ain't got so much to sell," she warned him. "I'll be back soons I kin, but you bes' git workin' on that pass."

"I'll shur try, May, if'n I hafta go to the Colonel hisself," he replied earnestly.

They returned to the sutler area as the sun reached its highest point and the wagons were being packed. He knew she had to see to her goods, but he was reluctant to part from her. She turned to face him for good bye.

May let one hand caress his cheek. "I'll see you in a few days, Josh," she said softly.

He stroked her face and hair as they let fingertips express their feelings. Josh choked out a "bye", and May turned toward her wagon. He stood and watched as she pitched in with her father to hitch the horses and secure the remaining goods. May climbed onto the wagon seat beside her father and he jerked the reins. The horse began to trot, she glanced back with a smile, as the wagon took her down the road.

A muddle of feelings churned inside Josh as he returned slowly to the mess. This time with May had thrilled, but worried him. He learned that he could not control himself around her. But he enjoyed losing that control, guided only by his passion.

Though she thwarted his bold attempt, he found peace with her. He pictured May's sweet face warmly, stumbling on something as he neared the campfire.

"What you so dreamy 'bout," Hugh prodded, "yer grinnin' like a damned fool." The question brought Josh up short.

"Jes feelin' happy is all," Josh replied not wishing to share his thoughts and trying hard to remove his natural smile.

"You gonna be real happy when we break camp," Davy said harshly and Josh glared back in disbelief. "Got orders fer a place called Goose Creek, 'bout five miles east o' here, near the River."

The news provoked a renewed round of grumbling from the mess, but the information hit Josh hard. He had just promised May to get a pass, but that would be unthinkable while the Regiment moved camp. He silently cursed the army. His sour feeling must have shown as the others bemoaned the upcoming change.

"What's the matter, Pard," Zeke said to him, "you look like a man's been punched in the gut." Josh turned to his friend with a sick smile, not trusting himself to reply sensibly, and stalked off, angered at the change to his plans.

He walked only a few steps, blinded by his rage, when he collided with Jasper Welburn.

"Mind where you walk, Private," Welburn commanded haughtily as he gathered himself. Josh tried to continue on his way when Welburn cracked, "You must salute an officer."

Josh was not in the mood for the Third Lieutenant's arrogance and he whirled to face the man up close. "Jasper, this ain't no time fer yer foolishness," he said angrily.

Welburn shifted to allow more space between them. "You'll not take such liberties with a Second Lieutenant," he said hurriedly.

"I ain't heard you bin promoted," Josh questioned.

"Barnett is bein' sent home. I'm in line fer his spot," Welburn told him. The company Second Lieutenant had been wounded in the recent battle, but was expected to return. Welburn had news ahead of the camp grapevine.

"That mean you'll be out front o' the next charge, Jasper," Josh taunted.

Welburn stiffened, his face coloring. "I was in that charge," he declared hotly.

"I didn't see you in the first rank," Josh rebuked.

"All officer's can't be in front," Welburn explained weakly.

"Bein' promoted ain't gonna give you no backbone," Josh said without thinking. He immediately regretted his charge of cowardice to the officer.

"You retract that remark, Campbell," Welburn said loudly.

Josh realized he had provoked the challenge and matters were getting out of control. He had spoken in anger, but he could not back down from this upstart.

"You figure to git me in a duel, Jasper," he said with a wry smile, hoping Welburn would shy from the consequence of his demand.

Welburn glared at him, but understood that Josh had rightly gauged the usual consequence of honor.

"Dueling is forbidden in the army, Private," he said with some relief. "But you will regret your words," he added menacingly.

Josh smirked at the claim and swept past the shorter man to end further conversation. He refused to glance behind as he walked away, though troubled by the feeling that he had provoked Welburn to retaliate. Josh knew he could handle a physical confrontation, but he also knew Welburn would not take that path. Welburn would find some way to slight Josh and as an officer, he had more means to do so. Josh would have to watch his step in coming days.

Damn this army life he thought to himself, suddenly craving the freedom of a civilian.

15

The 17th Mississippi struck tents and broke camp in early November, anticipation high that change would be good. Camp at Leesburg had grown squalid, walking paths worn to mud and latrines reeking. A new camp held fresh promise and the men responded eagerly.

Goose Creek joined the Potomac a few miles south of Leesburg, but north of Edwards Ferry. The only feature of military significance seemed to be a narrow wooden bridge over the Creek. The hope for better living conditions evaporated as the 17th arrived to find a ground broken by gullies widening toward the running water, scrub growth and spongy earth.

An area near the bridge was cleared and tents sprouted quickly. Rations were issued, hot meals prepared. The soldiers stoked fires to blaze away November chill and persistent dampness. Men soon began to grumble about their new surroundings. Returning patrols reported little of interest up or down the Potomac and the Yankees seemed quiet on their side of the River. Soldiers resigned themselves to renewed monotony.

Then a curious change occurred. The weather turned mild, making life more bearable. The Regimental band played many nights and the men joined in song. Officers mounted theatricals that generally became comedies as the performers, some dressed as females, stumbled over lines or parodied army life. The Federals roused enough to banter across the River with invitations to 'come on over', and were greeted with good natured replies from the Virginia side.

Josh noted the change as if the wind had turned and embraced the new mood to finally overcome his troubled thoughts. The battle was relegated to the past, no longer a topic of discussion in the mess. Zeke injected levity at every opportunity, sometimes playing a clown or mimicking officers to everyone's delight. Miller began to share some of his knowledge on a variety of subjects with a more receptive group. Riley could be counted on to spark stories of home, recalled in a welcome way. Only Walter Tucker remained melancholy in the absence of his brother, though he always joined the campfire gatherings.

A disturbing note for Josh was an increasing familiarity between Jasper Welburn and Lucius Bradwell. As word of his conduct in the battle spread, Bradwell had become a pariah, friendly with no one. Bradwell had stood extra duty for fighting and men were wary of the hulking brute quick to take offense. Josh had noticed Welburn in idle conversation with the surly Bradwell. He had no clue as to why the two should be friendly, but he could not shake a feeling that such an alliance did not bode well.

Josh had lost any desire to cross paths with Bradwell and was by now unsure of his feelings toward him. The man had killed in cold blood, but killing Yankees was their sworn duty. Josh was bothered that Bradwell had taken pleasure in death, but he could only condemn the excess of results from that blood rage, not the means with which Lucius, or any other soldier, chose to fortify his courage. With such doubts, he could not rightly question another's conduct and resolved to simply distance himself from Bradwell.

A far more memorable event occurred during their stay. The Rangers were ordered to patrol upriver from camp one day. Jasper Welburn was officer in charge and led those fit enough for the assignment, just less than half the company. Josh and his mess participated, having defied the rampant maladies that sometimes

1861 A TIME FOR GLORY

arose before a difficult duty. The frosty day was clear and warmed surprisingly during the march. The patrol followed a worn trail along the River, never far from the bank, with a good view of the other side. They had just turned about on their way back in early afternoon when several men cried 'Look a thar.'

Josh was roused from a mindless stare to follow everyone's gaze to the sky above. By now the entire group had halted and lowered their rifles to gape at the apparition. Slowly rising above the trees was a large round object unlike anything Josh had seen. It rose higher until a small basket shape, tethered to the round ball, appeared below. He could make out a figure in the basket and long ropes trailing toward the ground. As men wondered aloud at such a sight, Miller Cummins supplied a description of what they saw.

"Must be a gas air filled balloon, boys," he exclaimed to no one in particular as he too fixed his stare upon the sphere. "I read about something like that, but didn't know the Northerners had any such thing," he added absently.

"You reckon them Yanks'll shoot at us," Joe Crawford asked suspiciously. Welburn had joined the throng around Cummins to hear his response.

"Likely, there's only one man in the basket, and he's up there to look about," Miller told them, keeping his eyes on the floating ball. "He'd be more afraid of gettin' shot at, than shootin' back."

"We should be movin', to report back to the Colonel," Welburn said, though not one man responded. Sergeant Ferrall took control.

"Form up, lads, nothin' more to see here," the Sergeant ordered and men now began to shift into marching order. Welburn bellowed in his high pitched voice, "Forward, march" and the column began moving again. No order could prevent sideways glances, however, nor stifle remarks of wonder. As they continued toward camp, the balloon grew in imaginations as it receded from view. The strange object provoked great speculation around the nightly campfires.

Josh heard the speculation, but kept his thoughts private./ Miller assured everyone the balloon could not carry a cannon and that, if it was hit by a bullet, the air inside would leak out, forcing the balloon to fall. Josh was not sure what purpose the balloon would serve if it was so vulnerable. But the hard fact was the North had such a thing and the South did not, and that did not bode well for the Confederacy. The Yankees were liable to come up with something that could be used to fire on troops and wreak all kinds of havoc. Josh could only hope the Confederacy was working on some surprises of its own.

In late November, the Regiment was ordered to return to camp near Leesburg. Spirits soared as the men broke camp at Goose Creek, though sorry to leave the place behind. They would be on familiar ground when December began, the belief widespread that their present camp would be home for months to come. The Mississippians were resigned to spending winter in Virginia.

After weeks of adjournment, the renewed session of Congress began in early December, 1861. The Union's military situation dominated thoughts and discussions among members. Doubts had resurfaced after Balls Bluff to fracture the unity of resolve so carefully constructed after Manassas. While some of those returning to the Capital wondered what could be done, some few Senators and Representatives had a firm grasp on the future.

Elihu Hawthorne counted himself among this select group that many referred to as the 'Radical' Republicans. In the weeks before Congress returned, he had sounded out other Representatives on a Congressional committee to oversee the military and found many receptive. Ben Wade had been doing the same with his Senate colleagues. Thus, the first order of business in the Congressional session would be the creation the Joint Committee on the Conduct of the War.

The Committee was approved without public dissent, and the Radicals anticipated no private misgivings either. As he expected, Hawthorne was included in the membership of the Committee, though more senior Congressman grumbled at his sudden rise in status. With his appointment, the member from Massachusetts had irrevocably cast his lot with the Radicals.

Hawthorne concentrated on the work of the Joint Committee to the exclusion of other matters. Determined that the Committee would not be sidetracked with procedural matters in the beginning, Hawthorne worked closely with Wade to prepare for the first session. The direction of the Committee was clear. Military action would be reviewed with a fine tooth comb, starting with Balls Bluff. Committee leaders judged George McClellan, as commander of the Army of the Potomac, untouchable for the moment. Colonel Edward Baker, darling of the White House, had been removed from the Committee's reach by death. The Radicals set their sights on the nominal field general during the ill-fated action, Brigadier General Charles Stone. Behind closed doors, Committee members wondered aloud whether the administration and military would rally to Stone's defense, or offer him as a sacrificial lamb. Hearings began without certainty as to how these factions would react.

On a chilly, gray December day, Representative Hawthorne was approached by an army captain as he descended the Capitol steps. With pressing business, Hawthorne thought to simply be polite and keep moving. But as he neared the officer, recognition dawned and he slowed his steps.

"Young Robert, it is good to see you," Hawthorne opened, extending his hand cheerfully. He had not seen Lowell since that day before Bull Run when the junior officer had briefed him on the coming battle.

Lowell took the offered hand firmly, if not enthusiastically. Hawthorne noted the young man's reticence. He asked after

Robert's family and the Captain responded tersely that they were well, without elaborating.

"Unfortunately, I have a prior engagement and must not tarry," Hawthorne commented. "It was good to see you. . ."

Lowell cut in. "I need to speak with you, sir. Perhaps I could walk with you to your destination."

The Congressman was surprised, but agreed to allow the persistent Captain to accompany him and they set off toward Pennsylvania Avenue. Hawthorne decided to let his young friend explain the purpose of this meeting on his own terms. An awkward silence intruded before Robert composed himself to speak.

"I have been asked to contact you by an officer whose name I am not at liberty to divulge," Lowell began, with great effort.

"May I assume that you have some position with General McClellan's staff," Hawthorne inquired pointedly.

Captain Lowell flinched and looked sharply at the Congressman. Hawthorne glared back, demanding a response. Lowell appeared to ponder the question, a perplexed look on his face.

"I would suppose my current duties are easily determined," he noted. "Yes, I am assigned to Army Headquarters, but I beg you to allow this simple statement to satisfy your inquiry." Lowell paused to read Hawthorne's reaction, and the Congressman decided not to press the matter.

"What do you wish to tell me, Robert," Hawthorne demanded impatiently, for he now understood the Captain had been sent as an emissary.

"The General's staff has learned some information about the Joint Committee on the Conduct of the War, of which you are a member," Lowell continued cautiously.

"We have been given to understand the Committee will hold hearings on the incursion at Balls Bluff. We also understand that troubling questions will be asked of General Stone." The

Captain paused to measure his next words and Hawthorne allowed him to continue at his own pace.

"General Stone will not be assigned any further command in the Army. General McClellan has lost faith in his ability to command men, though he will not publicly reprimand the Brigadier." Lowell choked out the last words, the burden of his assignment bearing hard upon him.

Hawthorne halted and turned to his young friend as he realized the import of the Captain's message. "Am I to understand that McClellan will not dispute the censure of Stone by the Committee," he asked, almost rhetorically.

Robert averted his eyes in shame. A knowing smile creased the Congressman's face.

"Stone will be sacrificed to the Congressional wolves," Hawthorne mused. "Presumably on the hope the Committee inquiry will not implicate anyone in headquarters, including the commanding General." The full impact of McClellan's offer became evident.

Robert Lowell slowly turned his head to meet Hawthorne's eyes, the guilty look upon the young man's face confirming the Congressman's conjecture. Hawthorne's mind raced through possibilities the army's offer entailed.

"You must understand, Robert, that I do not chair the Committee, but I do have some influence," Hawthorne assured him. "You may tell those who sent you that I will bring this information to the attention of the Committee and I will suggest that the Committee confine any punishment to General Stone."

Lowell seemed relieved that his task had been successful, but Hawthorne could see the young man was bothered by his assignment.

"You are ashamed of this political maneuvering my young friend," Hawthorne said evenly. "Your impulse does you credit," he added spontaneously.

"This must seem a sordid business to you, to surrender a military officer to the Congressional lion's den. You may be assured his fate was already sealed, so McClellan has given up nothing. In return, the Young Napoleon's star can remain untarnished. But the General will do well not to forget this accommodation." A misting rain began to fall as Hawthorne concluded.

Robert Lowell pulled his overcoat tighter, unsure whether to express gratitude or dismay to the Congressman. Hawthorne read the struggle in the Captain's face and added one more thought.

"With all due respect, Robert, you must also tell whoever assigned you this task that I will not communicate with you again about Committee affairs. If headquarters desires to discuss some matter before the Committee, I will expect someone of higher rank." Hawthorne cocked an eyebrow as he spoke, to be sure Lowell understood his message.

The Captain seemed angered at first and attempted to explain that he was chosen because of his acquaintance. He ceased his response abruptly as he realized Hawthorne was trying to save him from any more such missions. As that thought penetrated, Robert smiled weakly in gratitude. He sought the Congressman's hand and shook it vigorously. Then he bade Hawthorne good bye and walked back toward the Capitol.

Elihu Hawthorne stood for a moment in the falling rain, ignoring his waiting appointment for the instant and reflecting on the change in his political fortune. Some six months ago, his reception at McDowell's headquarters had been decidedly cool, his inquiries barely tolerated. Now, his counsel was actively sought by army headquarters. George McClellan had 'come a courting' and Hawthorne perceived a distinct advantage with his new found friends.

The cares of a busy day subsided and the weather seemed less miserable. Congressman Elihu Hawthorne was fast becoming a political force in the war torn nation. He quickened his step toward his appointment, unsuccessfully suppressing the sly grin on his face.

>< >< >< >< ><

The last month of 1861 began brightly amid seasonable weather for the 17th Mississippi. The soldiers set about preparing shelters for winter. More than planking for floors was needed. The men scrounged or purchased materials to construct knee walls and chimneys for tents. The camp took on a more permanent appearance with these improvements as fall waned.

Drilling resumed with some regularity. Patrols and guard duty remained constant. Rumors of Yankees were plentiful, but sightings none. Weather was the impending enemy. Chilly winds and damp rain infiltrated the camp on gray days, and Mother Nature promised to be a formidable foe.

Winter weather was not the only visitor to camp in late fall. As men sought the comfort of extra clothing and declined to bathe in the cold, they experienced persistent irritation. With some embarrassment, Riley had gone to the surgeon seeking a remedy for the itching and burning he felt. He returned with word that his malady was lice, and the surgeon reckoned the whole Regiment was infected. Davy relayed the name other soldiers used for the condition, calling the hard to see critters 'gray backs'. The only prescribed remedies were lye soap and removing the vermin by hand for burning.

The stay at Goose Creek convinced Josh he was ill prepared for the coming cold and he had written home to send warm clothing. He shared the Yankee overcoat with Zeke, taking turns to wear it on night guard duty. He secured an extra blanket from Ferrall for the cooler evenings and stayed near the fire when he didn't have duty. Sleep in the chilly nighttime air proved difficult, however, even with improvements to the tent. Josh began to fear colder weather more than the Yankees.

The 17th received its new uniforms at the beginning of December. None too soon by the look of many, for every man in the Regiment sported torn, frayed and dirty pants and jacket.

Shoes were a dire need, but hard to come by despite repeated requests from the officers. A shipment came in with the uniforms, but the Rangers were not among the companies to share in the bounty.

A rumor of furloughs swept camp, brought to the mess by an unusual source, Dutchie. He had the rumor before Davy, a fact that caused Davy to express sincere doubts about authenticity. Dutchie spent some considerable effort to be among the first allowed to return home, eagerly seizing upon the news and convinced of its truth.

Josh noticed Dutchie had been more anxious since the battle. He had little good to say around the campfire and grumbled about every part of army life. The diminutive corporal pined for home as if he feared for his return. They were all treated to the particular glories of his Greta, her cooking, housekeeping and mothering. Homesickness infected everyone from time to time, but Dutchie refused to shake the feeling and seemed to take comfort in his misery.

Josh had confronted Dutchie one day about his melancholy mood, on the vain hope he could help the Corporal through its grip. The man was not inclined to speak with him, though Josh eventually prodded him to respond. Besides his dissatisfaction with anything involving the army, Josh was taken with one particular remark. Dutchie told him there were Federal soldiers like himself at Balls Bluff, men of German heritage who had been taken prisoner. The gray clad corporal had spoken with them in his language, and learned they were not so different than he. He also learned that many had enlisted to serve the Federals and there were whole regiments of German soldiers. Dutchie was troubled that he might have killed a fellow countryman and felt he could not shoot at Yankees again for fear of hitting one of his kind. Josh could offer no solution to the problem, though he quickly understood Dutchie would be disobeying orders if he refused to fire. The consequences of such an act were severe.

Sergeant Ferrall appeared at the campfire one evening on a

promise of hot coffee. The sustaining brew had become scarce and some in the Regiment cut the rations with burnt acorns or parched corn. The mess had a pure reserve hoarded by Riley and supplemented with stock purchased from sutlers. Davy poured a cup of the dark liquid and handed it steaming to the genial Irishman, then proceeded to relay some news he had heard to the mess.

Since the 13th Mississippi Regiment had been detailed to the Leesburg area before the October battle, that regiment had been officially added in November to General Evans Brigade. The news of December was that the 21st Mississippi Regiment would replace the 8th Virginia, for an all Mississippi Brigade. As Davy conveyed this information, the natural question was who would command.

"They don' figger to leave no Carolinian like Evans in command of Mississippi boys," Zeke noted.

Davy had the answer. "I hear we got a gen'ral from Mississippi gonna take over fer Evans. Likely to be General Richard Griffith, oncet the change is approved by Beauregard. He had the 12th Mississippi."

Ferrall had stood quietly as Davy rambled on, his face neither affirming nor disputing the news in the low fire light. Davy moved on to another subject.

"Hear the boys in the Guards're complainin' bout havin' to give up their cooks. Some has servants doin' their cookin' an the Captain said they got to cook fer the whole comp'ny."

Josh was mildly interested at the news, for he had not spoken to Lem Morse in recent days.

Davy continued. "Whole comp'ny's on extra guard 'til they agree to give up private cooks." There was little sympathy for their friends in the Guards among the mess, since the Rangers had cooked their own meals from the beginning.

Davy finally turned to the subject on everyone's mind of late. "Heard some talk 'bout liberty fer the enlisted, Sergeant," he asked Ferrall directly, "but hard facts is scarce. You know anythin' 'bout it."

"If you ain't learned by now, lad, rumors an soldiers go hand in hand, natural as a bee to honey," Ferrall remarked pointedly to Davy, though with a smile. "You'll be knowin' I don't have the ear of t'officers."

Davy was not discouraged so easily amid the curiosity of the others. "Word is we kin go home on furlough an collect a bounty on signin' up fer the duration," Davy exclaimed, relating the most reliable information he had heard.

The Sergeant hesitated, surveying expectant faces, and knew they wanted him to contribute. "Aye, lad, that's what I've bin told, though it depends on the President in Richmond to agree," Ferrall confirmed, now suspecting his coffee came with the price of information.

Josh brightened at the hope of seeing his family, but Ferrall had more to say.

"The furloughs could begin in winter, but you'll not be tastin' home cookin' before the year ends." This information was not well received and he added something else to dampen anticipation. "They'll not be lettin' more than a few at a time go home. No tellin' how they'll figure who'll be first to go."

The Sergeant's reasoning was sound and hopes visibly deflated. Davy could offer nothing to dispute Ferrall, and the others glanced accusingly at him for prodding the Sergeant to deliver this news.

A stony silence reigned until Ferrall finished his cup and thanked Davy for the coffee. He started to take his leave when he asked Josh to walk with him a ways. Josh wondered at the invitation, but of course scrambled in place beside the shorter man.

Directly, Ferrall said, "Might be there's room fer a new corporal, lad," once they were out of ear shot from the others. Josh stared at the Sergeant, wondering why he was being told.

"Dutchie's asked fer a discharge, an the Captain is likely to grant it," Ferrall explained as they slowed their pace. Josh was surprised, for a discharge proved nearly impossible to get, though he knew Dutchie was surely unhappy in the army.

"There's no fight left in the Dutchman. He ain't bin hisself since the battle at the River," the Sergeant confirmed.

"Fact is, I think you could wear that extra stripe," Ferrall added. "You've a good head on yer shoulders and t'others'll listen to you. And you've learned a bit 'bout bein' a soldier," the veteran of two armies noted.

Josh puffed at the rare compliment, keeping a careful silence. His mind grappled with the implications. Ferrall smiled and clapped him on the shoulder.

"You'll be keepin' this under yer hat, lad, for the discharge's not been signed. I've had a word with the Captain and First Lieutenant, though, to keep your name in mind."

Josh grappled with the right words to express gratitude. Sensing his dilemma, Ferrall continued in the awkward moment.

"There's a bit more you'll find to yer likin', lad," Ferrall said, looking directly to the young man. "You may be gettin' that pass you want so dearly. Seems the Colonel remembers how you doctored his horse this summer. If we've no duty elsewhere, there could be leave for you after the new year."

Josh suddenly felt lightheaded. He steadied himself, a simple smile playing across his face as a picture of May flashed in his mind. He impulsively reached to shake the hand of his Sergeant, but Ferrall stopped him.

"Before you let yer mind go, you'll be knowin' there's no leave 'til the furloughs are sorted out," the knowing soldier added.

Ferrall bid him a good night, leaving a stunned Private behind. Josh struggled to calm his feelings and turned back toward the campfire. As he neared his friends, he realized they would be full of questions about what the Sergeant had told him. Josh thought quickly. He could not reveal the possible promotion. His pending pass was not certain, and likely to rouse some jealousy among his friends, so he could not speak of that. He settled on a lie to downplay any significance in his meeting. He would mention that Ferrall wanted him for some vague detail to stifle further inquiry. Josh smiled privately with the knowledge that soldiers rarely questioned another's misfortune in extra duty lest they be given some themselves.

16

Rumors of festivities for the 17th in recognition of the charge at Leesburg had circulated since the battle, whirling through nightly campfires and refusing to succumb with time. Jefferson Davis would journey to their camp, to recognize them for their glorious service. If not Davis, then Beauregard, some argued, or perhaps Brigade Commander Evans others concluded. Colonel Featherston would receive a medal, or be promoted general some whispered knowingly. All sorts of honors would be given the men and officers from Mississippi, including home leave in the most enticing version.

As with so much of army life though, rumors proved more satisfying than the actual event. A general order was issued for Regimental formation the weekend before Christmas. The 17th would parade in full dress for assembled dignitaries and the citizens of Leesburg. A shoot was decreed, involving the best marksmen from each company for an unspecified prize. No regimental honors were specified.

Josh sought out Lem Morse three days before the parade, as night fell on a cold, rainy day when drill had been cancelled and men kept to their tents. Hoping his friend from the Guards would have heard more about the upcoming event, he bundled into the Yankee greatcoat and made his way to Morse's company area. He found Lem huddled inside his abode against the chill weather.

"Y'all hear who's gonna be here fer the grand parade," Josh asked after greetings had been exchanged. He had noted the absence of a cook fire and omitted a request for coffee, though none was offered.

"Gen'ral Beauregard's comin', likely with his staff," Morse told his visitor, watching him settle into a dry space near the canvas tent flap. Two other men lay sleeping on blankets, uninterested in Josh's presence.

"Reckon the fine citizens of these parts will be in attendance," Lem continued. "I hear they gonna roast a pig an serve hot cider to mark the festivities."

"Hope the sun shines," Josh remarked evenly, "I ain't much fer paradin' about in this kind o' weather."

"Beauregard s'posed to present us a new regimental flag, to replace the one Featherston got us before Manassas" Morse confided, though Josh had already heard this. However, Lem knew more. "Hear it has a blue cross on a plain background, from corner to corner like an X, with a star fer each o' the Confederate states. A sutler saw one the 8th Virginia got, said it looks grand."

Josh tried to picture the flag in his mind, but knew of nothing like what his friend described. It sounded far different than the red and white bars of the old flag.

"Who y'all puttin' up to shoot," Morse asked with some interest.

"Ain't heard yet," Josh replied. "They won't find a better shot than Zeke Owens, though," Josh continued as the thought occurred.

"We got a boy named Taylor who's gonna stand in for the Guards," Lem explained. "Feller could knock a tick off a hound at fifty paces."

Josh smiled. "Ain't no use to even have a contest, then," he declared and Morse smiled back.

The visitor changed subjects. "Yer mess gonna have a Christmas celebration?"

"Boys're talkin' bout makin' a nog if they kin git the eggs

an spirits," Lem told him. "You'd be welcome to stop by, have a cup."

"I might jes come a visitin', we don' have some ourselves," Josh remarked as he rose to leave.

"Thought you might take the holiday to see that gal o' yers," Lem called after him.

"Cain't git a pass 'til after first o' the year," Josh replied as he dropped the door flap. He traipsed back toward his quarters in the slippery mud, rain falling steady now, pulling the coat tight about him. His cap was wet and moisture seeped through his shoes. Seemed no matter how he dressed, the Virginia chill cut through him. Walking was a chore, but warmed him.

He encountered Zeke, Davy and Walter huddled in blankets beside a sputtering fire. They were covered by a half shelter the mess had constructed with brush for a roof. The shelter leaked in heavy rain, but was tolerable in the light rain falling now. Josh joined his friends underneath and crouched to warm his hands by the sparse fire.

"Jes talkin' wi' Lem Morse 'bout the big doin's. Told me about the flag Beauregard's gonna present to the Regiment."

"Ain't no news," Davy said testily.

"You find out who's gonna shoot fer the Rangers," Josh challenged, barely able to see Davy's face inside the blanket.

"I reckon I am," Zeke cut in, and all eyes turned toward him.

"Cap'n Franklin asked me this mornin' after roll. Ain't thought to tell y'all." Zeke glanced to Josh in direct apology.

"Ain't nobody in this company better with a rifle," Josh rejoined confidently.

"You git anythin' fer winnin'," Walter asked through chattering teeth.

"Cap'n wouldn't say," Zeke responded. "Jes said winner'll git somethin' special. And course ever one's gonna know who's best shot," he added with a sly grin.

Davy pushed some wood on the fire and conversation

paused. Josh turned away as partially wet sticks began to smoke in his direction. Half turned, he asked Davy about Riley.

"Still feelin' poorly," Davy said. "Got some kind o' flux 'cause ever thing he tries t'eat cuts right through him. He ain't bin right fer near two weeks now, but he won' go see the surgeon."

"We sher could use his cookin'," Zeke noted. "Takin' turns wi' the meals ain't done much fer mah appetite."

"Joe Crawford ain't cookin no meal fer me, agin," Davy declared to the agreement of all. "Burnt ever part o' dinner."

"Ain't never seen taters burnt so bad," Walter commented and joined the others to laugh about the blackened spuds. The meal had been ruined so that everyone just had coffee and hardtack, though Crawford had eaten his fill.

Preparations commenced in earnest as the weather cleared the following day. Uniforms were washed and mended as needed, caps brushed, mud scraped from shoes. Rifles were cleaned and every scrap of brass polished. Drilling resumed in afternoons as the 17th reacquired marching and turning in formation. Confidence began to show among the officers.

Zeke found time to practice as did other contestants and the camp resounded with infrequent gunfire.   Good natured taunts were traded between companies and betting followed. The Rangers promoted their nominee shamelessly and even the officers were rumored to have wagered a few dollars.   Zeke appeared unfazed by his supporters, concentrating on the task ahead. He made his own lead shot, carefully shaved to a personal standard, and prepared his own cartridges. Zeke's Mississippi Rifle, with modifications he refused to reveal, shot as true as any weapon in the Regiment.

The long anticipated day dawned clear and warmer. Just before noon, the Regiment formed to march to the parade ground. Numbers for all companies increased as the sick and ailing were turned out, if they could stand.   In their uniforms made in Leesburg, the Regiment marched to a field just outside of town where a reviewing stand had been erected.   On arrival, the men formed in ranks and were ordered to stand at ease. From the first rank Josh easily surveyed the scene before him. Townspeople gathered on either side of the stand opposite the Regiment. Smoke swirled off to one side where tables for food and drink had been set. On the opposite side, bales of hay were stacked for the shoot. Perusing the crowd he hoped to glimpse May's familiar face, and noticed the Marlowe clan prominently positioned in the front row. He turned to tell Zeke, but his friend seemed distracted and Josh resolved to mention Anne after the contest.

Mounted men in uniform approached the gathering as orders were barked to form at attention. Company officers with dress swords appeared in front of the straightened lines and Colonel Featherston trotted his mount to center front. General Beauregard and his staff rode onto the grounds, dismounting in unison. Leesburg's citizens formed a receiving line to greet the hero of Sumter and Manassas.

Josh watched the diminutive Confederate General with his distinctive mustache, outfitted in gray cloak and red banded kepi, make his way along the line of admirers. Offering salutes to men, he paused to greet some of the ladies by hand. The gallant Louisianan moved persistently through the crowd then nimbly mounted the stand, swept his cloak aside and assumed a chair placed there for him. Once seated, the crowd stilled and he simply nodded toward Featherston.

The Colonel raised his sword in front of his face and glanced toward the Regimental band now positioned on one side of the spectators. The band broke into a jaunty rendition of 'Dixie'. Featherston walked his horse to the Regiment's left and officers retreated into the ranks. As the last notes of the Southern anthem faded, drummers beat out marching formation. Ranks turned to column of fours with rifles shouldered and the 17th stepped off behind its Colonel.

The Mississippians marched to the left, then, on command, turned right and right again. The column now passed in review before the crowd and General Beauregard, progressing to the far right, before turning twice right to bring the column to starting position. Drums ceased and officers barked orders to form in four rows, now nearer the General than before. The men were ordered to parade rest and rifles slipped neatly beside legs. Colonel Featherston returned to the space before the commanding General and shouted, "General Beauregard, the 17th Mississippi Regiment at your service."

Men, women and children around the stand responded with applause and cheers. Beauregard stood and slipped his cloak off as an aide appeared by his side with a small package. He raised his hand to quiet the crowd, then stepped to the edge of the stand to address the Regiment.

"Gallant sons of Mississippi, your countrymen are justly proud of the glorious service you have rendered to our noble cause. You have contributed to the victory of our arms at Manassas and, most recently, swept the hand of Northern aggression from the very doorsteps of these good people."

Sweeping his arms wide in gesture, the revered son of Louisiana paused to give his words full effect. The aide quietly opened his package and unfurled a flag between outstretched hands.

"My courageous soldiers, I bring you a new standard of my own design, emblazoned with the name of your great victory at Leesburg. May our Northern foe tremble before the battle flag of our valiant 17th Mississippi."

A beaming Beauregard paused while the aide held the flag high and whirled to show the banner to soldiers and civilians alike. Josh craned to see the new banner from his spot in the ranks. As Morse had described, two blue bands, edged in white, were crossed on a pale, light, red-tinted background. Twelve white stars adorned the flag, three in each quadrant of blue radiating from the center. 'Leesburg' had been painted in white on the blue intersection as a battle honor.

From the edge of the regimental formation, an officer called three cheers for General Beauregard and the men responded loudly. The last cheer faded as the General departed from the stand. From his mount, Colonel Featherston announced, "Good people of Leesburg. A shooting competition among the Regiment has been organized and refreshments have been prepared. Please join us in celebration."

An officer barked "Dismissed" and the formation dissolved with cheers and yells. Bidding Zeke luck as his friend started toward the shooting area, Josh stacked his rifle with others and worked his way toward the dispersing crowd, hoping to find May. He was ambushed by Anne Marlowe, bundled in a becoming fur trimmed coat and stylish hat, who waylaid him with a playfully harsh tone.

"Shame on you, Joshua Campbell, for not calling upon me again," she challenged, a mock frown upon her face. As he started to reply, she held up a gloved hand. "And spare me your excuses for such ungentlemanly conduct."

"If I cain't defend myself, then I'll jes surrender," he declared with a good natured smile, forcing a grin from her pouting countenance. "Sides, I thought you joined the cavalry," he countered with a sly wink.

"Mah friendship with Captain Marston does not preclude acquaintance with our valiant men from Mississippi," she replied pointedly.

Josh smiled and began to parry with another teasing remark when he spotted May among the crowd some distance away. He waved to catch her notice, breaking his attention from Anne. She was quick to note his distraction and turned to follow his eyes, spotting the lithe, homespun clad girl instantly.

Anne laced her arm in Josh's and guided the surprised soldier away. "Ah hoped you would escort me to some refreshment."

Once she had diverted his attention, Anne remarked critically, "Ah see you have discovered some of the more common attractions of our town."

At first puzzled, Josh now understood that Anne intended

to direct him away from May. He stopped after a few steps, disengaging his arm from hers, prompting her to turn and face him with an insistent look.

"I value your acquaintance, Miz Marlowe," Josh said formally, if sternly, to the compelling dark haired beauty, "but I don' need yer say so to see my own friends."

Anne's expression hardened and Josh regretted his tone. Struggling for the right words, he continued, "You kin count me among yer many admirers, though I ain't gonna pine over you. We're both free to go our own way," he concluded reasonably.

"Ah have thought of you fondly since that day in Manassas," she croaked, color rising to her cheeks, "but I shall cease such thoughts if mah presence is an imposition. Our future acquaintance will be observed with strict propriety."

The young Virginia woman turned abruptly and stalked off, leaving Josh perplexed by the exchange. Had the Leesburg beauty expected more than a casual friendship, something she had never indicated before today. Surely her family would put off connection with an enlisted man from the deep South. At that instant, May Turner appeared by his side, quelling any thought of pursuing Anne.

"Ain't that Miss Anne Marlowe you was speakin' with," May asked. "How come you to know such as her," she questioned, and Josh did not mistake the insistence in her voice.

"We met 'fore Manassas, at a parade somethin' like this," he replied, "Zeke fetched her some water when she wuz in a faint."

Not wishing to dwell on Anne, he hurried on. "Sher glad you got my message to come down fer the day." He wrapped his arms around May and she responded for a fleeting moment, knowing further affection would be unseemly in public.

"If you ain't hungry jes yet, we ought to git over to the shoot 'fore it starts," Josh blurted. Sensing no hesitation in May he took her arm, guiding her toward the contest.

"Zeke's shootin' fer the Rangers," he advised her, "an' I

got a little money ridin' on mah pard." As they walked, they exchanged news of the past few weeks, May rambling on about her family and the upcoming holiday. Josh said little, taking comfort in hearing of family life and more than once thought of his own.

They wedged into a space to view the contest as the 17ᵗʰ's Major recited the rules. Each man would have one shot at a target in the first round. The five closest to center would shoot again in the second round. Then a final round would be held between the two best shots and a winner declared.

One by one, the men stepped forward to a mark, and took aim at a round target painted on wood some eighty paces distant. After each shot, a tender chalked the hole of the shooter with his company. The first round moved slowly on with each man loading, steadying, firing and then peering for his mark. Josh watched the first two, then, seeing Zeke nearly last in line, let his gaze wander about the ground while May held tight to his arm, craning to keep a good view.

Soldiers milled with citizens all over the grounds, the largest congregations at refreshments and the shoot. Some distance from where he stood, he noticed a large tent surrounded by officers, the new regimental flag flying high above. Inside he could see General Beauregard, Colonel Featherston and staff officers with food and drink. Company Captains ducked inside the tent to meet the General briefly. A delegation from the town hovered nearby, presumably for an audience. Josh could see Randolph Marlowe, Anne's father, in the group, though he recognized no others.

May nudged him as Zeke stepped forward to take his shot. He watched his friend handle the rifle confidently, pause just a moment in aim, and fire. The target tender yelled out 'Near center', and it seemed likely Zeke would continue. Josh joined other Rangers dispersed in the crowd with hearty cheers for their favorite.

A last man shot, and as the smoke cleared, men for the

next round were announced. Zeke had made the group, with Taylor from the Guards and three others. They huddled to choose lots for shooting order and Zeke drew second. More quickly than before, the men stepped to the mark in succession to take their shot. No word came from the target tender and as suspense mounted, Major Lyles walked down range to learn the two finalists. He conferred with the tender, looked at the target, then returned to announce the names of Owens and Morgan.

Zeke broke a grin and the other man, from the Burnsville Blues out of Tishomingo County, let out a quick whistle. As Major Lyles readied the finalists to shoot, members of their respective companies traded catcalls and taunts in support of each man. Josh chuckled at some of the rudest, but did not join in with May at his side. Instead, he was relieved at Zeke making the final two, and the Guards entry having lost out. Zeke would at least be best shot in Marshall County.

When the two men had finished loading their rifles, the Major designated Zeke to shoot first. He toed the mark, raised his rifle, hesitated just an extra moment, and fired. With a determined look the Blues man followed suit, but as he sighted down the barrel, his nerve flickered and he lowered his rifle, then took aim again. The rifle cracked and the shooter stepped back from the mark. Major Lyles strode through hazy smoke down range again, but returned quickly.

"Winner is Ezekial Owens of the Rangers," he announced to wild cheers and applause. Josh rushed forward to congratulate the company favorite. Then the Major drew Zeke apart and Josh watched the pair walk toward the officers tent he had seen earlier. Zeke was going to be presented to General Beauregard!

He remembered May and found her easily.

"I wuz hopin' to spend some time with you 'fore I got to leave," she reproached. "I didn't come all this way jes to see a shootin' match."

"Had to watch my pard, May. I reckon we'll have some time fer sparkin' now," he chided in response.

Gazing about for some privacy he noticed a glade behind the reviewing stand. He squired May in that direction, but the pair were waylaid by Hugh and Charlie, with Miller in tow. They cackled about Zeke's win and the money they would collect, but Josh checked his enthusiasm and disengaged after a few minutes with a now restless May.

They had only taken a few steps when Josh was diverted by a familiar voice raised in disagreement near the officer's enclave. He spotted Zeke surrounded by several officers, shaking his head. Sensing trouble, he asked May to wait and double timed toward his friend.

Major Lyles and Captain Franklin stood before Zeke while the Regimental Adjutant and Lieutenant Abernathy held each flank. Junior and staff officers formed a half circle around the lone enlisted man. As Josh neared the group, Jasper Welburn broke away from the assembly and stepped in front of him.

"Your presence has not been requested, Private," the Third Lieutenant commanded, bringing Josh to a stop. Josh tried to ease around Welburn with the salute the man so often craved, but the Lieutenant blocked his path.

"You take another step an I'll see you don't git that Corporal stripe," Welburn declared.

Josh hesitated, staring at the shorter man, then made his decision. "I'll see what I kin do fer Zeke," he said, pushing his tormentor aside with his forearm.

From behind, Welburn hissed "I'll not forget this, Campbell." Josh fought the urge to turn, reminding himself why he had come.

Josh slipped amongst the group of officers quietly, but at a spot where he was able to get Zeke's attention. The officers paid no attention to Josh, but Zeke nodded slightly as he caught sight of his friend, relieving some of the tension on his face.

Josh was not sure what he could do to help Zeke, nor did he know what the fuss was about. He heard some of the officers talking low, but could make out on a word or two of what they said. Major Lyles paced back and forth in front of Zeke and began to speak loudly.

"Colonel Featherston has ordered the winner of the shooting contest to carry our Regimental colors," the Major reminded everyone, glaring at Zeke. "However, Private Owens has seen fit to refuse this honor."

"Major, I ain't goin' into battle with no flagpole in mah hands. If them Yanks is shootin' at me, sir, I want somethin' to shoot back," the young marksman said defiantly, but respectfully.

Lyles turned in disgust and Captain Franklin began to say something about the pride of the Rangers. Suddenly, General Beauregard and Colonel Featherston appeared in their midst and everyone snapped to attention.

"May I meet the young man who is your best shootist," the commanding General asked, Cajun accent prominent in his speech. Colonel Featherston gestured toward Zeke, saying "Private Owens, sir." Remaining stiffly at attention, Zeke raised his hand to salute the commander.

Featherston noticed Josh and directed a questioning glance toward him.

"I am informed you have won the honor to carry your Regiment's colors," Beauregard began. "You have accepted, no," the respected Louisianan inquired. In the pause that followed, all eyes turned to Zeke, every officer hoping to hear acceptance.

Josh could sense his friend's uneasiness, his struggle with the proper reply to the most famous man in Confederate uniform.

"Gen'ral, sir, I don't mean no disrespect, but I kin do more fer the cause with a rifle in mah hands," Zeke said slowly, hoping he was right to speak plainly. He appeared to want to say more, then stopped, realizing he might be insubordinate.

Beauregard gazed up at the taller enlisted man, officers around him holding their breaths. Then the hero of the South smiled, the famous handlebar mustache rising on each end. He tapped Zeke on the shoulder with an open gloved hand and tension eased slightly.

"This young man has discovered that the essence of war is to kill the enemy," Beauregard announced to all. "The South needs such men," he declared. Turning to Featherston, he said, "Surely Colonel there must be some other deserving man to take the colors."

"I am sure we can find a substitute, General," a more relaxed Featherston replied. "We need trouble Private Owens no longer."

Beauregard turned to face a visibly relieved, and smiling, Zeke Owens. "Is there some other token you would accept in honor of your victoire, young man," the General asked.

A now exuberant Zeke cleared his throat, hesitated just a moment, and blurted out, "I'd shur like to git me a finer cap than the one I'm wearin', Gen'ral."

All eyes suddenly shifted to the poor specimen atop Owens' head. A bemused Beauregard nodded, then said, "We shall see to that." The General spun on his heel and walked back to the tent, Featherston joining him as everyone else shifted to attention.

Everyone seemed momentarily rooted in place. Josh stepped toward his friend and tugged the sleeve of Zeke's jacket. Zeke stepped back with Josh, saluting broadly to cover every officer in sight. The two Privates slipped quietly away before the blank stare of each officer.

Beyond earshot of the officers, Josh whistled low. "You shur know how to put them fellows in a lather, pard," he whispered with a sly, but relieved, grin.

Zeke was still miffed. "I flat told that Major I ain't interested when he first told me 'bout carryin' that flag," he said angrily. "But he took into his mind to force me. I don' see none o' them officers volunteerin' to give up his weapon," the young Private observed.

"I reckon they'll find some glory boy wants to be out front," Josh commented. "You bes' keep yer distance from them officers for a spell, though." He noted the advice for himself, at least where Jasper Welburn was concerned. The thought caused him to look over his shoulder, but the troublesome officer was not in sight.

"Anne Marlowe was here about," Josh said quickly, hoping to divert Zeke's attention to something more pleasurable. He scanned the people who remained on the parade ground without seeing Anne.

Zeke nodded recognition at Anne's name and followed his firend's gaze without success. As the smell of roasting ham greeted them, Zeke turned to satisfy an urgent desire, but Josh begged off, noting he had left May alone earlier. He located her near the reviewing stand, speaking with an older man. Josh stepped quickly to catch her up, arriving as the man departed.

"May, I'm real sorry to be so occupied," he apologized, "we got us some time now."

"I got to git goin', Josh," she told him with a pained expression. "I come down with mah uncle and he's ready to leave."

Josh reached for her and pulled her to him. She responded without hesitation, returning his embrace. He took the opportunity to kiss her warmly, half hidden as they were by the stand.

"I think about you ever day," he told her and she beamed with the compliment. "I hope to git a pass first o' the year, an come see you," he said as she nestled into his arms.

The older man returned and cleared his throat from a distance. May broke slowly from Josh's embrace. "You bes come soons you can," she told him. "I'll fix it with my Pa."

She walked away, bundling the rough woolen coat about her and pulling a man's cap down on her head. Josh noted the unfeminine look of the garments and strained to recall the shapely body within. She smiled goodbye as she climbed into her uncle's buggy, then was gone into the failing light as he waved to her.

Though disappointed for wasting his time with May, he realized he had not eaten and wandered toward the food area hoping to catch Zeke. His friend was no longer there, but he managed to wrangle some cooked meat and bread, washed down with some cider. As he walked to where his rifle had been stacked, Davy joined him with his rifle and they began to walk back to camp, most of the Regiment having preceded them.

Davy rattled on about the presentation by Beauregard, saying the 17th Mississippi was the bravest Regiment in the whole army. He related a rumor he'd heard about Featherston being promoted to general and put in charge of a brigade. Josh listened absently, not bothering to remind Davy that other regiments had fought at Leesburg and likely received a similar flag. In a moody silence, he began to think of May and turned his mind to how soon he could get a pass to visit.

When they returned to camp, he joined the mess to celebrate Zeke's victory. Ferrall came by to congratulate Zeke and to laugh over his refusal to carry the colors. He informed the obstinate soldier that Featherston held no grudge, but Major Lyles was yet in a forgiving mood.

Davy prodded Ferrall for comment on some of the rumors he'd heard that day. The genial Irishman could add nothing to what Davy related and mildly protested that he was only a Sergeant. He did reveal interesting news that rations were being held in Leesburg and would not be brought to camp. This generally signaled a move by the Regiment.

"You'll be movin' to winter quarters, lads," Ferrall told them. "The Regiment has been offered a place at the Swan plantation."

Zeke let out a shrill whistle. "You say Swan's, Sergeant," he asked absently. Turning to Josh, he said loudly enough for all to hear, "Swan's is out near the Marlowe place."

Josh now understood his friend's interest.

"Aye, lad, the Swan house is on the River side of the Marlowe place," Ferrall confirmed. Zeke's grin stretched ear to ear, but the other men resisted any enthusiasm for what would surely more backbreaking work to construct new quarters.

Ferrall noted the move would be made first of the year and took his leave.

Josh wandered off to bed, leaving Zeke in a happy state of mind and Joe Crawford grumbling about the upcoming change. Rolled in his blankets he remembered the excitement of the parade and Zeke's encounter with Beauregard, and mourned his lost chance to be alone with May. She had taken an easy place in his mind and just the thought of her brought a good feeling. But he remained puzzled by Anne Marlowe's actions, and the Virginia beauty was on his mind as he surrendered to sleep.

17

Christmas day broke clear and frosty. Many in the Regiment attended Chaplain Owen's morning service to begin the day. With all drills cancelled, men began revelries early. Officers congregated by themselves, leaving lower ranks to their own devices. By evening, vast quantities of spirits had been consumed, though the mood was peaceful.

After attending the service, Josh visited acquaintances around the Regiment, avoiding those in a melancholy mood for being so far from home. Zeke joined him for a while until Hugh talked his friend into slipping out to town. Hugh was keen on a girl in the village and painted Zeke an alluring picture of bountiful female relatives gathered for Christmas feast. Josh doubted Hugh's version of the evening, but Zeke was in no mood for reason and the two left before dark.

Josh visited until he had enough to eat and drink. Feeling light headed, he returned to the mess campfire where a sullen Dutchie and solemn Charley, perhaps thinking of home and wives, played indifferent hosts to occasional visitors. Joe Crawford lay snoring on the cold ground, an empty jug nearby. Charley told him that Riley had come out for a cup of egg nog and retreated to his tent. Josh thought to cheer the ailing soldier. He found Riley stretched on a rough bed with eyes closed, but the reclining man roused when he entered the tent.

"You feelin' better," Josh asked in greeting as he settled on the closest blanket.

"Better today than yesterday, but I'm still weak as a kitten," Riley replied.

"You hold down some o' that nog, you mus' be better," Josh said, glancing at the half full cup with a smile.

Riley grinned back. "I reckon it don' kill me, I'll be ready to git back in this war," he drawled slowly.

Josh noted the weakened man's labored speech. "Jes wanted to see how yer doin', I'll leave ya to rest," he said, rising to go, but Riley turned on his side to stop him.

"Set a spell an talk, Josh, I ain't had much company lately," the young soldier pleaded and Josh could see his friend craved a chance to converse.

Riley lay back and looked to the ceiling before he continued. "Had me a bad dream two nights ago," he declared, "an it troubles me still. I cain't seem to shake the feelin' it put on me."

Josh was struck by the concern in his friend's voice. "You'll git over it once't you git back on yer feet regular," he replied evenly.

"T'is hard to shake pictures in my mind plain as day," Riley continued, then turned his head to look at Josh. He paused, deciding whether to explain his vision, but feeling the dream might fade in the telling, he went on.

"We wuz in a battle, all the Rangers, an the Federals were chargin' at us," he explained. "Yankees as far as the eye could see, an we shot ever one comin' at us. The dead Yanks was scattered ever which way. An still they came. Blood was all over, till all I could see was red. I kept loadin' an' firin', an killin' them Yanks. We all did." Riley paused to catch his breath.

Josh felt his friend's torment and it chilled him, but did not interrupt.

"My rifle got so hot in mah hands I threw it down. Thought I'd git shot, but I realized no one was firin' at me. The Federals were jes runnin' at us, without firing their rifles." Riley paused again and Josh, thinking the story was over, cleared his throat to speak, but Riley held a hand up, signaling more.

"I looked round an Davy was standing there, pale as water, like some kind o' spirit. Not a mark on him, but not a sound from him neither," the now trembling man related.

"Somethin' bad's gonna happen to Davy, Josh, I feel it. But I cain't tell him 'cause it'll jes scare him," Riley finished in a sputtering cough as he explained his dilemma.

Josh waited through the coughing fit, troubled by the vision just related. He tried to ease his friend's mind, and his own.

"Dreamin' somethin' don make it so, Riley. You was sick an that fever got yer mind confused," Josh said reassuringly.

Riley glared at him in the pale light, nodding his agreement. "I know yer right, an I keep tellin' myself the same, but I cain't shake the sight o' Davy like a ghost."

Riley fought the grip of fatigue. He rose on one arm with great effort, opening his mouth to speak, then lay flat, exhausted.

He turned toward his visitor with an intent look and Josh wondered if there was more to the story, but Riley smiled helplessly. Then he said, "Ain't much use to dwell on it. I thank you fer listenin' Josh," before he turned away, eyes half closed.

"Git some rest an git back to cookin' our meals," Josh said good naturedly, patting the silent man on his shoulder as he rose to leave.

Outside the tent, a breeze slapped his face and he noticed fluffy specks floating down from above, disappearing on the ground. He moved toward the fire to rid himself of chill in body and mind, but Riley's tale had dampened his spirits. Josh passed the remainder of his evening at the campfire, thinking warmly of his family and trading remembrances of home with Charley and Dutchie.

On the final day of 1861, the Rangers were ordered to picket Edwards Ferry. They drew two days rations and prepared to stay the night, marching in late morning. A glowing sun warmed spirits, but had no effect on a cold day. The company passed the old camp at Goose Creek and arrived at their destination in mid afternoon, relieving men from the 13th Mississippi. They were divided into squads and assigned a watch. First watch took their places above and below the Ferry and on the approach road. The second and third watch established camp and prepared the dinner meal. Josh and Zeke were assigned second watch, from evening to early morning.

On schedule, they were assembled to relieve those on duty. The irksome Welburn was in command and their watch numbered a dozen men, including Hugh, Charlie and a surly Bradwell. Josh and Zeke were assigned to a spot near the Ferry with a good view of the Maryland bank under a bright moon. They surveyed their surroundings, Zeke wisely placing some dry leaves and brush along the path the Sergeant of the Guard might trod so they would not be taken unawares.

Fires were allowed against the chill river air and the two men stoked the dying embers from first watch with fresh wood. Josh was fortified against the cold in flannel underclothes and shirt received from home. Zeke could muster few extra garments and wore the captured Yankee greatcoat by agreement.

Zeke also sported a brand new cap, delivered the day before, courtesy of General Beauregard himself. He had quickly discarded the worn out, misshapen castoff he had worn since Manassas. His new kepi was dark gray wool with a band of black along the edge and sported a leather chin strap above the short brim. The cap was easily the finest in the company and Zeke was quick to point this fact out to all who admired the headgear, along with the name of his benefactor. He claimed there was no amount of money in the entire Confederacy that would make him part with such finery. Amid a barrage of teasing and threats to steal the cap, he had worked the day to shape the hat and curl the brim until he was satisfied with the fit.

They took places either side of the fire and Zeke's head began to nod before long. Josh had agreed to remain alert if his friend dozed, to avoid the punishment that would be meted out if either were caught napping on guard. Josh noted picket fires on the Federal side, though he saw no soldiers, and the thought occurred that there would be no alarm this night.

With the year about to end, he began to think about what had happened to the Rangers since they departed Holly Springs. Memory of that warm, spring day brought a smile to his face. The boys had become a hardened lot, used to the discomforts of camp life and seemingly restless in the absence of combat. He realized with some surprise that his comrades had changed from the fellows who had mustered in.

Zeke had acquired the useful habit of being able to catch sleep in any condition, as he did now in chilly weather on hard ground. Though Riley had been on the plump side at home, he was now much thinner, more so after his recent sickness. Yet he remained as even tempered as ever and a fair hand with their provisions. Davy had become the news gatherer, and quick to take offense if someone acquired information before he did.

Hugh had not changed from the ladies man he had been before, though he had acquired the bothersome ability to shirk his duties, leaving others to carry the load. Charlie held to his religious ways, but he became determined in battle, ready and willing to dispatch Yankee souls to purgatory. Walter had been forced to grow up fast. Without his brother, he held mostly to himself, but he pulled his share in camp and battle.

Joe Crawford had become a skilled forager, bringing sometimes hard to find items to the mess. Questions about the source of this bounty ceased as the commissary proved less reliable. Josh had not known Miller well before the company formed. But he always enjoyed his conversation with the thoughtful, educated man. Miller could be counted on to help everyone understand their part in the War a little better.

They had been part of an army for many months now, taken part in two battles, and, he noted with pride, charged the Yankees with fearless courage at Ball's Bluff. They had marched until their shoes were worn through, and suffered the privations of three seasons in northern Virginia. The Confederacy had seen fit to glorify their courage with a battle flag, while often ignoring their basic needs for decent food, clothing and shelter.

In the course of seven months, the men he'd mustered in with had become part of a regiment, and then a brigade and an army, yet they still referred to themselves by company and mess. A 'band of brothers' as described in the 'Bonnie Blue Flag' and superior to their enemy, though Josh suspected the Federals were not so very different. He knew Ferrall would laugh to call them soldiers, but they had all learned the soldier's duty and lived the soldier's life.

He turned his mind to home. The holiday just passed had brought warm memories, though Christmas was not a day of celebration in the Campbell house, rather one for religious reflection. His family would be safe and warm, far from the presence of conflict, and for that he was thankful. He had written when the Regiment returned from Goose Creek, but he vowed yet again to write more often to let them know he remembered. He was glad to have conquered homesickness and he enjoyed the freedom of army life. Temptations beckoned, and he had sampled a few, but he was grateful for the experience.

Josh was jolted from his reverie by a rustle in the bushes and he prodded Zeke awake.

"You bes' set up 'fore the Sergeant catches you," Josh whispered, pointing in the direction of the noise he heard, "you ain't s'posed to sleep on duty."

"Aw, Haskins ain't comin' till end of watch," Zeke grumbled in a hushed voice. Second Sergeant Haskins was well known to partake of spirits on cold nights and to be extremely casual about his obligations as Sergeant of the Guard.

They listened a moment more as some creature made its way through the bush and then Zeke settled back in frustration. "I cain't git no sleep if you gittin' skittish on me," he growled.

"Don' hurt to be careful. We both be on report, they catch

you dozin' " Josh responded.

"You don' wanna lose that corporal stripe 'fore you even git it," Zeke chided. Josh cut him a sharp glance, but he made out a thin smile on his friend's face. They had known each other too long not to poke fun at each other.

"You reckon' to sign on fer the duration, git the furlough," Zeke asked. Rumors had continued to fly in camp, but there had been little chance until now to discuss the subject by themselves.

"I ain't thought too much on it, but I reckon we ought ter see this thing through," Josh responded. "I shur ain't gonna have this much fun if I go home," he added wryly, breaking a sly smile.

"I kinda got used to this mill-e-tary life," Zeke drawled. "Leastwise, there's a sight more to do than wrasslin' a plow an watchin' the backside of a mule."

"But ain't nobody shootin' at ya plowin' a row," Josh noted with some seriousness. He caught Zeke's involuntary nod in agreement.

"Seems like most of t'others are fixin' to stay on, so I figure we kin, too," he added. Josh realized he had spoken for his friend, but Zeke simply nodded again and the matter seemed settled.

"You ain't lookin' to part from that golden haired gal jis yet, neither," Zeke prodded.

Josh grinned at his friend. "Seems like you got a stayin' feelin' since you heard we wuz gonna camp near Anne Marlowe."

Zeke colored with the jibe, but did not respond.

"You think them Yankee boys're awake over there," Josh said after a pause, looking across the river.

Zeke followed his gaze. "Them that's on guard likely doin' the same as us, tryin' to keep warm an thinkin' on better times.

"Why you reckon they don' quit this fight," Zeke posed. "We keepin' to our side. All we want's to be left alone."

"I figure they won't go home til they have another try at us," Josh explained. "We licked 'em twice pretty good, but Miller figures this Gen'ral McClellan will have to git whupped 'fore

Lincoln learns we ain't gonna be beat."

"Ain't gonna be no fightin' in winter though, so they'll have to make their move in springtime," Zeke noted, relaxing his posture and pushing his well worn cap forward. "That'll likely give us a few months to step out with these Virginia gals," he added.

Suddenly, both men tensed, clutched their rifles and looked across the river as they heard a deep rumble. No other sound immediately followed and they relaxed slightly.

"Yanks mus' be celebratin' the new year comin' in," Josh remarked, not completely certain he was right.

Congressman Elihu Hawthorne had been invited to witness the dawn of a new year in the camp of a newly arrived Massachusetts regiment posted along the Potomac. He accepted the invitation partly for political reasons, but also to spend some time away from the hectic atmosphere in the Capital. Journeying early on the 31st, he reached the regiment's headquarters near Poolesville in time for evening meal. He was shown to comfortable, and warm, quarters. After a leisurely dinner, well supplemented with fine wines, the evening festivities included a company inspection and cannon firing at the stroke of midnight.

Hawthorne was received with a measure of deference among the men. The district commander, a brigadier general, joined the regimental officers for dinner, and his manner was positively fawning. Hawthorne knew without question that his revered status stemmed from the Joint Committee. These military men seemed intent on creating a most favorable impression on the visitor from Washington. The Congressman had learned not to dissuade such impulses.

He inspected a well equipped and eager company of men. A young corporal was introduced to him as a constituent and in the course of a short conversation, the fellow mentioned twice how his comrades respected their officers. Hawthorne was privately impressed by the skillful orchestration behind his visit.

As the midnight hour neared, he was escorted to the nearby Ferry on the Potomac. He had a clear view of the Virginia side. A mere glance in that direction brought forth boastful declarations from his companions about the future. The current cry was "On to Richmond" and Hawthorne found himself stirred by their confidence. He was tempted to believe that next year would bring complete victory.

Hawthorne noted the sentry fires on the Virginia side. The rebels were not asleep. Their foe was aroused and prepared for the coming year. Progress would be difficult and only purchased in blood.

A smartly uniformed gun crew stepped to a cannon aimed across the River just before midnight and expertly loaded the piece under crisply shouted commands. When loading was completed, the gunnery sergeant prepared to touch fire and all eyes turned toward the officer in charge. That officer consulted a pocket watch for a few moments, nodded toward the sergeant and the gun roared.

A thunderclap roar shattered the still night air, the sound echoing along the River before it died away. The momentary silence that followed was broken by scattered rifle shots and faint cheers from both sides.

Hawthorne noted to the gathered officers that General McClellan could not report 'All quiet along the Potomac' as was the General's custom. The military men hesitated momentarily, unsure whether to condone the sarcasm, then joined the Congressman in a hearty laugh.

1861 had passed in to history and Elihu Hawthorne began the new year in a good humor.

Amid the noisy new year celebration Josh grabbed his

friend's free hand and shook it, relieved that the firing they heard was done in merriment.

"We ain't got no spirits to mark the night, but here's to whuppin' the Yanks and goin' home," Zeke shouted with his rifle raised high. Josh leaned toward his friend to yell another sentiment.

The shot cracked into a tree trunk a step away from Josh, bark flying as both men dove to the ground. An echo followed from down river.

"Damn Yanks is gittin' careless," Zeke whispered.

They slowly raised their heads and peered across the Potomac, but could see no rifleman on the darkened Maryland side. Clutching rifles, they rose to a kneeling position and gazed up and down the River to be sure no Federal force was on the water. Satisfied no enemy lurked nearby, the two men stood, watching for moving shadows on the water or the Virginia bank.

The wild firing had subsided. Quiet reigned on both sides of the Potomac.

Zeke stepped closer to see where the bullet had hit. Light from their campfire played on the tree trunk and he located the spot quickly, about shoulder height from the ground. Josh watched his friend stand near the spot and turn in several directions.

"Wrong side o' the tree fer a shot from the Yanks," Zeke said in a low voice as he joined Josh. "That ball come from our side."

Josh took a moment to digest this information. "You think one o' our boys let go to'rd us," he asked excitedly. Josh nearly turned a circle looking in all directions.

"Ball come from that direction," Zeke told him, pointing down river. "Take a five hundred yard shot to travel the right angle from their side. I don' believe the Yanks got a rifle kin do that."

Josh felt uneasy. "That ball was right close to doin' some damage," he noted, his throat suddenly dry.

"You almost made it home the hard way, pard," Zeke declared, trying to hide the worry in his voice.

Zeke suggested a scout down river and slipped off in that direction. He was back in a matter of minutes, shoving something in his pocket and forcing himself to show no concern.

"Ain't much we kin do now," Zeke said. "If anyone was out there, he's gone, and ain't nobody goin to fess up to this."

Silence intruded as they realized their helplessness, though the danger seemed to pass. Taut smiles creased the faces of both men, rifles ready, nerves tensed, as they started with any movement.

1862 suddenly threatened trouble from friend and foe alike along the Potomac River.

AUTHOR'S NOTE

The recruits of 1861 joined for many reasons, but most would have listed their respective 'Cause' foremost. Few had the luxury of deep thought about morality or national issues. Instead, politicians, newspaper publishers, religious leaders and assorted opinion makers exerted their influence on popular thought to bring the country to a shooting war.

Both sides quickly committed to a military solution, though neither side was ready to achieve such a result. Many thousands marshaled at various places for rudimentary training, in new uniforms, clutching a variety of armaments, and called themselves soldiers. Their military leaders were as often chosen for political connections as for military knowledge or experience. Helmuth von Moltke, chief of the Prussian general staff in the late 1800's, famously dismissed the Civil War as two armed mobs roaming about the country. There is nothing about the military actions of 1861 to refute the charge.

Manassas was garrisoned to protect a vital rail junction, situated as it was, near the Federal capital. The Confederate force was increased through early summer until it became a threat to Washington, though the South formulated no offensive plans. Instead, political and popular agitation forced the Federal army to attack before it could adequately prepare. Thus, the engagement along the Virginia creek called Bull Run on the broiling summer day of July 21, 1861.

The 17th Mississippi was part of David Jones Brigade on the right flank of Beauregard's army. In the original Confederate battle plan for that day, the 17th would have crossed Bull Run at McLeans Ford and been part of an attack on the Union left flank. The early morning attack by the Federals on the Confederate left preempted this plan and forced a change in disposition for the 17th. They would be marched and countermarched until late in the day, when the brigade was ordered to attack the Federal left. Along with the 18th Mississippi and 5th South Carolina, they maneuvered into position facing a Federal battery and infantry commanded by Henry Hunt, who would later become Chief of Artillery for the Army of the Potomac. The woefully uncoordinated attack accomplished little before Hunt's battery withdrew under orders from the Federal command. Casualties for the 17th were few, though the 18th Mississippi and 5th South Carolina suffered greater numbers of killed and wounded, in some instance due to friendly fire.

The scene of this action and the jump off point for the brigade lies outside of the National Military Park. The topography of the area is little changed, though one is hard pressed to see either the open, or forested, spaces that would have existed in 1861. McLeans Ford is unmarked and unknown in modern times, the exact location requiring expertise beyond the means of a casual wanderer. The north side of Bull Run is part of a Virginia Regional Park and affords the visitor a pleasant walk along the bank. Those interested can start at the sign marking Blackburn's Ford and head south along Bull Run.

The site of the 17th's attack is much harder to discern. The stream and hillside exist, but only to lend some perspective to that particular afternoon's activity. The action is neither marked nor recognized in most accounts of the battle and was noted only by those engaged in brief reports. I have embellished the pursuit by Confederate forces after the skirmish.

The Congressman of this book is fictional, though his capture is modeled on an actual event. Of the many spectators at the battle, Representative Alfred Ely of New York had the notable misfortune to be captured by the Confederates. He reported a harrowing experience during his capture when his life was threatened by a drunken colonel, to be spared by other clear thinking officers. His capture apparently damaged his political career, for he was not renominated by his party in 1862.

The 17ᵗʰ had a more active role in the Battle of Balls Bluff. This episode should have been a minor footnote in the War. Bungling by Federal officers, defense of an indefensible position and an attack that swept the field insured the battle a more prominent position in the history of the War.

Winfield Scott Featherston was a commander of some ability. A native of Holly Springs, Mississippi, he had gained military experience in the war with Mexico. Ordered to the site of battle by Brigadier Nathan 'Shanks' Evans, he arrived at the scene with his regiment, quickly analyzed the situation and accepted control of the 18ᵗʰ because its Colonel had been mortally wounded. Featherston seized initiative at the proper moment and turned the tide of battle. With steady promotion, he would rise to general rank and command a division in the Army of the Tennessee. He survived the War, and apparently revised his order to attack at Balls Bluff on later reflection, claiming that he said "drive them into Eternity" rather than "into Hell."

Ball's Bluff is also part of the Virginia Regional Park system. The heart of the site is preserved, though difficult to locate within suburban sprawl. Visitors can follow a well marked trail that includes commemoration of the 17ᵗʰ's attack. The River bluff remains, but covered in dense undergrowth. It requires a leap of imagination to see the field as it may have existed in October 1861.

Many an unexperienced novice received his baptism of fire at this battle, including a young lieutenant from Massachusetts named Oliver Wendell Holmes who would become Chief Justice of the Supreme Court. Among the many senseless casualties, one death stood out and echoed in the White House. Colonel Edward Baker, a personal friend of Lincoln, was killed during the fight. Hard questions were asked of the military after the battle and the political ramifications would echo throughout the War.

As a direct result of Ball's Bluff, Congress formed the Joint Committee on the Conduct of the War. In an instance of political hindsight, Congress began to review military activities and strategies and would continue to do so during the War. The Joint Committee naturally had a chilling effect on the military and would ruin the reputation of many Union officers, beginning with General Charles Stone.

I have consulted many sources in the preparation of this book. *A Life for the Confederacy*, the diary of Robert Moore, proved to be a reliable resource for daily life in the 17th Mississippi Regiment. *The Longest Night*, by David H. Eicher contains an excellent summary of all Civil War engagements. The periodical *Civil War Times* is a continuing source of intriguing and analytical articles on every aspect of the Civil War. For some perspective on the Southern experience in the Civil War, Gary Gallagher's *The Confederate War* is a valuable asset. The library of Civil War works is vast and contemporary and those who have an interest in this episode of American history need not toil in darkness.

Josh, Zeke and most of their mess have survived the year. In spite of initial assurances, the Yankees have been bested, but not beaten. The sections remain at War, though hard campaigning will only commence in better weather. As 1861 gives way to 1862, the time for glory has ended, to be replaced by a more terrible year than any could imagine. The second year of civil war will forge men on both sides as soldiers, in a crucible of battle.

ACKNOWLEDGMENTS

An undertaking such as this is simply impossible without the valuable assistance of family and friends. I owe a deep debt of gratitude to an energetic proofreader and editor, Diane Preisinger. Her critical comments were enlightening and helped me avoid many mistakes. Thanks to family and friends who read the manuscript for comment and criticism. The book is better for each of their efforts.

My continuing gratitude to longtime friends who have provided inspiration and critical analysis on the Civil War. Warm thanks go to Greg Compton for accompanying me on a chilly walk along Bull Run. Thanks also to Steve Kane for challenging historical analysis on Civil War battles. Special thanks to Steve Greenwalt who helped kindle my interest in the Civil War and has been a life long source of knowledge and discussion about military history. For this project and more, I also want to recognize Kari Greenwalt who represents the next generation of Civil War enthusiast - keep that fire burning.

Many aspects of publishing this novel were beyond my simple abilities. My sincere appreciation to Dave Greenwalt and Ad Pro Mark, Inc. for assistance in publishing and publicizing this book. And my deepest appreciation to Brett Greenwalt for his technical expertise. I am in awe of his ability with a computer.

Finally, thank you seems an inadequate expression to my wife and children. Son Brett and daughter Julie deserve much more for persevering through countless battlefield visits and dinnertime history pop quizzes. But an extra special thanks to my wife Mary Carol who served as sounding board, editor and inspiration.

To all of you, thanks for believing.